This book is dedicated to my two little jackpots,
Isaac and Anna

So incredibly original and refreshing, it has all the elements that make it a fabulous read including witty dialogue, romance, humor, a remarkably original plot and wonderful characters. *Jackpot!* is a novel that readers of authors like Emily Giffin, Sophie Kinsella and Jennifer Weiner will adore!

-Danielle Smith, Chick Lit Reviews

Jackie Pilossoph definitely hits the jackpot with her sophomore novel. With snappy dialogue and loveable personality traits, the two main characters will become your friends. Add in a heart clenching plot twist and plenty of scenes that will leave you laughing out loud!

-Samantha Robey, Chick Lit +

JACKPOT!

Jackie Pilossoph

Lisa

You hit the jackpot twice!

Jackie Plough

A big thank you
to the following people:

Christine Reiter Salah for editing this book for me, Mia McNary for her amazing artistic ability, Dina Silver for giving me the guts to actually go through with this, Anne Paul Clarke for being my on-call attorney, Jackie Langas for becoming a PR agent for HOOK, LINE AND SINK HIM, Sandy Sroubek for schlepping to LA with me for the HOOK, LINE AND SINK HIM book launch, just to be by my side, Kathy Jeffery for attending multiple book events (and working booths) with me, Jamie Gelb and Ruby Kang for flying here to come to the HOOK, LINE AND SINK HIM launch party, the wonderful Glenview community who supported me and gave me an overwhelming turnout for the launch party, all the people who came to multiple book events for me just because they knew I needed a crowd, the editors from Make It Better and Patch for publishing my articles, Lisa Kappes for bringing her entire book club to the NBC 10 show to support me, Chris Blackman for getting me on the

NBC 10 show, Mary Beth Wilkas for driving me to my book signings in Philadelphia, Mike Hamernick for the WGN appearance, Shana Drehs for giving me the confidence that Jackpot was a really great book, Matt Balson for building me an awesome website (really quickly), all the people who took time to read my manuscripts: Lynn Bruno, Jennifer Devine, Keri Williams, Melissa Uhlig, Laura Harris, Holly Hamburg, Susan Slutzky, Cindy Klaja McLaughlin, Melinda Boutsikakis, Alixe Small, Christine Reiter Salah, Anne Paul Clarke, Susan Palkovic, Liz Becker, John Fitzpatrick, Julie Kadish, Kate Weaver, Kristin Portolese, Mitch Galin, Sue Pilossoph, Frieda Pilossoph, Robin Pilossoph and Vicki Pilossoph, all the women who hosted me at their book clubs over the past year, the Cinnamon 7 whose friendships are so dear to me, my family who continues to stand by me and support all my nutty ideas, my dad for his everlasting encouragement and words of support, my mom for being my best friend, my boyfriend, Mark, who always makes it clear he's rooting for me, and of course, my kids, who continue to give me overwhelming joy and happiness every day.

Although I have problems and issues (just like everyone else), I truly feel like in life, I've already won the JACKPOT!

JACKPOT!

From *The Chicago Tribune* obituaries,
December 21, 1982

Jacobson, Seth Alan

Seth Alan Jacobson, 27, of Chicago, passed away on December 18, 1982. A funeral service will be held tomorrow at 12:15 at **Shalom Memorial Funeral Home,** 1650 W. Dundee Road, Northbrook, IL. He is survived by his loving wife, Francine (Frankie), his son Danny, 5, and his daughter, Jamie, 3.

Prologue

The year 2011...

Jamie

"How much are these again?"

The shoe salesman answered with slight annoyance in his voice, "Four ninety-five."

As Jamie Jacobson looked once again in the two foot mirror that was on the carpet of the *Saks* shoe department, she continued admiring the strappy gold *Jimmy Choos* on her feet. The thought of spending almost five hundred dollars she didn't have for a pair of sandals was semi-ridiculous, therefore causing her major anxiety. On the other hand, she knew she looked hot hot hot!

Jamie turned her right foot about 5 degrees to appreciate the side view. Then she did the same with her left foot. 'I can think of at least five occasions I need them for,' she sold herself.

She could actually hear her mother's voice inside her head. 'No one looks at your shoes, they look at your eyes.'

Jamie spoke to herself again. 'I've had a rough week. These will really put me in a good mood.'

Again she heard her mother. 'You're getting married soon. That doesn't put you in a good mood?'

'My feet look like Halle Berry's,' was Jamie's best selling point. Her mother had no response.

"I'll take them," Jamie told the salesman.

"Very nice," he responded, instantly perking up and transforming into a cheerful guy, "How are you going to pay for these?"

Suddenly Jamie was offended. "What?" she snapped, "Do I look like I can't pay for these?"

"All I meant was credit card, cash or check?"

"Oh," Jamie responded humbly, "Visa."

Jamie's new *Jimmy Choos* sat in her closet for exactly two hours before she decided to wear them out for dinner with some friends that evening. Walking down Michigan Avenue, she felt confident in her slinky black halter dress, but it was the shoes that made her feel like a movie star. With her head held high and her shoulders back, Jamie strutted down the block like she owned it. Several men noticed her. She noticed them noticing, and smiled as she thought about how glad she was that she bought the shoes and didn't listen to her mother.

When she reached a stoplight, she stopped walking and waited to cross with a handful of other pedestrians. That's when she heard something awful. It was a sound that actually made her cringe. A toddler was screaming and crying. Before Jamie even turned around to find out where the annoying noise was coming from, a baby stroller pulled up next to her and she saw the little terror. 'Please God,' she prayed silently, 'make the light turn green quickly.' Then she gave the kid's mother a fake, sympathetic smile. The light remained red.

"Here, sweetie," said the brat's mom to her son as she handed him the McDonald's milkshake she was holding, "Will this make you feel better?"

Jamie rolled her eyes and looked at the boy with disgust. 'Thank the Lord this will never be me,' she thought, as she saw the light turn green. Then, just as she was about to take her first step across the street, she felt it. Cold, thick, sticky liquid on her feet. She gasped when she looked down and saw the milkshake the toddler had just thrown on her sandals. All she could do was stand there with her mouth hanging open.

Danny

Outside a Lincoln Park *Starbucks*, a beautiful girl sat at one of the tables drinking a venti skim misto and reading the *Chicago Tribune*. She kept to herself until she saw a really good looking, dark skinned, dark haired guy come out of the store. They exchanged smiles, and then he approached her.

"Mind if I sit here?" Danny asked.

She answered amenably, "Not at all."

It took a mere ten minutes for both to decide there was enough chemistry between them to take things a step further.

"What do you say we continue this little meeting on the patio of *Que Rico*?" Danny suggested, "A couple of margaritas, some chips and salsa?"

Now the girl, whose name was Kate, seemed hesitant. "I'd love to but..."

"Don't tell me you have a date," interrupted Danny, with his best puppy dog face, "I'm a pretty fragile guy."

"No, it's just…"

'What's her deal?' Danny thought to himself, 'A second ago she seemed to be digging me. Why is she backing off now?'

Then he heard, "Mommy!" and saw a little girl running toward them.

"Hi, sweetie!" answered Kate.

Now Danny realized the woman he was hitting on was a mom, too. He watched the little girl give her a tight hug. Boy, she was a cute kid, he thought. Looked just like her mom, in fact.

"Danny, this is my daughter, Sophia," Kate said proudly, "Sophia, this is my friend, Danny." Sophia smiled shyly, which made Danny smile.

"Hi Sophia!" he exclaimed.

There was a moment of awkward silence, broken by Danny introducing himself to Sophia's babysitter, who he thought was quite a looker, too. Then, a second later, the actor looked at his watch and began to act. "Hey, I just realized, I have a 5:30 audition," he exclaimed with fake surprise in his voice. He felt guilty about the lie, but he had a policy, and that was never to date women with children.

As cute and sweet as Sophia seemed, Danny always resisted getting involved with single moms and their kids. He actually looked up to the moms immensely, and had tons of respect for them, not to mention that 99% of the time they were smokin' hot! But it was himself he doubted, because he knew he didn't have the ability to make them happy.

First of all, he could barely take care of himself, both emotionally and financially, let alone try to support a family. Then there was the commitment factor. Obviously, if a woman had a child, she had most likely been in a committed relationship at one point, and probably wanted that again. Danny was smart enough to realize that his picture should be next to the word commitment-phobe in the dictionary (if commitment-phobe was actually *in* the dictionary.) So, no offense to Sophia, or her gorgeous mom, but he had to bail.

Before anyone could respond, Danny was already standing up. "It's been really nice talking to you," he said to Kate. "Nice meeting you, Sophia!"

Danny never turned around to see the confused looks on all their faces, but he wasn't confused. Things were very clear to him. It was clear that he was a huge jackass.

Frankie

The smile on her face was huge, but inside, Frankie Jacobson felt like crying. There she stood, holding a big plate of noodle koogle, watching yet another one of her friends' grandchildren get circumcised. This was Marilyn Grazer's third grandson, and the third briss of hers Frankie had been to in the last four years. It seemed like all of her friends' kids were reproducing, while Frankie's own two selfish offspring weren't even close.

When the Moyle performed the actual circumcision on poor baby Noah, the child wailed. Then everyone shouted "Mazol Tov," and immediately afterward the contest began.

"Guess who's expecting number three?" Sheila Katz beamed to a circle of women standing around eating lox and bagels.

All of the women turned their attention to Sheila, already a grandmother of seven.

"Joshie!" she exclaimed.

"Oh my God, Sheila!" responded a woman.

"Honey, that's wonderful," said someone else.

"I wish you the best, Sheila," replied Frankie, who wanted to scream with frustration, but instead continued to eat, while mingling with the other grandmothers.

Sheila's announcement caused all of the women to quickly put down their plates of food and begin digging through their purses, pulling out baby pictures, and showing off the grandchildren.

"Look, here are David's kids, Lilly and Jeffrey," Marcy Rothberg proudly declared.

"Very nice," faked Frankie.

A woman leaned over to have a look. "Absolutely gorgeous!" she exclaimed.

As the contest of who had the most grandchildren continued, Frankie looked across the room at Marilyn, who now had baby Noah contented in her arms. She thought about Marilyn, how her kids had married well and had given her so much joy with the births of their babies. Didn't every mother deserve to be a grandmother? Wasn't it one of the only benefits of getting old? Now on the brink of sixty, Frankie felt like she was getting up there. She also felt she deserved grandchildren more than any woman here, simply because her husband had died when she was so young, robbing her of so much happiness. Frankie wasn't bitter, though. She had ended up living a good life, thanks to her two children, who had both given her great joy when they were younger.

Jamie and Danny were both healthy, beautiful, smart and driven, all the characteristics for which a parent hopes. Frankie was proud that both of her kids graduated college, were registered voters, and even managed to donate blood every six months, which they knew pleased their mother. Somewhere along the line, though, Frankie's son and daughter had lost all sense of what was important in life; family. Neither was interested in long-term commitment or babies. All they cared about were their careers, which according to Frankie were self-serving narcissistic ones.

True, Danny was a teacher and a basketball coach for one of the Chicago Public Schools, a very noble and selfless profession, but his first love was acting, and thirteen years after college, he was still modeling for print ads with hopes of getting discovered. Her daughter, Jamie was the lottery number picker for WGB. Frankie didn't understand this. Didn't she want more out of life than being an on-air celebrity? Where had her kids gotten the desire to be in the limelight? Certainly not from her.

As she continued to glance at all the grandmothers in the crowd, Ester Cohen must have been reading her mind. "Is Jamie still dating that lawyer?" Ester asked her.

Frankie gleamed with pride. "Oh, yes! I'm waiting, any day for their engagement," she answered. Frankie wondered if she sounded convincing enough. She knew in her heart her daughter would probably never go through with a wedding to her current boyfriend, Max, even though Frankie adored the boy. Still, she could dream, right?

"Mazol, Frankie" replied a woman.

"Yes, honey. You deserve some good news," added Marcy Rothberg.

"What's that supposed to mean?" the woman asked in Frankie's defense.

"I just mean," said Marcy, "it's her turn. You know, for marriages..." she hesitated, "and babies."

"From your lips, Marcy," said Frankie.

At that moment, Marilyn Grazer walked up to the crowd, proudly holding sleeping Noah in her arms. "Sid says he looks exactly like me. What do you think?"

All the women responded on cue and made a fuss once again over Noah. Frankie couldn't muster up the strength for more fake praise, so she opted for the job of photographer, grabbing a disposable camera from a nearby coffee table. "Let me get a picture, Marilyn," she called out as she focused in on grandma and baby.

"How's that gorgeous son of yours, Frankie?" yelled out Sandy Greenberg.

"Danny? He's fine," replied Frankie, who spoke of him as if she barely cared. She did care. She was just irritated and frustrated because she knew her son was a playboy who could not have been further from diaper changing and bottle feeding.

"Is he seeing anyone?" asked a woman.

"I really don't know," replied Frankie.

All of a sudden, the earth shattering scream from across the room could have given any one of these woman a heart attack. "Guess who's engaged?" the screamer screamed, "Neil!"

Dramatic gasps could be heard from all the women, staging their responses as they congratulated the screamer and talked about it amongst themselves. All except for Frankie, whose smile returned but whose insides were burning with envy. Three of her friends watched Frankie while they talked about her.

"Poor Frankie" said Sandy Greenberg, "Lost her husband at such a young age and now all she's got is a divorced daughter..."

"And a son who will never settle down," finished Marcy Rothberg. Marcy looked at Sandy and another woman, who didn't know Frankie very well. "He dated both our daughters," she said.

Sandy validated the statement with a firm nod.

They all knew how badly Frankie wanted babies. But they also knew her children, and it was a well-known fact that Jamie and Danny Jacobson were about as far away from marriage and family as the earth was from the moon.

"I'm sure Frankie will have grandchildren someday," the woman added, "Eventually, everyone settles down."

"She doesn't understand," said Sandy to Marcy. Then she looked right into the woman's eyes for dramatic effect. "If you knew Frankie's kids, you'd agree with what I'm about to say." Marcy was nodding in agreement while Sandy continued, "Frankie Jacobson has a better chance of winning the lottery than she does of ever becoming a grandmother."

Chapter 1

I tried to sound as excited as I possibly could. "One…five… seven…three!" I shouted, easily fooling my audience with the fake enthusiastic tone I'd perfected over the years. Walking to center stage, I finished up the daily lottery with the sugary smile I'd practiced hundreds of times in the mirror. I forced out plenty of phony passion and added some much needed drama.

"There you have it," I exclaimed, "One five seven three for the pick four, and once again, three eight seven for the pick three. Thanks so much for watching WGB, the official station for the Illinois Lottery. Have a wonderful afternoon and remember…" I upped the drama even more at the very end, "Somebody's got to win. Why shouldn't it be you?"

"Okay, we're clear!" Richard, our producer, shouted the second we were off the air.

Instantly, my charming grin vanished. A look of annoyance took its place. "Suckers…" I mumbled as I took off my microphone and headed back to the office I'd recently been complaining about to management. It was too small for the lottery girl, who in my opinion deserved much of the credit for the consistently steady incline in WGB's ratings.

Following me like a puppy dog was Drew Conrad, one of the camera operators. I hate to sound conceited and egotistical, but I have to be honest and say that Drew was madly in love with me. Everyone at the station knew it. I didn't really get why he liked me so much, probably because back then *I* didn't like myself so much, but I have to say, I secretly loved the attention.

Most of our co-workers had a theory as to why he was so gaga. According to them, it was the chase. I was unattainable, due to my serious boyfriend, Max. And Drew, the handsome dark-skinned guy with the deep green eyes and jet black hair was on a mission to sleep with the one woman in Chicago he couldn't have.

I'd heard the rumors about Drew's motives, but I didn't care. He was really was nice to me, and he was entertaining. And looks wise, I hated to admit it, but with better clothes and no goat-tee, Drew Conrad was truly adorable.

Drew dated tons of girls and was very non-committal, but he was also a sweet guy. He had the potential to become a great boyfriend. I truly believed that someday, Drew would meet the right woman and she would transform him from a sweet-talking, sex-crazed, playboy to a "take home to mom" kind of guy. Not a "take home to *my* mom" kind of guy, however.

My mother, Frankie Jacobson, didn't want me with handsome, charming, or charismatic. She wanted her daughter with career driven, money making, nice (which I translated as not good looking), and most importantly, Jewish. Everything Drew Conrad was not (except nice, but not Jewish). And because Frankie drove me nuts and made my life miserable when she didn't approve of someone I was seeing (which was every man in my life except for Max), I had always chosen to view Drew strictly as a platonic friend, even during the times when one look from him melted me. There were several other reasons for keeping away from him, though. I had no desire to get into an inner office romance, I had no interest in a womanizer of any kind after my cheating husband divorced me, and I wanted no part of anyone who was so smitten with me, in hindsight, because I had major self-esteem issues and again, really wasn't that crazy about myself.

Drew would follow me into my office every day after the lottery and make small talk. Over the years, the two of us had talked about pretty much everything under the sun, including politics, sports, celebrity gossip, Chicago hot spots, my career goals, his career goals, and his love life.

The conversations always stayed casual, very friendly and superficial, and that wasn't by accident. I made sure to keep Drew at arm's length, letting him get to know me only to a certain extent, and never taking things even to a remotely more serious place. Drew was my colleague. He was an acquaintance. And even though I sometimes wondered (quite often, actually) what he looked like naked, I saw no point in dipping my pen in the company's non-Jewish, non-committal ink.

All that said, seeing Drew hang around my office pleased me immensely, to the point where I was dependent on his visits. I thought of him like the little pink spotted teddy bear I had when I was two. Just like with *Pinkie* (that was its name), I always felt the security of Drew by my side. Sure, if I was occupied by some task or project, I would forget about him temporarily, but if Drew happened to take a day off from work and didn't make an appearance at my office door, he was definitely missed. Today, as usual, he came by.

"So, are you watching the Cubs game tonight?" he asked, standing in the doorway.

"Uh…maybe," I replied, barely looking up, pretending to be more interested in checking my e-mail.

"What do you mean, maybe? Do you realize that this is game two of the playoffs and that the Cubs haven't made it this far in over fifty years? Doesn't that mean anything to you?"

"I guess," I answered nonchalantly while reading e-mails on my computer screen.

"You should be ashamed of yourself," he joked.

Finally, I looked up. "Yes, I care about the Cubs, okay? They're just not my number one priority in life right now."

"Well," said Drew, as he inched his face up to mine and gave me a wide grin, "Maybe you'd be a happier person if you moved them up on your list."

I was now forced to look right into his eyes since they were so close. Was it my imagination or did his green eyes look especially green today? My heart started to pound as I thought about how if I moved just a few inches closer, my lips could actually touch his. Did I want that? Panic began to set in. Could Drew see that a window had briefly opened up, and that if he planted a kiss on me at this moment, I might surrender?

I quickly looked away and once again focused on my computer. "Yes, I probably should pay more attention to the Cubs instead of focusing on how much rejection I'm getting from agents who don't know a good screenplay when they see it. Listen to this…" I then proceeded to read Drew three rejection e-mails from Hollywood agents.

"They're all a bunch of idiots," said Drew, "Someone will see your talent someday, Jamie. It's only a matter of time." He smiled and literally patted me on the back. "You'll see."

4

"You are a total sweetheart!" I wanted to gush. Instead, I gave my friend a polite smile and went with, "Thanks," keeping things status quo.

It was a good thing Drew Conrad believed in my ability to become a screenwriter because I was starting to lose faith. Flipping lottery numbers was never my long term career goal. I had gone to school to become a film maker, and instead had met the station manager of WGB at a Bulls game several years earlier. The guy instantly wanted me for the lottery drawing. Why? I had no clue. Rumor at the station was that I had a good voice and a nice butt.

I had always wondered why having a nice butt qualified someone to be the lottery host. Did anyone even see it on camera? Nevertheless, I had taken the job because I got to quit my then current position, which was a production assistant for the *Jerry Springer Show*. Plus, part of the job was to write and edit news stories, and that was something I liked doing. I swore to myself, though, that this would only be temporary. Half a decade later, I was still here.

"Hey, isn't your birthday next week?" Drew asked, "We should go out and celebrate."

"How do you know when my birthday is?"

"I know a lot about you."

The traffic guy was walking by and happened to hear Drew. "If you know a lot about her, you know she's not interested in you."

"Shut up" said Drew.

"It's true, Drew," I said, my tone sympathetic.

"No, it's not."

"Does the name Max mean anything to you?" I asked him.

"That lawyer guy you're dating?" he asked, "You're not into him."

"Not into him?" I asked defensively, "Just fyi, I am very into him."

"I don't think so."

We debated this point back and forth a few more times, and as much as I was trying to sell Drew on the idea that I really was in love, the person who really needed convincing was me. For a very long time, I had been trying to talk myself into the idea that Max was the one. I had a strong feeling I was getting engaged tonight, and the thought of it was making me physically sick. I had thrown up after breakfast and after lunch, and I wasn't sick, pregnant or bulimic.

I logged off of my computer and started to gather my things.

"Where are you going?" asked Drew, as I basically pushed him out of the way.

"Manicure appointment. Then dinner with Max later."

"Skip the manicure," he yelled after me, "Let's get a drink."

The traffic guy walked by again and mumbled, "Get a life, dude."

"Dude, shut up," he answered.

I stopped and took a few steps back to Drew. Now I was standing so close to him that I could smell what I suspected was his soap or his deodorant, and it was making me inappropriately weak in the knees. My heart began to flutter, and the look on Drew's face was telling me he knew this.

"Listen," I managed, my voice shaking a little bit, "I really am taken. In fact, I think I'm getting engaged tonight. I'm sorry. Please move on." Then I moved on. Quickly. I was walking so fast, I almost felt like I was jogging.

Drew yelled after me, "Congratulations!"

I never turned around.

The receptionist later told me that Drew made an announcement to the five people sitting in the newsroom, just after I got on the elevator.

"The engagement..." he called out, "It's never going to happen."

The receptionist also told me no one was really paying attention to him.

Chapter 2

As I was walking into *Morton's* to meet Max for dinner, I had the strangest thought. Why would he want to propose to me at a steakhouse? I didn't eat red meat. It made no sense. But neither did the fact that a ring was about to be presented to me, and the thought of that was making me feel worse than I did the day I found out Jennifer Aniston and John Mayer broke up (the first time).

When I reached the entrance to the main dining room, Max was already seated at our table, drinking a dirty martini and straightening his tie. I watched him for a second. He seemed nervous. Here was my guy, on the heavy side, but decent looking, with his dark, curly hair, dark skin, and kind eyes. He was sort of nerdy, but dependable, which was in hindsight, the main attraction.

As I watched my boyfriend for a second, nervously moving his diamond pinky ring back and forth on his thick finger, I thought about his other appealing quality, wealth. Max had serious cash, which made my mother fall in love with him unconditionally. Not me, though. Yes, his money was a huge draw, but honestly, the thing that had gotten me to where I was tonight, (about to be engaged) was that Max was sweet to me. He made me feel truly loved. He worshipped me. Again, a huge appeal to my mother, who always told me that my husband should love me more than I love him. But the question I kept buried inside the nine hundred dollar Prada bag he'd given me for Hanukah last year was, did I really love him?

Max was about to officially become my fiancé, and eventually, my husband. My second husband. I had been down this road before. I'd already made one mistake and couldn't help think I might be embarking on mistake number two.

Max would make a wonderful husband and father, but something was telling me it wasn't right. Max just didn't seem like the one. Still, these past few months, I had decided I would make him the one. With Max I felt safe and shielded. I'd had no father growing up, and a husband who lied and cheated, and that made Max the perfect catch. My ex-husband, John, was gorgeous. Max was not. John was charming. Max was not. John was soooo... good in bed. Max was not. John cheated. Max would not. That was the bottom line.

"Honey, over here," Max called to me while waving.

I gave him a big smile and walked up to the table. He was definitely a nerd, but a sweet one.

"Don't get up," I said, just before kissing him on the cheek and sitting down.

"You look amazing, as usual," he said with a nervous smile.

"Thanks," I answered. I had to admit, my heart wasn't into this, but I sure felt hot in my back-less red halter dress and *Manolo Blahnik* sling backs.

"I ordered mussels. Is that okay?" he asked.

10

"Perfect. How about some wine?"

Thank God, the waiter was on the ball. He had my drink order in no time, and quickly brought me a much needed glass of Pinot Noir. There was so much awkwardness it felt like a first date. For a second, I thought maybe I could be wrong. Maybe there was no ring. Suddenly, I began to have an appetite. That is until Max got up from his chair. That's when my heart went into my stomach. He actually got down on one knee.

"Jamie," he said, his voice soft and shaking, "I think you are the most beautiful, wonderful woman in the world."

A Tiffany's ring box appeared. The color in my face disappeared.

"Will you be my wife?" he asked, his sweet, round face filled with hope, "Will you marry me?"

'Where the hell is the waiter?' I thought. Couldn't he see my wine glass was empty?

I took a deep breath and managed with slight enthusiasm, "Yes, Max. I will." Then I gave him a big grin and hugged him. Diners at neighboring tables started to clap and cheer. I had to admit, it was really cute. I suddenly felt maybe I was doing the right thing. Maybe my doubts were normal for a girl getting married the second time around.

Max opened the box and pulled out the ring. Now my jaw fell to the ground. I was in shock. He had gotten me the most perfect three carat oval diamond I'd ever seen, set on a band of tiny oval diamonds.

"Wow!" I exclaimed. This time my voice was much more enthusiastic. "Thank you, Max, it's stunning."

Max put the ring on my finger, got up, and sat back down in his chair. The waiter returned with the mussels and I ordered another drink. The two of us ate in silence for a while, till my now husband-to-be reached for my hand.

"Let me see this again." He pulled my hand about half an inch from his eyes to get another glance at the rock. "This is gorgeous," he continued, "It cost me a ton, but I said what the hell."

"It's really nice, Max," I beamed.

Max's voice started to rise. "Nice? What do you mean nice? It's huge!"

Annoyance began to seep in. Yes, it was nice that Max sprung for the big rock, but was there really a need for praise, which I sensed the big spender was looking for? Again, where was the waiter when I needed him? Another cocktail was now a grave necessity.

"Yes, Max. It's huge. Okay?"

Max's voice went up another notch. "I would think you'd be happy, considering your first ring was the size of a pinhead."

"So what?" I responded, trying not to grit my teeth, "John wasn't making a lot of money at the time. That's all he could afford."

"Why are you defending your cheating ex-husband? Admit it, it was a teeny tiny pinhead ring."

The same people who were clapping and cheering were now watching with concerned looks on their faces. My drink finally arrived. I took a big swig, stood up, took the ring off and slammed it down on the table. "You're such a jerk!" I shouted. As I headed for the door, I could feel the stares.

Max stayed seated, but shouted after me, "Maybe you should get back together with your slimy ex-husband and get your teeny weenie ring back!"

As I was practically running out of the place, all I could think about was how angry I was at Max for the low blow. Why pick on John? Max should be thanking him. After all, it was John who led Max to me. John was the reason we met. Not that I was defending John, the lying, cheating, scumbag of the earth, but why would Max feel the need to bring up John, especially tonight?

Once outside the restaurant, I walked about half a block and then stopped. All of a sudden I felt ecstatic. Unbelievable relief came over me. I was off the hook! I was so happy I started to laugh loudly, almost to the point where people passing by were thinking I was a crazy person. One woman even stopped and asked if I was okay.

"You think this is funny?" Max said, interrupting my laughing attack. He had come after me. Sweat was dripping down his chubby cheeks and he had taken his jacket off.

"Max, if I don't laugh, I'll cry," I said, still giggling.

My response softened him and he gave me a huge hug, almost crushing me.

"I'm sorry, honey, about what I said," Max groveled, "Your ring, although very small, was I'm sure, a very good quality diamond."

I pulled away from the hug and started laughing even louder.

"Again with the laughing..." said Max, "Am I a joke to you?"

When I was finally able to contain my laughter, I managed to show some sympathy. "No, Max, no," I said sweetly, "I think I'm laughing because I'm so relieved. See, I don't want to marry you." At that moment, I hated myself because I knew I had just dropped a bomb on him. Still, I felt I was doing the right thing, fessing up now.

"What?"

I looked at him and said sadly, "You heard me." Then I waited for him to take it in.

"Why?" he whispered.

"I really care about you. You know that, right?"

Max nodded. I took a tissue out of my purse and wiped his forehead while continuing, "I already made one mistake marrying John, and the worst thing I could do is marry someone who I don't see myself with forever. I know that sounds harsh, but I'm just being honest."

He pulled my hand and the tissue away from his forehead. "But tell me why," he pleaded, "I need a more specific reason."

I thought about what I could say to make him understand and then it hit me. "Because you need someone who wants what you want. You want the suburban wife with the SUV, driving your two kids back and forth to Hebrew school."

"What's wrong with that?"

"Nothing, except that's the last thing I want. Max, I want to make movies. I want to write and direct, not pick balls out of bins until I'm nine months pregnant, and then become a stay at home mom. I don't know if I even want kids." I put my head down and finished, "I don't think I'd be a very good mother."

Now Max's sweet sadness turned to rage. "So what am I supposed to do now?" he demanded.

The fact that Max didn't respond with "Of course you'd be a good mother!" spoke volumes. I figured he agreed with me, and therefore he chose not to say anything about my parenting abilities. But part of me also knew that at this moment, Max was thinking only of himself.

A brilliant idea suddenly hit me. "You know what you should do?" I responded, "You should get back together with Bonnie." Bonnie was Max's girlfriend, who he'd dumped for the woman standing here breaking up with him.

Max looked at me like I was nuts. "Bonnie? How do you know Bonnie's still single?"

"You could call and find out."

Max was now completely pissed. "I don't believe this."

I continued trying to sell my idea, despite still absorbing the fact that my almost fiancé thought I would make a shitty mom. "Look, Bonnie wants what you want. I don't. Plus, Bonnie would do anything for you. I doubt that's changed."

Now Max's anger turned to a formal, unemotional tone. "Fine. Dump the fat guy."

"I'm not dumping you. I'm trying to do what's right for both of us."

He shook my hand, which I thought was really weird, and said, "Good luck, Jamie. When you wake up husband and childless at 40, I hope you don't regret this." Then he turned and walked away.

Instead of a serious relationship coming to an end, this felt like the conclusion of a bad business meeting. But as I watched Max angrily walk down the block, I didn't regret what I had just done, and I didn't feel sad or guilty. This might sound completely insensitive and rude, but honestly, the thought going through my head right then had nothing to do with Max. I was standing there trying to remember if I'd set the DVR to record *Entourage* four nights earlier.

Chapter 3

I took a big gulp of my Miller Genuine Draft. "Hey, what are you doing in there?" I shouted to Jennifer, who had been in her bedroom way too long, getting ready for our date.
"I'll be out in a second," she shouted back.
"Hurry! I need a kiss!" I demanded.
Stretched out on my girlfriend's couch, tired from the photo shoot I'd just come from, I was desperate for a smooch from her, the main reason being Jennifer was a woman. Not even an hour ago, I'd been posing on North Avenue beach half naked with a dozen other men, and had been asked to kiss a guy while a photographer snapped pictures for the annual Chicago Gay Pride Parade. So right now, I craved a female mouth on mine in order to quickly erase the memory of the dude's lips I'd felt earlier. Not that I had anything against gay people, I just wasn't gay, so it was weird. Plus, I hate to say this because the guy was really cool, but his breath freakin' reeked.
A moment later, my wish was granted. Jennifer dashed out, jumped onto my lap, and showered me with kisses and hugs. Thrilled beyond belief, I made an aggressive attempt to turn the kisses into passionate ones. In a matter of seconds, I was unbuttoning her

shirt. Hell, sixty minutes earlier, I had kissed a guy. It was time to attack my woman and validate my masculinity in a big way.

"Wait," she told me, "Slow down."

"Jen, I just made out with a dude. I need you." I kissed her again. "Now!" I opened her shirt and buried my face in her chest.

"Danny, can we just talk for a second?"

I was kissing her chest and trying to unhook her bra while I spoke. "Let's have sex and then talk."

Jennifer pulled away and got up. "Danny, I'm serious."

"Sorry. I'm just having a bad day. I need a little cheering up," I responded, trying to sound cute.

She looked at me with annoyance, and then began buttoning her shirt back up. "Why was it such a bad day?" she asked me, "You're getting jobs, aren't you?"

I frowned. Now I knew I wasn't getting any sex.

"Do you know how many actors would kill to get the jobs you get?" Jennifer went on. She spoke with authority, which was appropriate since she was not only my girlfriend, she was my agent.

I got up and headed to the kitchen for another beer. On one hand, I knew Jennifer was right. Then again, I felt like it was okay to feel sorry for myself since my resume as an actor wasn't even close to what I wanted it to be.

I had graduated from Syracuse thirteen years earlier with a degree in Elementary Education and a minor in drama. If it would have been up to me, I'd have done the reverse, majored in drama and then taken some teaching courses, maybe enough for a minor. But my domineering mother had insisted I get a degree in something practical, and truthfully, part of me wanted to be a teacher. But I also had the acting bug big time, and even now, all these years later, I still had it.

Shortly after college, I moved to New York City and got a job as a teaching assistant at an elementary school in Brooklyn. I also moved there in hopes of becoming an actor. But after five years, I managed to get only one credit under my belt. I played a criminal being hand-cuffed by a New York City cop for the ad campaign Giuliani implemented to get more recruits for the NYPD.

Fortuitously, a producer from Chicago happened to see the commercial and offered me a job posing as a rapist for a print ad for The Chicago Bureau for Self-Defense. When I flew back to do the shoot, I decided to permanently stay in Chicago, so I quit my teaching job and moved home.

I started interviewing at several schools and a few weeks later, I was offered a teaching position at Martin Luther King High School, a Chicago Public School in a rough neighborhood. I was excited beyond belief by the challenging position, but decided I wasn't ready to give up on my first love; acting. I still had hopes that acting would someday replace my teaching career.

Shortly after I started my job at MLK, millions of posters were distributed and placed all over Chicago. The caption read, "Your Attacker Could Look Like The Boy Next Door." Under it was none other than me, lurking behind an innocent woman walking alone on a dark side street.

The Superintendent of The Chicago Public Schools wasn't too thrilled that one of his teachers was the poster boy for rape, but eventually he got over it, especially when I brought the posters into my classroom and explained to the kids that I was also an actor, and that I felt I was doing the world some good by participating in such a good cause.

The Chicago Bureau of Self-Defense ads ended up attracting the attention of Jennifer, who was a relatively reputable agent. Within a week of seeing me, she signed me as a client. At first, our relationship was all business. Jennifer and I got along great. She got me a decent amount of work, and even though I had a full time teaching job, I was going on a fair amount of photo shoots and being paid, which was great since teaching at a Chicago Public school wasn't exactly making me a wealthy guy. So, in addition to all the exposure, the extra money was a big perk.

Jennifer made me feel important. She made me feel talented. She made me feel good. And I always knew I should be grateful, but I was growing impatient. When was I going to be discovered? When would my big break come?

I wanted to be more than just "the before guy" for the sales literature for Hair Removal Treatment Centers of Illinois. I wanted better jobs than the Warts-Be-Gone guy people commented on while paging through the Chicago Tribune on a Sunday. I felt like I deserved more than posing as a down and out guy for Gamblers Anonymous, which was what I was presently trying to explain to Jennifer, who didn't understand how I could be so unappreciative.

"Do you know how many actors would trade places with you in a minute?" she asked me, "At least you're getting jobs."

"That's not the point," I replied, as I headed back toward the couch. I sat down and took a big gulp of my new beer. "Just once, I'd like to play a doctor, or a teacher. Something good." I sighed, "Maybe a fireman."

"How about a dad?" asked Jennifer, who was now seated in an upright, uncomfortable looking position.

I thought about it for a second. "Yeah, a dad..." I started to get excited. "That's perfect! I would play a dad!" I exclaimed with a smile, "Now you're talking. What's the part?"

Jennifer grabbed the beer bottle out of my hand and took a big sip. "Danny..."

"Jennifer, this is good," I said, as the wheels began to spin in my head. I was getting more and more psyched. "A dad..." I was truly thrilled, and felt like a 10 year-old kid whose parents just told him he was going on a hot-air balloon ride. "Are you sure I don't look too young?"

"No, you're definitely not too young."

"This is great, Jen, thanks!" I scooted over to be closer to my favorite agent. "Tell me more. Who is it? When's the shoot?"

She took another gulp of beer. "Danny..." she said before taking a deep breath, "I've been thinking, I want to have a baby, and I want YOU to be the father. Will you do it?"

"What? I don't get it."

Jennifer took another big inhale and exhale. "I'm 37. I'm getting up there. I want a child. And I want YOU to have one with me." She put her arms around me and finished, "You'd be a great dad!"

I wasn't sure how long I'd stopped breathing. One minute I was dreaming of a possible break-out role to jumpstart my acting career, the next I was sitting in a catatonic-like state.

"Did you hear what I said?" Jennifer's voice had gone up an octave.

Now my head was pounding. How could Jennifer and I be on such opposite ends of the spectrum? I was having fun, she wanted to start a family with me. How could we be so far off? I had a quick flashback to the first time I slept with Jennifer. It was only a couple of months earlier. There had been sexual tension between us for years, but I purposely never acted on it because I didn't want to change the dynamics of our relationship. I liked it the way it was. Jennifer and I were polite to each other. We treated each other with respect.

However, after four dirty martinis, and seeing Jennifer in a tight pair of True Religions one night when we happened to run into each other at Hub 51, this theory didn't hold much water. I woke up in my agent's bed the next morning. Instantly, I knew I screwed up. I realized I didn't have romantic feelings for Jennifer, and that the combination of booze and stupidity had caused the hook-up. Nevertheless, I wasn't a total jerk, and I did enjoy being with Jennifer and her perfect body, so I just sort of fell into a relationship with her. It was convenient. Plus, I figured maybe she *would get me some better gigs now that I was her boyfriend, too. But I'd always been honest with her. In fact, we weren't even committed to each other. She had told me just weeks earlier that she'd had a date with some guy she met at her gym.*

"If you don't say something I'm going to hit you over the head with this bottle."

Softly, I managed, "Jen, I can't have a baby. No way."

"No way?"

"Look, I'm a history teacher. I make twenty-five thousand dollars a year and some pocket change on the side from the jobs you get me."

"Danny, I make A LOT of money. That's not an issue."

"That's not the only reason."

"Then why else?" she asked.

"What about us?"

Her eyes welled with tears. "What about us?"

I gave her a gentle smile, "I think we both know we're not in love."

Now the tears started to stream down her face. "I know that, Danny. But we like each other, right? Please do this for me."

I took a deep breath and then I hugged her and said, "I'm sorry, Jen. I can't do it. It wouldn't be fair to you, or to the baby."

Jennifer pulled away from the hug and I watched her face go from sad and somber to psychotically angry. "You know what, Danny? You are an evil person!" she screamed, "After all I've done for you, you won't even consider giving me the one thing I really want!"

"Jen, we've been dating for two months! Plus, why do you feel like I owe you this? You get commission from my jobs, don't you?"

She stood up, went to the front door and opened it. "Get out!" she shouted.

"Please don't do this," I urged, "Let's talk about it."

"No! You've shown your true colors. I'm not good enough to have your baby."

"Jen, that's not it. I don't want ANYONE to have my baby right now. I really like kids, but I may never want a baby. I'm not sure. What do you want me to do?"

"Nothing," she said bitterly, *"Just continue being your selfish, self-centered, womanizing self."*

Now I was getting pissed. The nerve of this girl! *"Look, I might be a little selfish,"* I said, *"but I'm not going to feel guilty about this. I'm not doing anything wrong by not wanting to get you pregnant in the next ten minutes."*

"Get out of here! You make me sick!" she shouted, *"And by the way, consider yourself agent-less!"*

"Fine," I said, walking out the door, realizing you can't reason with an unreasonable person.

As I rode the elevator down to the lobby, I found myself feeling sorry for Jennifer. For her to ask ME, a guy she'd been romantically involved with for a little over 60 days, to father her child, she was obviously desperate. If I was her best option, that was sad.

I wasn't sure I meant it when I told Jennifer I may never want kids. Of course, I wanted kids. Someday. Just not today, or next week, or next year, for that matter. I had a complicated life. I was a hard working history teacher, trying to mold rough, city high school kids into moral, upstanding adults. And I was proud of that. I really felt like my work made a difference. And it was a great feeling.

I was also a struggling actor with ambition and dreams of being wealthy. I felt guilty about wanting to trade in a life of selfless work for what my mother called a narcissistic, egotistical career. But I also wanted to have fun. I liked acting. I liked being in the spotlight. I wasn't hurting anybody. I was just trying to enjoy my life as much as possible. After all, I was 34 years old. And although that may seem young to some people, my dad died when he was 27, so my theory was, anything can happen. Better enjoy yourself! So, along those lines, for some *chick that I'd been dating for the blink of an eye to pressure me into having a baby, that was just purely unacceptable. But the bummer of it all was that I'd lost my agent, the person who was getting me jobs and exposure.*

I got off the elevator, walked through the lobby, thinking how glad I was to be getting the hell out of this building, when suddenly, as I opened the glass door to leave, my eyes met the eyes of a woman walking in, and she literally took my breath away. She was beautiful. Dark skin, black wavy hair, and big gorgeous full lips. When she smiled at me, I think my heart stopped.

I suddenly understood the meaning of the phrase "love at first sight." Of course, I wasn't in love with her, but yes, I was definitely in love with her face. Not just because it was pretty, but because it lifted me, and made me light up like a Christmas tree. I wasn't thinking I wanted to nail this girl, or even that I wanted to try to go out with her. It was strange, but just seeing her face, and the way she looked at me gave me inspiration and hope that love really did exist.

And ironically, I was leaving the building where I assumed she lived. Then again, I was leaving Jennifer's building as well, and any sane person would have told me to sprint out the door after what she'd just asked me to do.

I held the door so Miss Stunning could walk in and then I walked out, briefly turning around to watch her walk to the elevators. She also turned around, saw me, and gave me another one of her dashing smiles. I thought about going back in to talk to her, but because of what had just happened with Jennifer, I thought it was best to leave it be. Yes, I could be a jerk, but I wasn't a total asshole. I had feelings and I knew Jennifer was upset right now and probably still crying. And I felt sad for her. The last thing I wanted to do was hit on some chick who lived in her building. So I took a deep breath and started to walk, severely bummed out that I may have just passed up someone pretty damn significant.

On the walk back to my apartment, I thought about calling Jennifer to see if she was okay. I didn't, though. I thought I should leave her alone tonight. Plus, I hate to admit it, but all I could think about was the girl who with one smile, had just stolen my heart.

Chapter 4

It was a tradition in my family to have Shabbat dinner every Friday night at my mother's condo. Frankie didn't cook brisket or buy challah bread, though. Instead, we ordered Chinese. We'd been doing it for years, and although both my brother and I looked forward to the food; spring rolls, crab Rangoon, Kung Pao Chicken, and pork fried rice, we couldn't stand the conversations. They were exactly the same, week after week after week.

For example, Frankie would ask Danny (in her most sarcastic tone), "So, who's the lucky girl of the month?"

Danny would then reply by saying one of three things. "No one special, Ma," "Let's change the subject, Ma," or my personal favorite, "None of your business, Ma."

When it came to me, it was all about Max. "How's Max?" or "Are you ever going to marry that sweetheart of a guy?" And every week, when I walked into the condo, before I even had my coat off, it was the same question. "Why didn't Max come tonight?"

It's funny. I had never brought Max to one of our Friday night dinners. Not one. Max and I took my mother out for dinner quite a bit, but for some reason, I chose to keep the Shabbat dinners as a threesome. Asking Max to join us just never seemed quite right.

On this particular Friday night, I took off my coat, realizing that Ma's question, "Why didn't Max come tonight?" would never be asked again. Ever. Frankie didn't say a word about it. In fact, she didn't say anything at all, and after a few minutes I realized that my break-up had disappointed her so much, that for the first time in her life, Frankie Jacobson was perhaps speechless.

I had called her that morning and told her that Max and I were through. My hand was shaking as I dialed my mother's number.

"Hello?" Frankie answered the phone.

"Hi Ma, it's me," I said, realizing that my voice was shaking too. Breaking the news to Frankie seemed scarier than breaking the news to Max.

"What's wrong?" she asked immediately. The funny thing about Frankie was that she could actually read my mind. Danny's too. The woman was completely intuitive when it came to us. She was able to detect voice inflection, tone, and meaning behind everything Danny and I said, and even what we didn't say! That was why I was dreading the conversation that was about to take place.

"Nothing, why?" I answered, knowing full well this was a pointless response, since I wasn't going to fool my mother.

A moment of silence followed, before Frankie spoke again. "Oh my God!" she exclaimed.

"What?"

"You broke up with Max," she said in a sad voice.

It was truly amazing. The mind-reader already knew. And all I could think about was my poor mother. There wasn't a woman in Chicago who wanted grandchildren as much as she did, and now her chances of that had just gone from slim to slimmer. A future filled with sweet little voices, visits to the park, and trips to Costco for diapers and formula was more distant than ever. While her friends would continue babysitting their dozens of grandchildren, Frankie would remain a mother with two very independent, non-committal children.

My mother was fifty-four years old. My dad had died when I was a toddler, and Frankie had never remarried, or even dated, for that matter. She had lived alone since I left for college, clinging to the hope that someday, when we got older, Danny and I would expand the family. Frankie used to tell me her goal was to be a grandmother by the time she was 50. When I got divorced, I realized she would not hit her objective.

"How did you know?" I asked her, regarding the news I'd just delivered.

"A mother knows," said Frankie in her self-pitying voice.

"I'm sorry, Ma." I sat there wondering why I was apologizing to my mother for not marrying a man I didn't love.

"I just don't understand," Frankie began, "Max is such a good man. He's smart, he's rich…"

As Frankie went on with a list of Max's good qualities, I stopped listening and began to think about how much I had disappointed her over the years when it came to the men in my life.

"I'm just so disappointed, Jamie," was the next thing I heard her say. I realized now, that just like Frankie could read my mind, I could read hers, too.

"Ma, I've got to go. I'm late for work," I lied in a desperate attempt to end this conversation that was showering me with guilt I knew I didn't deserve.

"I love you, Jamie," she said.

Now I knew my mother felt badly about making the disappointment comment, and I realized her disappointment was in the situation, not in me. I also knew Frankie really meant it when she told me she loved me. And that's how I was able to tolerate my mother and have a good relationship with her. I loved Frankie dearly, and I wanted to make her happy. But I couldn't marry the wrong guy just because she wanted a Jewish son-in-law and babies.

I told her we could talk more about it more later, even though I had no intention of bringing it up ever again. Then I said good-bye and I avoided her calls the entire day, wondering each time I saw Frankie's number pop up, what people ever did without caller ID.

Dinner seemed like a poker game, everyone at the table wondering who was going to hold out the longest and who was going to fold by using the "M" word (Max) first. I was a bundle of nerves, while my brother was enjoying the fact that tonight the focus was on me, and not on his non-commitment issues for a change.

Just as the shrimp fried rice was making its way around the table, Frankie made a subtle move. "So…" she began in a casual, polite voice that both of us knew was forced, "Josh Katz's wife is pregnant with number three."

"That's nice," I replied, remaining calm, as I took a couple spoonfuls of rice and then handed the container to Danny.

My brother didn't respond to our mother's piece of gossip. Instead, he decided to stay silent and shovel rice onto his plate.

Frankie continued, "You know Josh. He's Sheila's son." She had stopped eating.

"Uh huh," I managed to respond while chewing.

Frankie waited a couple seconds before she spoke again. "And Neil Goldblum is engaged."

"Great!" I responded, sounding so fake I made myself cringe.

Danny added with a chuckle, "So, Neil decided not to come out of the closet, I guess."

I giggled.

Our mother did not. She shot Danny a dirty look and then turned to me and said, "I'll never understand why you two didn't hit it off."

"Because he's gay, Ma," said Danny.

"No," I joked, "Because he's a loozaaa..." Both Danny and I burst out laughing.

Frankie fumed. "You two are immature and selfish. That's the bottom line."

"Sorry, Ma," said Danny, "We're just kidding around." He patted her arm in adoration.

"Ma, we're just picky," I said, "I think Danny and I are both holding out for the right people." I turned to my brother for support. "Right?"

Danny nodded and I could tell he was just appeasing us. I knew deep down that my brother wasn't holding out for anyone. He had no intention of settling down in the next century.

"Is it so bad that I should want babies from my thirty-two and thirty-four year old children?" Frankie asked.

"No, but don't you care about what *we* want?" I asked.

The conversation had finally struck a nerve with Danny. He put his fork down and turned to me. "No. I don't think she cares what we want." Then he looked at Frankie. "Tell you what. Jamie will get back together with Max, marry him, have a baby, give up all her dreams, and live miserably ever after so you can have a grandchild."

"And what about you?" I asked him.

31

"Me? I'll knock some girl up and pretty much do the same thing..." He looked at our mother, "so you can have baby pictures to show your friends."

"What sweet children I have," Frankie answered bitterly.

I could tell Danny was angry now. What I didn't know at the time was what an extremely sensitive subject this was for him, having just been asked by Jennifer to impregnate her.

As we all ate in silence for the next few moments, I began to feel sorry for my mother. Frankie didn't deserve this. The way she felt about having grandchildren seemed natural and normal. It was similar to the way a thirty-something person should feel about being ready to have children. Unfortunately, I realized there were two thirty-somethings sitting at this table who weren't even close to being ready. I wasn't sure Danny would ever take that plunge, not because he didn't like kids, but because I wondered if he could ever commit to a woman long enough to bring the relationship to that level.

As for myself, I was two for two when it came to picking the wrong guy. And if I couldn't even get it right in the husband department, how the hell was I supposed to have a kid? But there was something else. I was very afraid of having a child, my reason stemming from my ex-husband constantly telling me I was too selfish to have kids. After having that drilled in my head for so long, it was hard to think otherwise.

I really did understand my mother's frustration, though. After all, Frankie had to deal with my divorce, which I knew horrified the woman. Additionally, she now had to accept the fact that Max wasn't going to be her son-in-law. When I looked at her and saw the sadness in her eyes, the guilt I felt was so overwhelming, it nauseated me to the point where I felt like undigested crab Rangoon might end up all over the dining room table. My mother really did have a lot to be sad about.

Frankie met her husband, Seth, in high-school and the two were married soon after. Seth attended a small college in the city, where he was earning his teaching degree at night. During the day, he worked at a shoe store. Frankie got a job as a secretary for a brokerage firm and was a waitress at night. Even with their hectic schedules and their limited time together, the two were very happy and very much in love, according to my mother.

They were living in a tiny studio apartment, which they didn't mind, till the place got a bit too small when Danny was born a few years later. The couple didn't plan Danny, but birth control back then was a little more difficult to manage, and frankly I was surprised they managed to remain childless that long. My parents were thrilled to have a little boy, only now, Frankie had to quit her jobs, which made money tight. Still, they managed to get by.

When my dad finally graduated, he got a job teaching at a suburban high-school and the three moved to a quiet little neighborhood nearby. I came along a couple years later, and things couldn't have been better for the happy little family. Frankie and Seth were living their lives with much joy and happiness, and experiencing the fun of little ones like all parents should.

Then tragedy struck. It happened on a Wednesday afternoon in December. Snow was falling pretty heavily and Seth was still at work around four o'clock. School had been out since 3:15, so all the kids were gone as were most of the teachers when they saw the snow getting thick. Seth chose to stay and get some work done, as he was enjoying the peacefulness of sitting in his quiet classroom alone. When he finally decided to head home, the roads were treacherous. Back then, no meteorologist could predict how much snow would fall, or how bad the conditions could actually get, so Seth wasn't too worried about driving.

As Frankie was preparing dinner and teaching us Hanukkah songs, she heard a knock at the door. She knew instantly that something was very wrong. When she answered the door, there were two policemen standing there. They told Frankie her husband was dead. He was twenty-seven.

"Don't worry," I said, putting my hand on my mother's shoulder, trying to comfort her, "I'd like to have a baby... maybe...someday, I think." I noticed she hadn't touched her food.

"You think?" she replied.

"Look, I don't have a lot of faith in my parenting ability," I said sadly.

"That's because your asshole ex-husband treated you like crap and made you feel bad about yourself," Danny answered.

Ma smiled at him for the first time that night. "You're right," she said.

Danny added, "And Max...well, the thought of having sex with that guy would turn any woman off of wanting a kid!"

I burst out laughing. My mother's wide grin turned into a frown.

"The other thing is," I said, "I need to focus on my career now. My writing. I want to make movies, Ma. Did you know that?"

Danny turned to me in support. "I respect that."

"Thanks. If I end up producing or directing anything, there's a part for you. You know that, right?"

Danny smiled back at me and then looked at our mother. "Do you even care about that, Ma?" Before she could answer he got up from his chair and headed into the kitchen.

"Where are you going?" asked Frankie.

"I need another beer."

"Beer. My son drinks beer," she said to nobody, "I shouldn't even allow it in my house." Then she looked at me. "I do care about that, honey. I just want you to realize the important things in life. Marriage, family, children. And Max would be such a great father." Obviously, she wasn't ready to let go of hope that there could be a reconciliation, which was completely out of the question in my mind.

"Can we change the subject?" I asked, "How was your day, Ma?"

"Fine. I took my morning walk with Sheila and then visited Mr. Fineberg. He had a hip replacement, you know."

"Yes, you told me."

"And then I bought my lottery ticket."

"Why do you play the lottery, Ma? Do you know what the odds are of winning?"

My mother giggled, "My daughter, the lottery host is telling me not to play the lottery."

"There's just no point."

"Well, I only play it on Fridays. For Shabbat."

I smiled at my mother's cute tradition. An instant later, we heard Danny shouting from the kitchen. "Holy shit!" he cried. "What is it?" I asked.

Danny dashed through the door with Ma's lottery ticket in his hand. He was out of breath. "The TV was on. I just saw…"

"You saw what?" I asked.

"Ma won the lottery!

From the front page of *The Chicago Tribune,*
September 3, 2011.

And The Winner is...

Frankie Jacobson of Chicago was last night's
winner in the Illinois lottery. Sources haven't
confirmed, but it is believed Mrs. Jacobson's
winnings are in excess of 17 million dollars.
A press conference is scheduled for today at
noon, outside the WGB studio on Michigan
Avenue. When asked in a brief phone inter-
view how she was feeling, Jacobson, 54, who
has been a widow for over thirty years, said,
"I'm fantastic. I'm loaded!"

Chapter 5

When I walked outside of the studio and saw my mother standing in the spotlight getting ready to answer questions from reporters, all I could do was grin. Here she was, a fifty-four year old multi millionaire. In my opinion, no one deserved wealth more than Frankie did.

My mother's financial status had changed so many times during her life. For most of it, Ma struggled when it came to money. Growing up, her parents owned a small grocery store and they lived pretty well. But when Frankie was sixteen, her father became ill and died, and my grandmother took over the business.

According to Ma, my grandma wasn't as successful as her husband at running the store, and a few years later she was forced to close it. Frankie and Grandma were broke. They sold their house and moved to a small apartment. Desperate to earn a living, my grandmother got some jobs cleaning houses to make ends meet. My mother told me she was horrified and ashamed that her mom was a cleaning lady, but nonetheless, she volunteered to help her after school. Ma said as long as no one knew how she and grandma got money, she was okay with things. And they were able to hide their secret for a long time.

Here's the story my mother told me a long, long time ago. It is perhaps one of my favorite Frankie stories.

Apparently, one evening, she and Grandma were cleaning the house of a very wealthy banker. My grandma was upstairs working in one of the bedrooms, while Ma was vacuuming the foyer. All of a sudden, she heard a knock at the front door. She shut off the vacuum cleaner and answered it. When she opened the door she saw two boys standing there. She recognized them from her school.

Now Frankie wanted to die. Not only because her shameful secret was now revealed, but because of her appearance. She was dressed in a pair of old jeans and a torn tee-shirt, her typical working attire. Her hair was pulled back off of her face and she was sweating a little bit. She never felt more dirty or ugly in all her life.

"Oh, thanks," said the boy who lived there, whose name Frankie knew was Alex, "I forgot my key."

"Sure," answered Frankie, who wanted to crawl into the nearest hole and never come out. As Alex whipped through the foyer and headed for the kitchen, the other boy just stood there staring at her.

"What?" Frankie asked this kid who she was sure was fixated on her because he thought she was disgusting. The truth was, he was in awe.

"I'm Seth. Seth Jacobson," said the boy.

"Hi," she replied shyly.

Then Seth gave her a big grin and said, "I already know you're your name. It's Frankie."

Ma told me that was the moment she fell in love with my dad. They were instantly a couple, and when the news hit school that Frankie was a cleaning woman (thanks to

Alex), Seth was the first one to support the profession and tell all the gossipers in the hallways that there was no shame in hard work. He even began helping Frankie and her mother clean houses. Dad was pretty popular, so if he thought something was cool, the kids were pretty forgiving. Plus, now that Frankie was Seth Jacobson's girlfriend, she was popular and accepted.

So now, the little girl who had worked so hard to get by, was majorly loaded. Here she stood, her shoulders back, her head held high, and a smile on her face the size of Texas. Ma was in her glory, the center of attention, and I could tell she was welcoming the opportunity of the press conference so she could live up to being the drama queen she truly was.

There were seven different cameras shooting her and twenty microphones in her face. Next to her was a huge, cardboard check with the amount of her winnings, "$17,500,000," boldly printed on it.

"What are the odds that the lottery girl's mother would actually win the lottery?" asked a reporter from WBBM. His tone was accusatory and at that moment, I noticed several other reporters waiting for my answer.

"Are you interviewing me?" I asked.

"Yes."

"The odds are pretty high," I said with a nervous giggle.

"Did you have anything to do with it?"

"Maybe you should have an attorney next to you while you answer questions, Jamie," said the traffic guy from the station.

"That's okay," I answered him. Then I turned to the reporter and responded, "No. I didn't rig anything if that's what you're wondering."

Right then, my producer, Richard stepped up to save me. "Actually, there's an investigation going on right now to make sure everything was done fairly. That being said, we're not concerned and we don't suspect any foul play by Jamie or any other employee at WGB. This was a total, utter fluke, folks."

The reporter was satisfied with that answer and the second he looked away I mouthed "thank you" to Richard.

"How are you feeling right now?" a reporter from *Craign's* asked my mother. It was the first question that began the live broadcast of the press conference, where the world got to see a sweet, older widow react to her new millions.

Frankie gave her a huge smile and said loudly, "Loaded!"

The crowd erupted with a laugh, and I realized the drama queen was truly in her element.

"Are you planning on taking the monthly payments or will you receive the winnings in a lump sum?" asked Kim Vatis from WMAQ.

Before Frankie could answer, a nerdy Jewish guy with glasses spoke up. "She'll be taking the lump sum benefit," he answered. Alan was the lawyer my mother had hired that morning. He was one of her friends' sons. The name actually sounded vaguely familiar when she told me about him, and then I realized Ma had set me up with him years earlier.

Sylvia Perez from WLS asked the question everyone was waiting for. "What are you planning on doing with the money?"

Following Sylvia's question came an extremely lengthy pause. In fact, it was so drawn out that the crowd seemed to be on the edge of their seats waiting for her answer.

Finally, she spoke. "Actually…" Ma began. The way she was dragging it out was painful. "I plan on re-decorating my condo, and the rest…" The anxiety in the room was so high it was almost funny. What she announced next, however, was very much not funny. "The rest will be given to my grandchildren."

Some of the reporters started to ask follow up questions, but a couple of them who knew me turned around to see my reaction. Anna Davlantes from Fox, who I knew pretty well mouthed, "Are you pregnant?"

When I tried to answer, I couldn't speak. My mouth was hanging wide open.

Chapter 6

Whenever I get really stressed out, I walk. And tonight, after meeting with one of my students, Angela Walker, a junior who had just informed me she was pregnant and thinking of dropping out of high-school, my level of anxiety and worry was maxed out. Angela, who was a smart, talented and beautiful girl, and who I secretly had hopes would end up being the next Oprah, was thinking of trading in a potentially extremely productive life for the life of a single mother without a high-school degree. The thought was depressing beyond belief.

So, I'd tried to convince her she could still have the baby and finish school. Apparently, her parents thought it was a better idea for her to stay home and get a job somewhere. I wanted to kill those people! I didn't want to judge them, but it was frustrating as hell because it was such a bad idea.

Because of my meeting with Angela, I'd missed my mother's press conference. Yes, I could have rescheduled it, but I didn't want to do that because Angela needed some guidance from her teacher. Plus, I figured I could DVR the press conference and watch it later.

Throughout the day, dozens of friends texted and left messages asking me if I'd knocked up a girl and if I was going to have a kid.

"What are you talking about?" I answered one of my buddies in a text message. He then informed me about the little announcement my mother had made on T.V.

So, while I waited to hear back and get an explanation from the new multi-millionaire, I decided to clear my head with a walk down Armitage Avenue, a quaint tree-lined street with little shops, boutiques, neighborhood pubs and restaurants. I lived just off the beaten path of Armitage on a quiet side street in the garden apartment, (i.e. the basement) of an extremely old brownstone. My street and the brownstone were beautiful and had lots of character. However, my apartment was the size of a shoe box. I loved it, though. It was close to a lot of night time hot spots. Plus, it was pretty cheap. My job barely paid the bills, and even with my acting gigs on the side, I struggled financially, living paycheck to paycheck. But that was okay. I was happy teaching. I was happier acting, though, and someday, hopefully, I'd get a break and land a decent role.

I walked by Ranalli's, an Italian restaurant that serves over 100 different kinds of beer. I thought about going in, but realized today was Saturday and Rachel was working. I had no desire to deal with Rachel tonight. We had hooked up several months back when I went in for a pizza one night. Rachel was my waitress. We flirted with each other all night, and when she got off work I took her home and spent the night at her place. It had been a great time. I liked Rachel. But I never got around to calling her.

So Rachel called me. She had gotten my last name and phone number off of my credit card receipt and left two messages on my voice mail that week. That weekend, I had a great idea. I thought I'd return Rachel's phone calls in person with a surprise visit. So I stopped into Ranalli's, prepared to get a warm reception from her. But instead of a nice hello and a smile, she threw a beer in my face.

Rachel went off on me, screaming and yelling, "How dare you sleep with me and then not call me!" A couple of the waiters had to hold her back because she began to get physical. She actually threw a few punches, but luckily for me she missed.

So that was that. 'Such a shame,' I thought, 'good pizza.'

I passed by a couple more storefronts, walking at a leisurely pace on this gorgeous evening, casually looking in the windows of each place. Lucky Brand was having a sale on men's jeans. Good to know. Sushi on Armitage was now offering half-price rolls on Tuesday nights. Not bad. It was the next window, though, that would perhaps change my life forever.

A new store was opening soon, the sign not even up yet. A large poster taped onto the window read, "Coming soon...YOU SEXY THING YOU-sexy lingerie for sexy women. And by the way... all women are sexy." I took a closer look inside the shop, peeking through the window just below the sign. What I saw made my heart stop. A gorgeous woman was dressing a mannequin. She was placing a pink lace bra and panties on the wooden model. The girl wore just a black tank top and jeans, and she was barefoot. I couldn't quite see her face, but I was somewhat sure she was a knockout. 'You sexy thing you!' I thought.

All of a sudden, I heard Sean Kingston's "Fire Burning" playing in the background. And then I saw a sight I'll never, ever forget for the rest of my life. The girl stopped working, and she started dancing. Actually, she began doing the exact dance Sean Kingston does in his video of this song. It was almost as if she'd watched the video several times and memorized the choreography. That's how down pat she had it. And she was great!

I was chuckling and laughing, fully entertained by what I was witnessing. I turned around to see if anyone else was watching her. It was amazing to me that no one else noticed what was going on. I turned back around to see more.

As she moved to the music, You Sexy Thing You looked like she was having a blast. I was dying to see her face. I still couldn't, though. Was it possible to fall in love in 15 seconds? Finally, she moved closer to the front of the store and that's when I got a full view. Now my heart was really pounding! The girl was the same girl from Jennifer's building. She was the same girl with the same gorgeous jet black hair, the same full lips, and the same curvy, sexy body.

I watched her for a couple more minutes, knowing the look on my face was that of a lovesick puppy dog. Then, You Sexy Thing You happened to catch a glimpse of me out the window. She froze for a second and then quickly ran out of sight. Next, I heard the music stop. I now knew what I had to do. I wasn't letting this girl get away from me a second time. So I went to the door and knocked.

"Uh, we're closed!" I heard her shout.

"Yeah, I know but..."

"We open next Saturday. Ten o'clock!"

I thought about what to say next. "Listen, can you just open the door for two seconds? I know you. I'm the guy from the other night...in the lobby of your building. Remember?"

The girl finally came to the door and opened it, just a crack. "How can I help you?"

It was hard not to laugh. "Is this your store?"

"Yeah," she said trying to be cool.

"Wow, that's awesome. Congratulations!"

The girl managed a smile. "Thanks. How can I help you?" she repeated.

"Well, I was wondering, would you like to go have a drink with me? Or coffee?"

"I don't think so."

"Why not?" I asked her.

She opened the door a bit wider. "Um...cause I don't know you? Thanks, anyhow."

She started to shut the door, but I put my hand up to stop it. I was desperate now. I wanted to get to know this girl. I would not let her get away a second time. Things with Jennifer were done. I hadn't heard from her. She hadn't answered my apologetic texts (even though I didn't really have anything to apologize for) so we were done. And I had every right to go after this girl.

"Wait a second. Will you just tell me your name?"

"Courtney."

"I love that name," I said. 'Not Jewish,' I thought. I didn't care, though. Ma would care, but I didn't care. I never cared about that. But if I didn't care, why every time I met a girl did I wonder about her religion?

"Thanks," she said with a kind smile, "But I really have to go."

As she started to close the door again, I felt even more desperate. I had to do something. So I blurted out, "How about I help you?"

"Help me?"

"Yeah. I'll make a deal with you. I'll stay here and help you unpack and clean and get your store ready, and I won't mention anything to anyone about what I saw. You know...Sean Kingston..."

"I don't know what you're talking about," she struggled, "I was just..."

"You don't have to explain. I enjoyed it," I said with a wide grin, "But I did snap some photos of you on my phone, and if you don't let me in, I might have to go public with them. You wouldn't want that, would you?"

Courtney looked amused and I knew I was winning.

"Look," I continued, "it's obvious you need some help here. I'm a guy. I can lift heavy boxes, hang things... I'll even clean the john."

When I saw the look on Courtney's face, I knew I'd just succeeded in my quest to get into her life. "Deal," she said matter-of-factly. She started to open the door wider but paused for a second. "What's your name?"

"Danny," I said with a smile. Then I pushed the door open and walked in past her.

"The bathroom is straight back and to the right, and the cleaning stuff is already in there."

I walked back to the bathroom, whistling and wondering how I could be so damn happy about becoming a restroom attendant.

The two of us worked and worked, and a few hours later the future site of "You Sexy Thing You" looked amazing. But the two people who worked so hard fixing it up looked like they had been in a gang fight. Both Courtney and I were hot, sweaty, smelly and tired. We had been moving things around, unpacking, dusting, cleaning, vacuuming and arranging displays. The dozens of merchandise-filled boxes that were sitting all over the store were now empty and stacked up against a wall, their contents now hanging on racks throughout the shop. The place was completely transformed and looked almost ready to do business.

"Hey, want to order a pizza?" I asked Courtney, who was organizing some bras on one of the tables.

"Sure," she replied, "How about Ranalli's?"

Yikes! I thought, as I remembered the Rachel factor. "Fine if they'll deliver."

"I'm sure they will," she replied.

When the pizza came, we sat and ate in silence for a few minutes, pretty much because we were both starving. We had worked long and hard, all the time while making small talk, laughing a lot and getting to know each other. I found out Courtney was into kick boxing, loved Jerry Seinfeld, had had her appendix removed a year earlier, had a white chocolate fetish, and the most shocking thing, Courtney, with her majorly non-Jewish name, was Jewish. And surprisingly, I found that a very attractive quality.

After inhaling a couple slices of pizza, I finally spoke. "So, I want to know more about you. Tell me something."

"Well, let's see," Courtney replied, "I'm thirty-six..."

"You cougar!" I joked, "I'm thirty-four."

"I'm not a cougar unless you and I are on a date."

"I'd call this a date, wouldn't you?"

"I haven't decided yet," she replied. I felt like she was flirting and I was psyched. "I have two questions for you. First, what do you do, and second, why were you in my building the other night?"

"Well, I'm a history teacher at Martin Luther King High School."

"I love that," she exclaimed.

"Yeah, it's cool, but I'm also an actor on the side. My agent lives in your building. Actually, my ex-agent lives in your building. She's also my ex-girlfriend. We broke up that night I saw you."

"Which is why you're here with me, the major cougar," she said with a giggle.

I smiled, but I didn't laugh. Instead, I stood up and walked over to her. I had major pizza breath and I couldn't even begin to imagine how I smelled after cleaning and lugging boxes around for four hours, but something in me didn't care. I took her face gently in my hands and kissed her lips. She kissed me back, and in my entire life I couldn't remember a better kiss, and trust me, I'd done my share of kissing.

"So why'd you guys break up?" she asked.

"Want to hear the truth?"

She nodded.

"She wanted me to get her pregnant and I said no."

"Really?"

"Yeah, she's 37 and she wants a baby."

"So she's a cougar, too."

I chuckled, "Yeah, I guess she is. The thing is, I've known her for years. She was my agent. But we'd only been together as a couple for a few weeks. I like her a lot, but I don't want to have a baby with someone I don't love." I gave Courtney a wide grin and said, "I'm holding out."

"For love?"

All I could do was smile and nod. I didn't want to speak, because I was afraid three little words would come out. I know it sounds nuts, but I loved her. I mean, not really LOVE since I barely knew her, but for the first time in perhaps my entire life, I understood how a guy could fall. And it was scary as hell, but frighteningly appealing, too.

"Good for you," she replied with a smile, "Good for you, Danny."

Chapter 7

"Why are you acting so weird?" I asked Ma over the phone a couple days after the press conference, "You still haven't explained that strange thing you said about giving your grandchildren the money. Do you have other kids that we don't know about, Ma?"

"No," she answered with a laugh.

"Ma, please don't play games. What's going on?"

At that moment, Drew appeared at my office door with a *Vanity Fair* in his hands. He was reading an article, waiting for me to get off the phone. I wondered why he was reading *Vanity Fair*, but I was more focused on how his arm muscles looked in the tight white shirt he had on.

"Listen," said Ma, "Can you come over tonight at 7:00?"

"Um…okay, sure," I answered, "Is everything okay?"

"Yes. We'll talk about things tonight. Got to run. Mwah!" Then she hung up.

I looked at Drew. "I can't figure that woman out."

"That's funny. You usually have her pegged pretty good," he said.

"I know. So what's up with the magazine?"

"I wanted you to see this article about Amy Adams. Did you know she worked at *Hooters* before she became famous?"

"Are you comparing a *Hooters* waitressing job to what I do?"

"No. I just thought you might find it inspirational." He handed me the magazine.

Right then, I wanted to throw my arms around him and tell him how much I appreciated his thoughtfulness. He really was a sweet guy. Hot, too. But as I always did, I kept my feelings to myself. "Thanks," I said.

"Sure. So, is your mom finally going to explain the grandchildren comment?" he asked.

"That's what I'm thinking."

"I have a good feeling about this whole thing."

This time I didn't hold back. With a wide grin I said, "You always seem to see the bright side of everything." I was dying to add, "And your biceps rock," but I didn't.

A few hours later, I knocked on Ma's door. For some odd reason I felt really nervous. I'd been knocking on that door for almost 15 years, and every time my mother answered I would hug her tightly. I really did love her. Sure, we had always had our differences, like the time I went to Aspen for the weekend with Kerry Wood (pitcher for the Chicago Cubs at the time) and Frankie had a complete fit, telling me I was going to end up labeled as a groupie-slut. Then there was the time I sat her down and told her I wasn't sure I loved Max.

Frankie's reply was, "What's not to love?"

"Ma, I know he's a good man. But I'm not sure if he's right for me. Shouldn't I feel more?"

"Feel more what?" asked Frankie, "More attraction? More lust?"

"Can I just shoot myself?" I'd replied.

"You see where that got you, right? You don't need another John. You need someone to take care of you. Max is that someone."

I knew my mother loved me and wanted to protect me, but we didn't always agree. In fact, we rarely agreed. Still, we had always been close. Besides seeing Ma every Friday night, the two of us loved to shop together, we liked the same movies, and for special occasions like birthdays or Hanukkah, we loved going to *The Drake* hotel together for tea.

Ma was great company. She was fun. She loved to gossip about Hollywood people, and I had no idea where she heard them, but she always told hilarious jokes. Perhaps my favorite thing to do with my mother, though, was to sit and talk about my dad.

I could listen to her stories for hours. They interested me. They comforted me. And Ma enjoyed telling them. She would describe everything very vividly about her life with my father. Because of her drama and the colorful details she shared, I felt like I was there. Often times, I'd ask to hear some of the stories over and over again. The details of how my dad proposed, or how my parents spent their first New Years Eve together had been shared by Frankie at least fifty times.

Danny had no interest in hearing about my parents past, not because he didn't feel love for his father, and not because he didn't miss him. I suspected it was just too painful for him to hear such good things about someone he never really knew.

"Danny feels like he was robbed when I talk about the good times I had with Dad," Ma would tell me, "and that's okay. He was."

I, on the other hand, could tell someone the life story of Seth Jacobson. Furthermore, I knew everything about

Frankie Jacobson. At least I thought I did. Now, because of how she'd been acting since she won the lotto, distant and vague, I wasn't sure.

The instant Ma opened the door, I felt the same weirdness I'd been feeling the past few days. Frankie hugged me hello, but she had this formality about her that I'd never seen before.

"Come in," she said.

No words were exchanged as I walked behind her into the living area of the condo. The silence was awkward. Then, when I saw Danny and Frankie's lawyer, Alan, sitting at the dining room table I began to see things more clearly.

"Have a seat please," Frankie said to me in a tone similar to that of a receptionist in a doctor's office.

"Hi," said Danny, who seemed puzzled.

I waved to my brother. "What's going on, Ma?" I asked softly, as I sat down.

"You know Alan, don't you?" she asked me.

"Yes." I gave him a polite smile.

"Hi, Jamie," said Alan.

Ma sat down at the table. "Alan, shall we begin?" she asked.

"Certainly, Mrs. Jacobson."

He started shuffling some papers. I looked at Danny and mouthed, "What's going on?"

Danny just shrugged. Then he turned to our mother.

"Ma, do you mind if I get a beer?"

Frankie was about to reply, but Alan beat her to it.

"Your mother would prefer if you gave up alcoholic beverages," he said.

Frankie added, "Except wine at Rosh Hashanah."

Danny stood up and got in Alan's face. "Hey dude, if my mother has issues with me, I think she can tell me herself."

"Sit down, Danny," Ma snapped.

Danny froze.

"Actually," she continued, "Alan will be speaking on my behalf for the remainder of the evening."

Danny seemed confused. He sat back down.

"Alan, please begin," said Frankie.

"Sure," he said, "As you probably heard at the press conference, your mother stated she will be giving her Illinois Lottery winnings to her grandchildren."

"Yeah, Ma, I don't get it," said Danny.

"Shhh. Just listen," Ma scolded, "Please continue, Alan."

Alan proceeded to pull out two copies of a lengthy legal document. He handed one to me and one to my brother.

"This document, signed by your mother, states that if either of you produce a child, you will receive a sum of eight million dollars."

I glared at the document for a few moments without even reading it. Then I stood up and exploded. "Are you crazy?"

"Nope," she answered flatly.

"Let me get this straight," said Danny, "You want us to have babies, and you're willing to pay us for that?"

"Yup," said Frankie.

"Why?" I shouted.

"Because all I want before I die..."

Danny interrupted, "Is to make us as miserable as humanly possible."

Frankie ignored him.

"So what are we supposed to do?" I asked, "Get married? Neither of us are even dating anyone!"

"The document doesn't state anything about marriage," Alan said, "just children."

Now I was fuming. "So, what? If we ever get around to having kids, like years from now, we become wealthy?"

"That's not it at all," Ma said, "Alan, tell them the interesting part."

As Alan nervously shuffled through some papers, something made me peruse the document. And just as I heard Alan clear his throat to speak, a certain paragraph on the page caught my eye.

"Oh my God!" I gasped.

Then Danny saw it too. "Oh shit!" he screamed.

Both of us looked at our mother, who was smiling.

"It says here we have one year to produce a baby!" exclaimed Danny.

"That's correct," answered Alan, "One year from today, if either of you have a child, either through a pregnancy or adoption, you will receive your inheritance."

I giggled bitterly, reading the document further, "It says here that the child will be tested through DNA."

"Yes," added Alan, "and if you adopt, we'll need to see the adoption agreement."

"So you basically want me to either start the adoption process, which I think we all know takes more than a year, or go out, find some guy, and get myself pregnant in the next three months?"

"Gives new meaning to the phrase the clock is ticking, doesn't it?" joked Danny.

I shot him a look. "Do you think this is funny?"

"No!" he defended, "I'm in shock!"

I turned to Frankie. "What about diseases?" I asked, "What about AIDS? Aren't you worried about that?"

"You're both intelligent, educated people. I'm sure you'll take all the necessary precautions to make sure your potential partners are disease free."

"Ma, you sound like one of those people who work at the department of motor vehicles, explaining the procedure on how to get a driver's license," said Danny.

"What have you turned into?" I shouted.

"I've waited long enough for you two to grow up," Ma responded, "Both of you are selfish, materialistic people. That doesn't mean I don't love you. I do. But it's time for you to realize what's important in life. Think of it this way. I'm giving you the incentive you need to settle down."

"You can't buy us," I said.

"I'm not trying to buy you," Ma replied bitterly, "I'm trying to buy babies. And guess what? Knowing you two, I think it will work."

I sat there frozen and watched my mother stand up and head for her bedroom. She turned to us and said, "Look, I don't want to get into a big discussion about this. My mind's made up. This is what I want. I love you both. Very much." Then she looked at Alan. "Please answer any additional questions my children might have. I'm going to bed." Then she was gone.

The three of us sat in silence for a few moments. Alan looked so nervous. I had a brief thought that maybe he was afraid Danny might start beating him up or something, but all Danny was doing was paging through our mother's ridiculous document. Not knowing what else to do, I did the same.

I couldn't believe what was happening. Adoption seemed impossible at this point. So who did Frankie think was going to father my child? Was she so desperate that she was willing to have her daughter go out and whore herself

57

around in hopes of getting pregnant? This woman, who I'd been so close to my whole life was now a complete stranger. I truly believed my mother had completely lost her mind.

"What are you going to do?" Danny asked me, "Get back together with Max?"

"I guess I have to consider it." It was repulsive to think about, but I had to admit it was a valid option at this point. Eight million dollars seemed like a reward that may be too good to pass up. With that money, I could make my own movie and not have to deal with the agents and producers who kept rejecting me. I wouldn't need them anymore.

But I'd have to be married to Max and have a baby. But so what? I'd be independently wealthy. I could eventually get divorced, be professionally successful, and get lots of help with the baby from my crazy, nutty mother, who I was trying so hard not to despise at this moment.

"How about you?" I asked Danny, "Any ideas?"

"Yup," he replied.

"Tell me."

He took a deep breath and grinned, seeming almost triumphant. "I know someone who will have my baby in a second."

Chapter 8

My heart was racing while I knocked on Jennifer's door and waited for her to answer. I was scared as hell that the girl of my dreams, who lived just down the hall might walk out of her apartment and see the guy she kissed a few nights earlier standing at his ex-girlfriend's door.

What was I thinking taking this risk? I wondered. I was really pissed at my mother right now. But I was more pissed at myself. My night with Courtney had been unbelievable and I'd barely been able to get her off my mind. But now, here I was at Jennifer's place, selling out to psychotic Frankie, by agreeing to have a baby with someone I didn't love. My rationale was, in nine months I'd be a multi-millionaire.

I wondered when I'd become so money conscious. Years ago, I wouldn't have cared about getting my hands on Frankie's millions. If I was a person who wanted wealth, I wouldn't have majored in education. I'd have become a doctor, or a financial planner, or a consultant of some kind. But I didn't. I became a history teacher and I'd always been satisfied with it, one because I felt like I was making a difference in kids' lives, but also because I was having fun acting on the side, and I always believed that eventually I'd get my break and the wealth might come anyhow. But nothing was really progressing in my acting career and now, getting older, I realized I wanted things. I wanted to take fun trips and go to nice restaurants, and was it so bad for me at thirty-four years old to actually want to own a condo or a house? I realized right then that I'd changed over the years, and although it wasn't making me very proud of myself, I couldn't deny it.

I thought about asking Courtney to have my baby, but I didn't for two reasons. One, what if she had a really harsh reaction to the idea and decided she wanted nothing to do with me because my character had offended her so much? She seemed like a pretty moralistic person. Secondly, even though I'd spent only a few hours with the girl, my gut instinct told me there could be a future for us and I didn't want to taint or spoil it by putting her under pressure to have my child. I wanted things to progress naturally with us. Of course, if she found out Jennifer was having my baby, did I really think she'd want anything to do with me? Still, with eight million dollars at stake, it was a risk I was willing to take.

I heard a door slam and my heart stopped. I looked down the hallway and prayed it wasn't Courtney. Lucky for me, it was one of Jennifer's other neighbors. The guy gave me a nod as he passed by, and then pressed the elevator button and stood there. I knocked again, wondering what was taking her so long. A couple seconds later, Jennifer opened her door.

"Hi," she said with a wide, welcoming smile.

"Hi." I tried to sound enthusiastic about seeing her, but in reality, all I could think about was how much I didn't want to have sex with her. The only girl I wanted to be with, both physically and emotionally, lived literally 25 feet away from where I was standing, and was hopefully not home at this moment.

"Come in," said Jennifer, leading me into the apartment I'd been in at least a dozen times, the same apartment that now felt like a prison cell for me. "Sit down. Want a beer?"

"I'm good," I replied.

"You seem nervous."

"Well, the thing is..."

Jennifer sat down beside me and put her hand on my knee. "Tell me why you're here, Danny. Why'd you call and ask to come over?"

I looked right into her eyes. They seemed to be begging for me to say what I'd come here to say. I could tell her I wanted her to have my baby and we'd probably be in her bedroom with our clothes off within thirty seconds. I'd have sex with her for a few weeks, hopefully get her pregnant, and collect millions of dollars. It seemed simple, effortless, too easy, almost.

"Danny, talk to me," she said, "I miss you. I miss being with you," she began to seduce.

I opened my mouth and was about to deliver the news that would make this woman the happiest person on earth. The words "let's have a baby" were inside me. Actually, they were sitting there in my throat, waiting for my mouth to speak them. But I couldn't get them to come out.

"What?" she said with a soft giggle, "just tell me."

"I think..."

"Yeah?" She looked like the anticipation was going to kill her.

"I think..."

She was smiling from ear to ear, and I now found myself looking not at Jennifer's happy, hopeful face. All I could see was Courtney's face, the face that made me want to be the best guy in the world.

"I think I should go." Then I stood up. Jennifer turned white and the look on her face instantly went from hopeful to appalled.

"Why?" she managed, tears already forming in her eyes.

"I'm so sorry, Jen. I came here to...well...forget it. I was thinking..."

"Thinking you want me to have a baby?" she said, standing up and taking my face in her hands.

"I thought I could do it, but I just can't," I said sadly. I took her hands away and kissed them. Then I walked to the door, and just before I left I turned around and said, "I hope things work out for you. I really do."

It made me physically sick to see her standing there crying when I left, but the relief I felt was almost overwhelming. I looked down the hall toward Courtney's apartment and I knew I did the right thing.

Chapter 9

As I walked down Wells Street in my Nine West sandals (since my Jimmy Choos were no longer wearable), I passed all the trendy restaurants I'd eaten at over the years. I'd had so many good times on this street with girlfriends, dates, my ex-husband, John, and even Max. But tonight wasn't about a good time. Tonight was a job. My task of the evening; meet Max for dinner at *Topo Gigio* and get back together. Not because I loved him and realized I made a huge mistake breaking up with him, but for a reason that was unimaginably unethical; collect my insane mother's money. The anxiety I was feeling at this moment was ten times worse than it was the night I was headed to *Morton's* to get engaged.

Walking briskly and with determination, I suddenly bumped into something that caused pain so sharp, I could barely catch my breath.

"Are you okay?" I heard a woman shout.

When I turned to look at her, I realized I knew her. She was Jill Goldfarb, one of Ma's friend's daughters, and I had just slammed into her baby stroller.

"Jill…hi!" I exclaimed in the sweetest voice I could manage, given the fact that my thigh was now throbbing. I wanted to ask her why the hell she would park her stroller in the middle of the sidewalk, but I didn't want to be rude.

"Are you okay? I'm so sorry!"

"Oh, I'll be fine," I said, trying not to think about the big bruise I knew I'd have in the morning.

"So, how are you?" asked Jill in the same tone someone would use on a person who just found out she had six months to live.

What I felt like answering was "Yes, I'm still single and I actually don't want to commit suicide." Instead, I went with, "I'm good, you?"

"Great!" she responded, before adding in a condescending tone, "Glad to hear you're well."

"How's your baby?" I asked, wondering why its stroller was here, injuring me, and why the baby wasn't in it. I got my answer an instant later when I heard the loudest, most piercing cry I'd heard in years. Up walked Jill's husband, holding their one year-old little girl. The two had just come out of *Lori's Shoes* (which has a bathroom and a changing table in it).

"She had a big poopie," shouted Jill's husband. He actually had to yell, so we could hear him over the screaming kid.

"Emma missed her nap today," yelled Jill, "she's a little cranky." She took Emma from her husband. "Don't cry, sweetie," she said in a high squeaky baby voice. Emma continued to wail.

I managed to fake sympathy, replying, "Aww…"

Then the most unbelievable thing happened. As Jill tried to comfort her, Emma punched her mother in the face. Jill gasped and Emma kept screaming. The husband just stood there, not knowing what to do.

Revenge can be so gratifying, I thought. "Well, it was nice seeing you guys," I shouted enthusiastically, "Nice meeting you, Emma!" Then, with a wave and a smile, I was off.

I practically ran down the block, the entire way wondering how the hell, after experiencing Emma, I could be doing what I was about to do. I was on my way to meet Max, get back together with him, and then get married and pregnant a.s.a.p. Was I going to have an Emma soon? The thought of that was making me crave a Xanax in a huge way.

It wasn't that I didn't like kids. Even with what Emma had just done I thought she was cute. It was just that I was afraid of them. Having a child seemed like being out of control of a lot of things; something I wasn't very good at. And let's not forget the drilling in my head by my ex that I wasn't meant to be a mom. "I was too selfish. I liked my freedom, my independence." Looking back, I realized he was talking about himself. *He* was selfish. *He* liked his freedom, *his* independence. He also liked to sleep with other women (which I didn't know at the time) so that gave him little time for kids. And even though I realized the damage he'd done to my mental state, it was hard to recondition myself that maybe I *could* be a good mother.

When I reached the entrance of *Topo Gigio*, I pulled out my Bobbi Brown Truffle lipstick and reapplied. I realized I was sweating, combination nerves and Emma. Once inside, the smell of good old fashioned Italian cooking should have been appealing to me. Instead, I felt nauseous. I looked around the room and saw Max, already seated and drinking a glass of wine. He waved me over. It was funny. This was sort of déjà-vu of the *Morton's* night, only for some reason, Max didn't look nervous. He appeared relaxed.

I took a deep breath and approached his table. This was going to be torturous. I was going to have to apologize, stroke Max's ego and perhaps even grovel to get him back. Not that I thought it would be difficult. I was sure he'd get back together with me. Nonetheless, I would have to falsely admit I made a mistake and then tell Max I loved him, which was also untrue.

"Hi, sweetie," I said, just before kissing Max's cheek and sitting down across from him.

Surprisingly, his reception was cool, almost cocky. "Hi," was all he said. It was obvious his defenses were up, and now I realized that selling the idea of getting back together might take some effort.

Max promptly ordered me a glass of Shiraz, and I joked to the waiter (I wasn't really joking) "a big glass please."

The waiter rolled his eyes and Max didn't laugh. It was so awkward, I wanted to shoot myself.

After a few moments, Max finally threw me a bone. "You don't have to be so nervous, you know," he said, his tone semi-sweet.

"Thanks," I smiled back, humbleness in my voice.

After another moment of awkward silence, Max blurted out, "You want to get back together, don't you?"

I suddenly felt amazingly relieved. "Oh Max, thank you for making this easy. I could hug you!"

"No problem," is all he said.

Things couldn't have felt more uncomfortable. "Look, I realize I've hurt you deeply. But can you find forgiveness in your heart?"

He didn't answer. He just sat there staring at me. Was he deciding what to say? What to do? This was absolutely brutal!

Lucky for me, a minute later my drink arrived, which I gulped down almost entirely in one sip. When I put down the glass, Max had a smirk on his face.

"Please talk to me, Max. Tell me what you're thinking."

The next thing I heard was a woman's voice. "Took forever to find a spot!" she exclaimed. Was she talking to *us?* I was confused.

I turned and saw that a big-boned, slightly overweight blonde had appeared at our table. She kissed Max on the lips and sat down. "You must be Jamie!" she exclaimed, as she stuck out her hand to shake mine, "I'm Bonnie. I've seen you on WGB. You're adorable!"

Suddenly I was dizzy, and the wine had little to do with it. Bonnie was joining us for dinner? Things were fuzzy. What exactly was going on?

"Hi," I managed to say. I looked at Max, waiting for an explanation. All I got, though, was a polite smile, which pretty much expressed the joy he was getting from this whole situation.

What happened next took things to an even more bizarre level. "So," said Bonnie, taking her left ring finger and practically pushing it into my face, "What do you think?"

My mouth was hanging wide open. This chick was showing me her engagement ring! Even more shocking, it was the exact three-carat oval diamond ring Max had given me just days earlier. *My* ring was now sitting on Bonnie's pudgy finger.

I turned to Max, almost afraid to look at him, and asked gently, "You're engaged?"

Max then got the satisfaction he must have been dreaming about for days. "Yup," he said in a most self-assured voice, "Bonnie is the perfect woman for me." Then he put his arm around his girl and looked right into my eyes. The happy couple was glowing and smiling at me for what seemed like ten minutes.

In all the years I'd known Max, I'd never met Bonnie. And Bonnie had never known I was the reason Max broke up with her. Max and I had met through my ex-husband, John. John was a trader at the Chicago Board of Trade and Max was one of his clients. It was actually through Max that I found out John was cheating on me. I had been suspicious, but never had proof until one day.

"Honey," said my husband in a most sincere voice, "I won't be around tonight. I'm meeting Max for dinner at *Tavern on Rush.*"

"Really?" I asked him in the disappointed tone I now used so often, "Again?"

"Listen, Jamie, I'm trying to make money for us and that means working. Do you think I want to go to dinner with Max? It's work, not fun. Don't you think I would rather be with you?"

"Of course," I answered, although not quite convinced. John's words sounded so rehearsed and at the time, what I really felt like saying is, "No. I think you're full of shit." I held back, however, and decided to take his word for it, rationalizing the situation by reminding myself that Max was one of John's biggest clients, and that it would be good for John to wine and dine this guy, who I knew had tons of money and loved to trade.

So instead of acting like a needy wife, I decided to make some plans of my own for the night. After all, just because my guy wasn't available, it didn't mean I had to sit home. I called a couple of girlfriends and made plans to meet them for dinner at *Sunda*, a hip new place in River North.

That evening, decked out in my best *Hudson's,* a gold halter top, and three inch heels, I headed to the restaurant. While waiting for my friends to arrive, I ordered a dirty martini. Just as I put the rim of the glass to my lips, I got the shock of my life. There was Max, standing a few feet away. My eyes wide, my body frozen, and my mouth wide open, I knew instantly that tonight's events were setting the stage for the beginning of the end of John and me. I took a deep breath and walked over to Max.

"Hi," I said, praying Max would tell me they had a change of plans, that John was here, and that he was in the bathroom. I knew that was a fantasy, though.

"Jamie, hello!" Max replied, "Are you meeting John here?" He obviously had no clue that he was my husband's alibi for the night.

Tears instantly filled my eyes.

"Oh my God," said a confused Max, "What's wrong?"

I told Max about the lie.

"Are you kidding me?" he responded. He seemed really angry.

As I began to cry, Max comforted me. I could tell how sincerely upset he was about the situation. It was so strange. Max made me feel very calm. He felt like a big brother to me that night, staying with me until my friends arrived, and then per my wishes, putting me in a cab. Max also offered to cancel his plans and go somewhere with me and talk, but I declined. Instead I went home and waited for my scumbag of a husband to walk in the door, which he did at 3:00 a.m. Actually he didn't walk in, he staggered in.

I waited until the next morning to confront the very hung-over jerk, and after a lot of screaming, yelling, arguing and saying cruel things to each other, we decided we needed time apart. John moved out two days later, and shockingly, I barely heard from him again, except for a few random phone calls regarding legal documents that had to be signed. I found out later that John's cheating had been going on almost the entire time we'd known each other.

A few days after John left, Max called.

"John told me you guys split up," he began, "I want you to know that I closed my account with him. I will never do business with John or his firm, ever again."

"Really?" I asked, feeling both surprised and impressed by his decision.

"Absolutely," Max answered, "Knowing what I know now, I have a hard time trusting that guy. And trust is pretty darn important when you're playing with the kind of money I play with."

Max's voice was soft and gentle and it made me feel relaxed and at ease. Also, the fact that he had more money than anyone I knew made me feel safe with him. Not that money was a huge priority, but after what I'd just been through, wealth and stability seemed to go up on my list of important qualities in a guy.

I don't know exactly when it happened, but I soon found myself very attracted to Max. He made me feel like a little girl with a security blanket. He wasn't drop dead gorgeous, but he was a big guy. He wasn't witty and charming, but he was kind and gentle. And he wasn't sexy, but he was someone I could depend on. So when he asked me out for lunch I agreed, making it clear to him that I knew he had a girlfriend and our relationship had to stay strictly platonic, which was convenient for me since I wasn't interested in dating him (or anyone) anyhow.

Lunch led to another lunch the following week, which led to coffee a few days later, and then to dinner, a few days after that. Max and I were becoming friends but nothing more, mostly because there was no attraction on my part, but largely due to Bonnie, who he was planning to marry. So why was Max continuing to pursue me? It wasn't like he was cheating on Bonnie, yet Bonnie knew nothing about our relationship. And although it seemed a little bit wrong, I didn't care that much because I liked my new friend, and as long as we weren't physical with each other, technically there was no issue.

I needed Max's friendship. He listened, he cared, and he made me feel good about myself. He idolized me, and that was such a foreign feeling. And according to my mother, who was Max's number one fan from day one, it was healthy.

Our get-togethers continued platonic for a couple months, until one night. I invited him to the U2 concert at Soldier Field. Someone at the station had gotten a bunch of free tickets and had offered two to me. For some reason, I really wanted to take Max. We had a great time. I was surprised at how much fun he could be. I was also impressed (and shocked) that he knew most of the songs.

After the concert, we decided to continue the festivities, hitting the bars until they closed. I couldn't believe it. Straight-laced, nerdy Max was actually really fun. I found myself having a great time. Max wasn't a stud or anything, but he was tall and big, and when I was next to him I felt protected. And after a few cocktails, and the lonely feeling of not having had sex for almost six months, I felt attracted to him. We ended up in bed that night.

Now, I have to admit, part of me felt sick about being "the other woman." I had been so disgusted by my cheating, slimy husband, and now I was just like one of the many women who slept with him when she knew he was married. Bimbo was the word that kept coming into my brain to describe myself. I also felt sorry for Bonnie, because she was me. She would find out that her boyfriend cheated on her, breaking a bond of trust that could never be repaired.

But when Max told me the next morning that he was breaking up with her, and that it had absolutely nothing to do with me, I felt a little bit better.

"Jamie," he said, holding my hands, "Even if I never met you, the fact that I was able to form a friendship with another women like I have with you, has made me realize that my emotional connection with Bonnie is lacking. I promise you, even if I'd never met you, I'd be ending the relationship."

"Are you sure?"

"Absolutely." He gave me a big grin and said, "I don't feel the spark with her. And every time I see *you*, I can barely breathe."

That day, Max drove over to Bonnie's place and broke up with her.

"Bonnie," he said holding her hand, "You know how much I love you, it's just that I need some time to go out there and have fun. I hope you understand."

Naturally, Bonnie was devastated. According to Max, however, she did make a bold statement. "You go out there and date around. I'm okay with that. You know why?" She looked him right in the eyes and said, "Because I guarantee you'll be back."

As fate would have it, and surprising to all three of us, Bonnie had turned out to be right. Here I was, sitting at a table with her, staring at the hand-me-down engagement ring.

Physically, Bonnie was nothing like Max had described her. Max made her sound like she was three hundred pounds and looked like Valerie Bertinelli (but blonde) pre

Jenny Craig. I couldn't have disagreed more. The woman sitting next to me had a nice body. Yes, Bonnie was a bigger girl, but she was very attractive. Plus, she was dressed well, had good hair with nice highlights, and was extremely well accessorized with three long silver chains around her neck and her Philip Stein watch.

Max was waiting for my response to his news, and was enjoying it oh so much. The first thing I did was put my ring-less hand up to call for the waiter. He came right over and I ordered another wine.

"Max, what do I want?" asked Bonnie.

This was so typical. Bonnie listened to everything Max said. Even more peculiar, she actually did everything Max told her to do. Literally! When she arrived at the table and said, "Took forever to find a spot," Bonnie didn't mean for her own car, she meant for Max's car. Max had actually asked her to drop him off at the restaurant and drive around looking for a spot while he came in to meet me. And she did it.

"She'll have the house Merlot," Max told the waiter.

"Isn't it beautiful?" Bonnie asked excitedly, as she stuck my old ring about an inch from my face again. "Max told me you were the one who said we should get back together. You're such a good friend to him! I'm so grateful I could kiss you!" she practically screamed.

"Then do it," said her commander.

So Bonnie reached over, grabbed my face, and planted a huge kiss on my lips.

I think I was more confused than shocked. All I could do was gaze at both my old boyfriend and his new fiancé. Max had a look of satisfaction on his face, and I realized just then how little I really knew him. He wasn't the sweet, loveable guy I thought he was. He was out for blood.

"You know what I love about Bonnie?" he gloated, "She goes along with anything I say." Then he kissed her on the lips. "I love you pookie poo-poo."

"Not as much as I love you, pookie pee-pee," Bonnie answered in a baby voice.

Nausea came over me. Pookie what?

"Pookie, I forgot my *iphone* in the car," Max said lovingly, "Would you be a pookie poo and go get it?"

"Anything for you, Poo."

What language were they speaking? I wondered. Pookinese?

Bonnie got up and when she spoke again her voice went back to normal, since she was talking to both of us. "I might be awhile. I parked pretty far away."

"You're the best, pookie," Max yelled to her as she walked away. Alone at last. Max didn't wait long before speaking. It was obvious he didn't want to waste any precious gloating time.

"Happy for me?" he asked me.

"It's only been a week!" I exclaimed.

"Hey, you're the one who said I should do it, remember?" "How could you give her my ring?"

"Actually, it's *my* ring. And now, it's *Bonnie's* ring."

I couldn't even respond. All I could do was continue drinking. I was fresh out of things to say. I wasn't hurt, I was surprised. And I wasn't angry, I was bummed. Not because I lost Max, but because if I wanted Frankie's money, I now had to go to plan B.

I could feel Max staring at me as I gulped down the last bit of wine left in my glass. Now the glass was empty, literally and figuratively. Not half empty, all the way empty. That is, until I looked up and saw Drew Conrad walk into the place and sit down at the bar. Now the glass in my mind was suddenly half full. The wheels started to spin. My depression suddenly turned to optimism as I watched the gorgeous camera man sit down at the bar. Even better, the waiter appeared with another wine for me. Now the glass was completely full, literally and figuratively and I was feeling better by the second.

"Thank you!" I said to the waiter with delight. Then I gulped down about half the glass. I was busy drinking, but I could hear Max mumbling something about me being a lush. But who cared what he was saying? I giggled to myself. I placed the glass down on the table and stood up.

"Good-bye, pookie poo poo," I smiled, "Have a nice life."

Max didn't look happy to see me go. "You're leaving?" Obviously he wasn't done rubbing it in.

I pulled out the *Bobbi Brown* Truffle again and put on another coat. Then I pulled my shoulders back, took a deep breath and said with all the confidence I could muster, "I've got work to do." Then I headed to the bar to approach my prey.

Chapter 10

For me to dress up like a chocolate covered pretzel, obviously I was hurting for money. Yes, me, Danny Jacobson, history teacher at Martin Luther King High School, 34 year-old upstanding citizen, was now spending my weekends dressed in a pretzel costume, handing out chocolate covered pretzels on Michigan Avenue.

I was working for **Pretzel Perfection**, *a tiny, no-frills candy shop, but nonetheless, a gold mine. Vito, the owner, kept the door propped open and the smell of chocolate that came out of there was delicious enough to explain the constant line of customers.*

On the sidewalk in front of the shop was where I handed out the samples. It wasn't a bad gig, except for the costume. I had to wear brown shoes, brown tights and a brown cap. The worst part was, around my middle was a big, thick pillow, shaped like a pretzel. The fabric was brown with multi-colored felt sprinkles pasted to it. I felt like a total idiot. Still, I needed the cash, so I did it.

"Chocolate covered pretzels...the best in Chicago!" I shouted, trying unsuccessfully to be enthusiastic. "Pretzels...chocolate-covered...delicious!" I continued to call out in a monotone voice, as I handed two of the little packets to a young couple.

How did I get here? I kept thinking while I worked. I'm a school teacher, one of the most respected professions out there, not to mention a gifted actor. Is dressing up like a chocolate covered pretzel the best job I can get? Would I ever get to play a respectable role? And now, with Jennifer gone, did I even have a chance at any roles?

"Delicious chocolate-covered pretzels..." I continued, realizing at that moment I might be the only person on earth who didn't like chocolate.

All of a sudden, wearing a chef's hat and an apron, Vito stormed out of the store.

"Listen, I can hear you from in there," he shouted in his thick Italian accent.

"So?" I answered.

"So you suck," he replied angrily, "Get a little more excited, would you?" Before I could respond, Vito grabbed the samples out of my hands, took over and started soliciting.

"Thick, chocolaty, creamy chocolate covered pretzels!" he shouted with extreme enthusiasm.

Two women passing by responded instantly, taking the samples with delight.

"Frighteningly fattening," he continued, "but oh...so amazingly delicious!"

"Thank you!" an older lady said as she took the sample and started to open it.

Vito handed the basket of the pretzels back to the pretzel. "Get it?" he asked me, "I thought you were an actor."

"I am."

"Then act!" he yelled, as he turned around and stomped back into his shop.

Vito was an older guy whose father (also named Vito) had started **Vito's Pretzels** on Chicago's south side in 1950. The first Vito had been in the candy business in Florence, working out of his

78

small kitchen and selling boxes of chocolate around the town. He had moved to the states after his brother, Frank (who had moved here a few years before) offered him a job as a baker in the small Italian grocery store he had opened. It sounded like a great plan. Vito even planned on continuing to make his chocolates and sell them in the store to make extra money.

However, when Vito showed up as scheduled at his brother's store, the sign on the door read "closed." Turns out, Frank's grocery store was a cover for what became a huge money laundering venue for the local mob. Frank ended up in jail. Luckily for Vito, his parents had given him some extra money to get by until he could stand on his own. So Vito ended up starting Vito's pretzels.

Vito had died a few years earlier leaving the business to his only son, Vito, who ironically was a bookie at the time, but had always paid attention to his dad's recipes. Vito junior quit his bad-boy profession and took over the business. No one could believe how talented he was in the kitchen. Plus, Vito was a great businessman. With no education past high-school and no legitimate business experience, Vito ran his dad's business better than any Harvard Business School grad could have. In fact, business was so good that Vito eventually moved Vito's Pretzels *from the south side to ritzy Michigan Avenue. And along with the new address came the new name,* Pretzel Perfection.

Knowing Vito's history, as much as the guy bugged me, I had respect for him. Vito took a very average business and made it extremely lucrative. Vito was a go-getter. He knew how sell himself. He knew how to find out what people wanted and he knew how to provide it. I couldn't help but think that if Vito was in my shoes, he'd find a way to get Ma's money. Unlike me, he'd figure it out.

As I tried to emulate Vito's sales techniques, I again wondered how things had gotten to a point where I was forced to dress up as Mr. Salty. I couldn't have felt worse. That is until I looked up and saw Courtney walking toward me with a big smile on her face. She was dressed in a black suit and high heeled pumps. Her hair was pulled back and she looked stunning.

"Do I get one?" she flirted with me.

I pretty much wanted to die. "Uh, sure." I handed her a sample, which she immediately opened.

"What's with the get up?" she inquired.

"I like dressing like this," I joked, "Girls dig it."

She giggled and right then I heard Vito shout from inside the store, "Hey pretzel man, enough with the ladies! Get back to work!"

Now I wondered if I should go in there and kick his ass or just kill myself, so I wouldn't have to face this intense humiliation.

"So, how are you?" I asked her.

"Pretty good."

"Sorry we've been playing phone tag."

"Me too."

I was just about to ask her out when I heard, "Time's up, pretzel boy!"

"Okay! Okay!" I shouted back. Then I turned to Courtney. "Look, when can we get together?"

"How about tonight?"

"Sure," I exclaimed, "I'll text you later. Does 7:30 sound good?"

"Sure," she smiled, "Can I have another pretzel?"

I handed her several samples and watched her walk down the block. This girl I barely knew was doing something to me and I didn't know how to stop it. And didn't want to. It wasn't just her physical appearance. There was something inside of her that felt comfortable to me. It felt natural. And at the same time, it was electrifying. Yes, Courtney had her hands on my heart, and I had no clue as to how that happened. Was it timing? Was it fate? Was it love? I wasn't sure, but I did know one thing. Courtney had awakened feelings in me I never knew existed. And I liked it. I liked it a lot.

"The most amazing, unbelievable, incredible pretzels you've ever had!" *I suddenly shouted out with more energy than I'd had all day (or all year, for that matter) thanks to Courtney's brief presence. I handed a few samples to passersby and then continued, "Pretzels that will please everyone's palate!" I went on, "Serve these at your next party and your guests will be begging you for more!" My voice was getting louder and louder, and I was really getting into it now, which was satisfying my boss.*

"Now that's a good salesman!" I heard Vito shout.

"There's only one word to describe these things," I continued. An older woman stopped, waiting for her sample, but also waiting for my word. When I spoke, she put her hand over her heart. With a laugh, I shouted, "Orgasmic!"

Chapter 11

The price of a hot dog at Rockit, *a trendy bar and restaurant in River North is sixteen dollars, no joke. The place does really well, though, and I don't know if it's because David Schwimmer is part owner and several celebrities hang out there, or if the dozens of different cutesy, frilly martinis on its menu attract customers. Whatever the reason,* Rockit *is a huge hot spot, and at the time, seemed like the perfect place for my first official date with Courtney.*

"This is so good," she said, as she munched on the popcorn rock shrimp that came with four different dipping sauces. I loved watching her chew. Those lips... As usual, she looked hot, wearing a brown sleeveless lace tank and jeans that looked like a size zero. In my opinion, Courtney had definitely mastered the art of dressing. She had a way of looking sexy, but not slutty, classy but not boring, and simple but not unoriginal.

"How's your hot dog?" she asked.

"Great," I replied, "Since all I've eaten today is a few chocolate covered pretzels."

Courtney smiled.

"Can I ask you something?"

"Sure," she replied.

"Does it bother you?"

"Does what bother me?"

"That I dress up like a chocolate covered pretzel and take shit from Tony Soprano."

"Why would it bother me?"

"Does it embarrass you?"

"Danny, are you crazy? I understand. You need the money. I respect that. And what I respect even more is that you're a history teacher. I want to hear more about that."

"Well, I really do like it. I feel like I'm good with the kids. They like me, I think. And I like the fact that I have the ability to make a difference in their lives."

"I admire that so much."

"It gets really hard at times, though. One of my best students is pregnant right now and she's thinking of dropping out. It's killing me. I have to find a way to get her to stay in school."

"That must be frustrating," said Courtney.

"And then there's the whole money thing. I mean, I like going out and doing things, and I'm getting older. I want to have the means to buy things and travel. And being a teacher, I'll never make any serious money. That's part of my attraction to acting."

"I could see that, but I think you'd miss teaching if you ever left."

"You think?"

"Sure. You're doing something productive. You're making a difference. You can go to bed every night thinking that you've done the world some good today. That's a gift."

I smiled at this awesome girl sitting across from me, beautiful on the outside, yes, but so sweet, so moralistic, pure, almost. She was so good for me. She made me feel good about myself. She made me like myself.

"Thanks," I smiled, "I have something to tell you."

"Okay."

"My mom...she won the lottery."

Courtney gasped. "That cute lady is your mother?"

"Yeah," I answered.

"Wow!"

I chuckled. "Yeah, I know."

"And...the thing is..." I was about to tell her about Ma's ridiculous bribe but the words wouldn't come out. I was afraid she'd judge me for even considering going along with it. And I was afraid she'd judge my mother. She'd have to be wondering, what kind of a crazy person would put this kind of pressure on her kids.

Courtney was ambitious, but she didn't strike me as the money-hungry type. She seemed like she believed in hard work and earning a paycheck independently, not taking money from your mother for knocking up a chick.

"Forget it," I said.

"No, tell me," she urged.

"No, it's okay. Tell me something about you. Something no one knows."

"That's easy," she said. Courtney then took a big gulp of her raspberry mojito, and suddenly I sensed nervousness. She waited a few seconds and then blurted out, *"I can't have kids."*

At first it didn't sink in. *"What do you mean?"* I asked.

"I can't have kids," she repeated. She began explaining that she had a condition that I might or might not have heard of called endometriosis, but I couldn't concentrate on what she was saying. I just kept hearing, *"I can't have kids...I can't have kids...I can't have kids."*

It now hit me. I was sitting here on a date with a girl I was nuts about, who I had hopes might someday have my child, who might help me collect Frankie's millions and at the same time, be my significant other. And now, that plan was shot to hell.

She continued, *"My chances of having a baby, even through in-vitro, are like one in ten thousand."*

85

I sat there semi-listening to her, but still hearing only "I can't have kids...I can't have kids..."

"Are you okay?" she asked me, "Say something."

"Like what?"

"How about I'm sorry, or what a bummer, or..."

"Or what?"

"Or it doesn't make a difference to me, I support adoption."

The truth was, I DID support adoption, and ordinarily, I would have been perfectly fine with having a girlfriend who couldn't have kids, not only because settling down and having kids was eons away for me anyhow, but because I didn't see the difference between a biological child and an adopted one. Either way, if a dude was a dad, he was a dad. Frankly, it didn't seem to matter to me where the kid came from. But now, under pressure and time constraints from my dear, sweet mother, who was on course to drive me to insanity, I wasn't sure if I was cool with the fact that Courtney couldn't give me what I now needed a.s.a.p.

I didn't want to upset this girl, who made me want to do cartwheels around the restaurant, so I answered, "Look, I have a lot going on right now, and I don't really want to talk about it. But, yes, that's true. It doesn't make a difference to me and I DO support adoption."

With tears in her eyes, she replied, "Thanks."

"And Courtney..."

"Yeah?"

"I AM sorry you can't have kids. It must be hard."

She gave me a really sweet smile, and at that moment I realized I had a huge dilemma, and that it all came down to one question. What was more important to me, money or love?

Chapter 12

Rockit has two eating areas, one upstairs and one downstairs. Drew and I were eating downstairs. I was enjoying my fried tilapia sandwich and he was eating a Kobe beef burger. I had no idea at the time that my brother and Courtney were right upstairs.

My date with the prospective father of my child was going pretty well, which wasn't surprising. There had been chemistry between Drew and me for years, so the odds that it would sustain itself in a bar/restaurant atmosphere were pretty good. That being said, I was nervous because the stakes were high. This date had to turn out fabulously. We had to hit it off, or at least *he* had to think we were hitting it off if I was going to seduce him and eventually have his baby.

Drew and I had ended up talking for over an hour the night I ran into him at *Topo Gigio*. In fact, the way we were flirting with each other, it would have been easy for me to take him home and sleep with him that night. I didn't want to do that, though, because I realized that getting pregnant took more than a one-night stand, unless of course, I was on *Days of Our Lives.*

I couldn't take a chance that Drew would think I was easy, possibly causing him to lose interest. That's why I knew I'd have to go the whole nine yards and feign a romantic relationship with him. So after a couple drinks that night, I told him I was tired. While kissing him good night on the cheek, I whispered in his ear, "I'd really like to see you again, and not just in the office." I actually felt like I deserved an Academy award for my genius seduction technique.

The next day at work, however, I was shocked. Drew didn't talk to me all day. No visits to my office, no following me around, not even in the minutes just before the lottery drawing when Drew was doing a white balance of me, did he mention anything about the night before.

It wasn't until late in the day that I heard from him. I was in my office checking my e-mail and scrolling down the list of new e-mails, past the daily rejection letters from agents and producers and past some junk, when I came upon one from: DrewC@WGBstudios.com. My heart skipped a beat. In all the years we'd worked together, Drew had never e-mailed me. There had never been a reason. Now, apparently, there was.

I clicked on it. It read, "I'd really like to see you again too, and not just in the office." And that is how Drew Conrad, a guy I swore I'd never go out with, ended up seated across from me at trendy *Rockit.*

"So tell me about Max," Drew said.

"What about him?"

"Why'd you dump him?"

"I didn't dump him. I broke up with him. There's a difference."

"Okay, why'd you break up with him?"

"Because I didn't love him."

Drew put his burger down and began clapping his hands.

"Stop," I said with a giggle, scanning the room to see if anyone was looking at us.

Drew laughed, "I'm giving you a round of applause for finally realizing that."

I smiled.

He went on, "And for realizing you and I needed to give it a shot."

My smile vanished instantly, the look on my face turning to terror.

"Why are you so afraid of me? Actually, why are you so afraid of men? Was your ex-husband that much of an asshole?"

"Yes, he was. Subject change. Did you hear about Kevin Beckerman? He's leaving the station and going to work for WLS radio."

"I don't give a shit about Kevin Beckerman," he said. Then he looked me right in the eyes and said softly, "Talk to me," and I pretty much found myself melting. I wanted so badly to open up to him. I couldn't, though. This was business.

"I'm not afraid of men."

"Well, you don't really like them."

"Why do say that?"

"Two words. Lucy Chi."

"What about Lucy Chi?" I asked, although I already knew he had me.

Lucy Chi was the entertainment reporter for WGB. About a year earlier, she was dating a guy she thought she was probably going to marry. She brought him into the station to meet everyone on a Friday afternoon, seeking approval from all of her co-workers. So on Monday morning, she popped her head in my office and asked, "What'd ya think?"

I stopped what I was doing (checking my e-mail rejection letters) to give Lucy my full attention, and said, "He seems great."

"What about looks?" she asked next, "Do you think he's cute?"

"Very," I said with lots of enthusiasm. He really was.

"Thanks, girlfriend!" Lucy said with a smile, as she moved on to hear other opinions.

At that moment Drew walked into my office. He yelled after Lucy as she walked down the hall. "He's a hottie, Lucy!"

Lucy turned around. "Thanks, sweetie!" She was ecstatic.

"I'm happy for her," he said to me, "The guy seemed pretty cool, huh?"

I barely looked up from my computer. "Looza..." I said.

"What?" Drew defended, "No! He seemed like a good guy!"

"Whatever," I said, apathetically and without looking up.

"Am I missing something?" asked Drew.

I finally looked up. "He seems too perfect. You know, too nice, too good looking, too...I don't know. What's the word I'm looking for?"

"Bitchy?" said Drew with a chuckle.

"What?"

"Sorry, I thought you were looking for a word for yourself," he joked.

"I just don't trust guys like that." And that was the end of the conversation.

Lucy Chi ended up marrying the guy. Currently, she's pregnant with twins.

"Okay, fine," I said to Drew, "I was wrong about Lucy Chi's husband. But there are a lot of jerks out there."

"And there are a lot of really great guys, too. Like me!"

God, he was cute! But he wasn't marriage material. He wasn't polished. Or ambitious. And he wasn't Jewish. Ma would hate him, I kept thinking. But I didn't hate him. I liked him. And now, I needed him. And as sad as it was to say, I needed his sperm. I wanted to kill my mother right now. I wanted to shout, "How could you do this to me?!"

But then I had a really nice thought. I realized right then, if Drew did end up getting me pregnant, and if I did have his baby, I wouldn't only get Frankie's money, but I'd get sweet revenge, as well, because if Drew was the father of my child, he would be in our lives forever. Frankie would have to see him all the time! That was the silver lining.

"So, how about you, Drew? Have you ever been in love?"

"Twice. My first love was Mrs. Lefler, my fourth grade math teacher, and the second was Monica McGrath." He paused for a second to reflect. "She broke my heart."

A girl breaking his heart? I couldn't even imagine, but he looked really somber at this moment. "Tell me about Ms. McGrath," I said.

"Actually, I was talking about Mrs. Lefler," he joked, "She wasn't that much older than me, you know. I was nine, she was twenty-five or so. It could have worked."

As I sat here laughing, I felt like I was out to dinner with a good friend. "So seriously, tell me about Monica," I said.

When Drew responded to the question by chugging his martini, I knew it was going to be a bad story. He began, "Monica and I met at a bar several years ago, and we dated for awhile. We were getting pretty serious. I mean, I went nuts over this girl."

"That sounds pretty good so far," I said.

"It was." He then took a deep breath before continuing, "Then I introduced her to my family. My dad and my brother."

Silence. It seemed as if Drew couldn't even go on.

"Oh, I get it," I said, "They didn't get along with her."

Drew let out a fake laugh. "Actually, it was just the opposite." He took a big chug of his drink. "Monica and my dad hit it off a little too well, and...they ended up getting married."

"What?" I asked in disbelief.

Drew just nodded and smiled sadly.

"Why didn't you ever tell me? I mean, I knew you then, right?"

"Yeah. I think it happened right before I started at the station. I kept it to myself. It was just really personal. And embarrassing."

"I'm really sorry," I said softly.

"Thanks. I'm cool with it. They're still together so I guess they're really in love."

"Can I order another drink?" I asked. Then, as if we were on cue, we both just burst out laughing. The two of us laughed and laughed for a long time. And it felt really good. And I think it felt good for Drew, too.

After we were able to control our laughing attacks, I said, "I still can't believe you've never said anything about her, in all the time we've known each other. Is that the reason you never have girlfriends?"

"I have girlfriends."

"Yeah, for like a week at the most. You're like my brother. He's a commitment-phobe too."

"I'm not a commitment-phobe."

"Drew..."

"Yeah?"

"I wish you would have told me," I said.

"It's okay," he said, looking right at me with a grin.

I put my hand on his. This was the best first date I'd had in years. I'd gone into this for sex, a baby and eight million dollars, never expecting to really enjoy the person I was using to get it all.

Then, just as I was about to suggest that we go back to my place, Drew pulled his hand away and began to hold his stomach. My first thought was that the story he'd just told me upset him so much, that he was going to be sick. Seconds later, he looked like he was in pain.

"Are you okay?" I asked.

"I'm fine." He was unconvincing. "Can I ask you something, Jamie?"

"Sure."

"Why are you here with me? I mean, why now, after all this time are you interested in me?" he asked.

"How do you know I'm interested in you? Maybe I just wanted a free dinner," I joked in an attempt not to blow my cover.

Drew smiled at my humor, but wouldn't give up. "Seriously. Tell me. Why now?"

I started to panic. What was I going to say? Lucky for me, I didn't have to say anything because Drew started to hold his stomach again.

"Are you sure you're okay?"

He stood up. "Actually, no!" Then he ran from the table and made a b-line straight for the men's room. I didn't want him to be sick, but I was hoping he wouldn't be back for a few minutes, so I could have time to make up a lie.

Chapter 13

In my opinion, food poisoning is the number one excuse to get out of a date. It's the perfect illness to get when you need a quick exit from a bad situation. It comes on quickly and doesn't last for more than twenty-four hours, so if you run into the girl or any of her friends the next night, there's no reason for them not to believe you're feeling back to normal and well enough to be out. I shared my theory with Jamie when she told me Drew got food poisoning and had to leave the restaurant the night before.

"I really don't think he was faking," she responded.

"Then why didn't YOU get food poisoning, too?" I asked her.

"We ate different things," she explained, "I had tilapia, he had Kobe beef. I've heard of a lot of people getting sick from that."

The two of us were sitting cross-legged on the wood floor in the middle of our mother's almost empty condo. There was barely any furniture left in her place, as Ma was executing her other post lottery winning plan; re-decorating her condo. She had hired a decorator and earlier in the week, the two of them had bought several floor samples from various furniture stores around Chicago. So, all new furniture was being delivered from Ethan Allen, Macy's, *and* Walter E Smithe.

As Jamie and I talked about the specifics of what Kobe beef really is, we could hear Ma talking on the phone in the kitchen.

"I'm interested in the Royal Ruby Metallic," she was saying.

"What's she talking about?" asked Jamie.

"No clue."

Ma spoke again. "Well, what colors do you have in stock?"

"It sounds like she's buying a car!" Jamie exclaimed.

"I am," answered Ma, as she burst into the room, the phone still up to her ear. "Sorry," she said into the phone, "I was talking to my children. What were you saying? I heard Golden Almond Metallic and Black something."

When I saw my mother walk in, I couldn't believe it. She looked almost transformed. Dressed in high heels and a very expensive looking suit, she strutted across the room with confidence, showing off her brand new look. Her hair was different, she had more make up on than usual, and she had this air about her that was filled with self-pride.

Don't get me wrong. Frankie had always been a pretty woman, especially when she was younger. And even as she was aging, she had always stayed thin, and she had always kept herself looking good. She didn't overdo it, didn't wear a lot of make-up, didn't buy expensive clothes, and wasn't into plastic surgery (unlike most of her friends) but she always looked nice. Ma was naturally pretty. She didn't have to try. And she would always say, "The women who have money to burn are the ones who look the best." Now, Frankie Jacobson was a woman who had money to burn and it showed. Nevertheless, as shocked as I was about her appearance, I had to admit she looked pretty damn good.

"Ma, what's the deal? New hair? New clothes?" I asked her.

Frankie put her hand over the mouthpiece. "Shhh, give me a second," she scolded. Then her hand came off the mouthpiece and she resumed her conversation. "Golden Almond Metallic sounds pretty. I'd like to see that one."

"You're buying a car?" I asked.

Frankie nodded as she wrapped things up. "That sounds great. I'll see you tomorrow at nine?"

Now I was flipping out. "Ma!"

"Shhh!"

"Thank you very much," she said, ending the call, "I'll see you in the morning."

"Hi kids. Get up. I can't bend down to kiss you."

Both Jamie and I obliged.

"What are you buying?" Jamie asked.

"A Lexus," Frankie said proudly.

"Why?" I asked.

"Because I can," she answered, sounding annoyed.

"You look so beautiful," said Jamie, "Your hair..."

"Your suit..." I added.

Frankie modeled her new look by giving us a quick twirl. "You like it? It's Chanel." Then she brushed the palm of her hand by the bottom of her bob. "And I got my hair done at **Elizabeth Arden**.*"*

She said **Elizabeth Arden** *like it was our first time hearing it.*

"You look nice, Ma," I smiled, "You really do."

"How's the baby-making coming along?" Frankie asked, "Any news yet?"

"Ma, it's only been a couple weeks!" Jamie answered.

Just then, Frankie's phone rang again. She looked at the caller ID.

"I need to take this. Tiffany's..." Then she answered, "Hello? Yes, this is Frankie Jacobson. Thank you for returning my call." She continued her conversation while she walked out of the room again.

Jamie and I sat back down on the floor. Now I was completely bugged.

"Why are we bothering to try to have kids?" I said loudly, in hopes my mother would hear, "she's going to spend it all!"

"*Do you remember when grandma first moved in with us?*" Jamie asked me.

"*How could I forget?*"

"*Nice attitude.*"

"*Sorry. Yes, I remember. Why?*"

"*I was pretty young and I don't really remember our lives before grandma moved in. But I do remember something very clearly; you, me, and grandma sitting on the couch...grandma in the middle... and she would be scratching both of our backs at the same time.*"

The memory of this made me grin. "*Yeah, I remember that.*"

"*And mom wasn't around that much. Where was she?*"

"*She was working.*"

"*That's my point,*" said my sister, "*She was working all the time. Think about it, Danny. She ran the gift basket business out of our basement, and she also worked for Dr. Schneider. Cut the woman some slack. She's struggled for money her whole life. Now it's time for her to spend HER money and enjoy it.*"

I realized my sister was right. The woman who had started and maintained a gift basket business out of our house, who was also a receptionist in a dentist's office, all to support us financially and to be able to send us to college, truly deserved the money she'd won.

"*Look,*" I replied, "*I'm happy for our nouveau riche mother. But I still strongly object to her using her new money to bribe us and ruin our lives.*"

"*How's that going for you?*"

"*Well, I'm totally into this girl and wouldn't you know, she can't have kids.*"

"*Really?*"

"*Ironic, huh?*"

"*I'm actually more surprised that you just said you're into a girl,*" said my sister.

"*I know. I can't believe it either.*"

"*So what are you going to do?*"

"Well, actually, I broke up with her."

I put my head down as I thought about how disgusted I was in myself. I'd called Courtney that morning and told her I couldn't see her anymore.

"I really like you, it's just that I've got major issues and I need to deal with them."

Her response had been like taking a bullet. She'd said, "It's because I can't have kids, isn't it?"

"No, I swear!" I'd defended myself.

"Danny, you don't have to explain anything to me. I'm really sad about this, but I'll be okay. I get it." She finished with a sad chuckle, "You're holding out." Then she hung up and I'd wanted to shoot myself.

"So I guess I'm choosing money over love," I said to Jamie.

"You don't have to," she said, pity in her eyes.

"Yes, I do," I replied, "I want to have money. I'm thirty-four years old and I live in a shoe box. I'm tired of struggling. I'm tired of dressing up as a fucking pretzel on the weekends. As far as women, it never works out with them anyhow. So I'm picking the sure thing. Cash."

When I said it never works out with women, Jamie knew exactly what (or I should say, who) I was talking about; Jillian, the only girl I'd ever loved.

I met Jillian while living in New York. It was at a wine-tasting event. Actually, Jillian was a guest at the event and I was a wine pourer. She tapped me on the shoulder and asked me for a pour of the 1998 Blackstone Cabernet I had in my hand. When I looked at her I went numb. She was so cute! I could tell by the look on her face that she wanted more than just a glass of wine. So I asked her for her phone number.

Typically, I'd have asked her to stay until my shift was over with the intent to take her home with me. But I wasn't in a hurry with Jillian. She seemed sweet and pure. Shit, how could she not be? She was a pre-school teacher! I was sure she'd never had a one-night stand in her life. So, as unusual as it was for me, I chose to ask her out on a date, not caring if we were going to have sex afterward.

We ended up going out and having a great time. At the end of the night, all I got was a light peck on the cheek, and that suited me just fine. We went out for the next five nights in a row, and every night I got a peck, until the fifth night. Jillian took me to bed. I finally got to touch this beautiful girl. And to my surprise, it wasn't at all what I expected. It was better. I was in love with her. I knew it right then.

We dated for a few months. Things couldn't have been better. Then, like an unexpected hurricane, Jillian's old boyfriend came back into the picture. The guy started pursuing her, calling all the time, sending flowers every other day, and showing up at her place, even when he knew I was there. In my opinion, the guy was a stalker and Jillian should have called the cops and had him arrested. She didn't, though. Jillian didn't see her ex as a psycho. She was actually touched by all his efforts. I couldn't believe how she kept defending him.

"Please don't hate him, Danny," she would say, "He was really confused when he broke up with me. He's different now."

Speaking of "different now", that's what I was starting to think about my girlfriend. She had no backbone. The old boyfriend had dumped her a couple years back and married some other girl. Now he was divorced and back to claim in his words, "the one who got away." Jillian was taking his side more and more, and things between us were becoming rocky.

Finally, one night when we got back from dinner, the guy was waiting in her lobby, holding up a big jam box over his head like John Cusack did in the movie, "Say Anything." The second he saw Jillian, he put the box on the doorman's counter for a second, pressed play and put the box back on his head. The song, "In Your

Eyes" began to play. I couldn't believe it. The doorman just sat there, and Jillian began to cry. Apparently, "Say Anything" was both Jillian and the guy's favorite movie. All I could do was walk away. The sad part was, Jillian and her ex didn't even notice me leaving. To this day, I can't even look at John Cusack.

When I moved back to Chicago, I was still heartbroken about Jillian. And looking back, I think I made a subconscious decision to take my pain out on every other woman in the world by keeping them at arm's length, never allowing myself to be vulnerable again. Yes, with women I was charming and sweet on the surface, but when it came to any kind of commitment, or being someone any girl could depend on for anything other than a good time under the sheets, I had mentally checked out.

Except for Courtney. She made me want to be one of the good guys again. Courtney had changed me from the guy who didn't care to the guy who cared deeply. But now, like my mother's sudden physical transformation, I'd quickly changed back to the coward.

"Look, Jamie, we're not talking about a few hundred dollars. This is EIGHT MILLION BUCKS. Yeah, I like this girl, but I don't even know her. Is she really worth risking that kind of money?"

"Only you can answer that," said my sister.

"My mind's made up. I made a few calls and I have three dates lined up this week. I don't want to do it, but I am." I put my head down in shame and added, "Just so you know, I hate myself right now."

All of a sudden, I heard a guy shout, "Jacobson?" I looked at the propped open door and there stood a guy holding a clipboard.

"That's us," I answered.

"Delivery from Macy's," said the guy, "I need a signature before I bring it in."

"I'll sign," said Jamie, standing up, "My mother's on the phone in the other room."

A few minutes later, two guys were coming through the door. "Hold her steady," I heard one delivery guy say to the other, "I'll back in." When I got a view of what they were bringing into Frankie's condo, my jaw hit the ground.

"Wait a minute," I shouted, "A woman with no grandchildren bought a crib?"

Jamie shouted bitterly, "It's against all principles of Judaism to bring a crib into the house before the baby is born!"

"Or before it's conceived!" I added.

My sister sat there, a hopeless look on her face. Then she asked me, "Does food poisoning really only last twenty-four hours?"

Chapter 14

I found myself checking my *Blackberry* for texts or missed calls all day. 'Would he call?' I kept wondering. Other than the sudden onset of food poisoning, our date had been great. So, of course he'd call! But When? I was feeling quite desperate to hear from him, and I hated to admit it but it wasn't all because I needed to have his baby stat.

When I got home from Ma's place, my phone finally rang and I figured it was Frankie calling to make sure I got home okay. It was a given that she checked in with me every time I left her place, just to make sure nothing happened in the ten minutes it took to get from her condo to my apartment. I looked at my *Blackberry*. "Unknown Caller," it read. That's how I knew it was Frankie.

"Hi Ma, I'm home," I answered the phone.

The caller disguised his voice to sound like a high-pitched older Jewish woman with a heavy New York accent. "Thank God honey. I was worried!" said Drew.

I giggled. "What's with the New York accent?" I asked him, "We're from here."

"I was just trying to do the Jewish mother thing," Drew said in his normal voice.

"Other than the accent, not bad," I responded, "She really does sound sort of sound like that."

"Maybe I need to meet her to see for myself."

"You want to meet my mother?"

"Why not? I've always heard that girls eventually turn into their mothers."

"Well, please shoot me if that happens."

"She can't be that bad," he replied.

I couldn't help but think that if he knew about the baby scheme, he'd retract his statement.

"So, how do you feel?" I asked.

"I'm okay. I pretty much threw up all last night and this morning, but I think it's all out of my system."

Danny's fake food poisoning theory flashed through my brain.

"So, are you free tonight?" he asked, "Want to get together?"

"Sure." My smile was so wide I was afraid he'd be able to see it through the phone.

"Pick you up at eight?" Drew asked.

"Okay," I said, dashing to my closet to start pulling clothes off hangers so I could throw prospective outfits onto the bed. "Do you know where I live?"

"What do you think?"

"Yes."

"See you soon," he said before ending the call.

I stood there for a moment and had a silent argument with myself. 'I'm using Drew and I hate myself for that.'

Myself answered, 'Yeah, but you're going to be loaded!'

'But he's a really nice guy, and he *really* likes you.'

'You'll pay him off,' myself answered. And that was how I rationalized for the moment that seducing Drew and having his baby was okay.

I ripped off my clothes and jumped in the shower. It was already 6:40, so I had an hour and twenty minutes to make myself look like someone Drew wanted to have sex with. Sad, but that was reality. The words con artist, manipulator and deceitful swindler were coming to mind, but I had to block them out. The words *eight million dollars* meant a lot more right now.

In the shower, I began to think about what was really going on, which was how much I was enjoying my potential sperm donor's personality. After all the years together at work, it took my mother's crazy dream to buy grandchildren to get me to go on a date with Drew. Ma was indirectly making me give him a chance, and part of me felt thankful to her for that.

On the other hand, who was I kidding? What were the odds that Drew and I would actually work out as a couple? Relationships with men never seemed to pan out for me. In fact, I wasn't sure if I'd ever been in love. I barely knew John when we got married, and Max, that was *security*, not love. I didn't have a lot of faith in myself when it came to men. That was the sad, sad, secret I kept to myself. John had really done some damage to me and my self-esteem, and I wasn't sure I'd ever have the guts to trust someone ever again.

I heard my phone ring, but I couldn't get it since I had shampoo in my hair. I knew this was Frankie's call, and I felt like telling her she should be more worried about her daughter's mental state, rather than if she made it home safe. Ma was turning me into a neurotic, conflicted mess.

After the whole hair process, which meant towel drying, applying two different kinds of hair gel, blow-drying, flat-ironing, putting hair crème on the ends, and spraying enough hairspray to become a fire hazard, I decided on a slinky black dress and silver sling-backs. I went heavy on the make-up but light on the perfume, because I didn't want Drew to think I was trying too hard. Around my neck, I wore a circular emerald, which ironically was given to Ma by my dad, thirty-some years earlier. Frankie had given it to me for my birthday, right after I got divorced. She told me that of all the things Dad gave her, this was the most special.

The story behind the necklace was that my parents had had a big fight about something really silly, but it was the first time they'd ever been so mad at each other that they didn't speak for a couple days. Ma told me that even though she knew she was right, she decided to give in and make amends. So she went out and bought her husband an "I'm sorry" card and left it on his pillow that night.

After my dad read the card, he apologized as well. They hugged and kissed and everything was back to normal, even though according to Ma, she had compromised her opinion to make peace. The next night, when Frankie went to bed, she noticed a tiny box lying on her pillow. She told me she was shaking while she opened it. Inside was the necklace. Dad told her he gave it to her to show how much he appreciated her willingness to make the first move to make up.

Ma told me that the necklace symbolized how much she and Dad meant to each other. So here I was, wearing this beautiful and valuable keepsake on a date I was going on for the sole purpose of tricking a guy into knocking me up. The necklace really was beautiful, but I wondered if I could hate myself anymore than I currently did, and if I was even remotely good enough to wear it.

At 7:55, five minutes before my date was to arrive, I poured myself a glass of Pinot and took one last look in the mirror. Without sounding like a bitch, I had to admit I looked really hot. It was perhaps the best I'd felt about my physical appearance in years. The sad part was, on the inside I felt like the devil.

But when I answered the door at 8:05 and saw Drew standing there dressed in jeans and a t-shirt, I felt like I looked stupid. I was dressed for a fancy dinner date, Drew was dressed for Taco Bell! He looked really cute, though, especially since he had shaved off his goat-tee. What a difference!

"Wow..." was the first word he said.

I smiled, realizing that the black dress was a fabulous choice.

"You look amazing, but..."

"What?"

"Would you mind changing? I'm taking you somewhere really awesome, but you might get cold."

"Wait a minute!" I wanted to say, "You want me to take off my perfect outfit? Not a chance."

Instead I just said, "No problem, I'll just go get a sweater."

"Look, would you mind wearing jeans and a sweatshirt?" he asked with a smile, "Trust me, where we're going, you'll be a lot happier in warmer clothes."

I had a mission. The dress was part of it. Now the dress was about to become history. I was being asked to wear jeans and a sweatshirt, not the clothing one wants to be in to seduce someone.

I'd have to make the best of it. The big dilemma suddenly became *True Religion* or *Rockin Republic*? The *True Religions* made my butt look better, but the *Rockin Republics* were a little more slimming. Before I even reached my bedroom, I chose to have the better butt for the evening. As I put on the jeans, along with a black t-shirt and a North face jacket, I thought once again about how wrong this was. Drew was actually romancing me with this mystery date. He was trying to impress me, woo me. He had no idea that his date had a goal, an objective. I felt horrible. Oddly enough, I chose to keep the necklace on, even though it didn't match my new outfit.

When I came back into the living room, I found Drew enjoying a glass of wine. "Perfect," he said of my new outfit. Then he held up the glass and added, "I hope you don't mind."

"Not at all," I replied. I liked the idea that he felt comfortable enough to pour himself a glass of wine without asking. Drew was so down to earth. He was the complete opposite of uptight. He wasn't tense, he wasn't edgy. He was easy going and calm. Being with Drew was like taking a Xanax.

After the wine and some casual conversation, Drew suggested we head out. I asked him where we were going, but he wouldn't say anything. He seemed really excited about it. I had to admit I was too, but I kept reminding myself of why I was really here. What had to matter the most was making sure the date went well enough to end it in bed. I loathed myself for thinking that way, but business was business, and this was a pretty big business deal.

In Drew's Jeep Cherokee, we headed down Lakeshore Drive, pretty far south. I started to put the pieces together when I heard rattling in his back seat. I turned around and spotted a cooler filled with ice. Beside the cooler were a couple of big blankets and another bag. Now I knew we were having a picnic, and I had a pretty good idea about where it was taking place.

A few minutes later, Drew turned into the parking lot of Soldier Field, home of the Chicago Bears. He took a spot right in front where the players parked their cars during games.

"I thought this would be more fun than eating at a restaurant," he said. Then he got out of the car, opened the back door and started taking out the cooler.

"How are we getting in there?" I asked.

"My buddy's working tonight. He's a security guard." Then Drew pulled out his cell phone and dialed a number. "Hey... Yeah, we're here... Okay, cool. Thanks bro."

He put his cell back in his coat pocket and continued getting all the stuff out of the car. I grabbed the blankets and followed him to a nearby entrance. We stood there for a minute until the door opened and a big huge guy, who looked more like a football player than a security guard appeared. Drew put the cooler down.

"Hey, dude," he said as he shook the guy's hand.

"Drew, what's up?" answered the guy.

"Eddie, this is Jamie. Jamie, my buddy, Eddie Walsh."

"Nice to meet you, Eddie," I said as I shook his hand. He seemed really sweet.

"Nice to meet you, too," he replied, "You look different than you do on T.V. You look thinner in person."

I frowned. He didn't seem so sweet anymore.

Eddie led us into the stadium and we walked for a long time, during which he asked me questions about the lottery. He wanted to know if I ever got stalked.

"The only stalker I've ever had is him," I joked, pointing to Drew.

"But all the stalking finally paid off," Drew answered.

"Yes, it did," I flirted. I rolled my eyes at the irony.

"Would you guys mind waiting to hit on each other till I'm gone?" asked Eddie.

We continued walking till we reached the field. It was eerily quiet, but I liked it. Only a few lights were on, and I felt like if the whole place was candlelit, this is exactly what it would look like.

"This is really something," I exclaimed.

Both Drew and Eddie agreed. The three of us were the only people standing on this gigantic field where tens of thousands watch the Bears, and millions of viewers watch on T.V.

Before tonight I'd been here only two other times. The first was when I was really young. The Bears were playing the Steelers and I remembered Ma telling me to keep shouting, "Go Bears!" And I did it, even though I didn't really know why I was doing it.

The next time I came to Soldier Field was for the famous U2 concert with Max, the night we slept together. Maybe history would repeat itself and I'd be sleeping with Drew tonight. I hoped.

"Well, I'm out of here," said Eddie, "Call me when you're ready to leave."

"Thanks, Eddie," said Drew, "We'll do."

"Thanks," I smiled, and Eddie was gone.

"Ready?" asked Drew.

"For what?"

"The fifty," he exclaimed with a smile, motioning to the middle of the field. When we reached the fifty yard line, I spread a couple blankets out and Drew began to unpack the cooler, taking out a couple beers and a bottle of white wine. The next items he pulled out surprised me.

"You brought sandwiches from Potbelly's?" I asked.

"Yeah, I hope that's okay."

"Sure," I exclaimed. Drew had chosen to bring dinner from my favorite sandwich shop, located a couple blocks away from the station. I was always telling my co-workers (including Drew) that if the line wasn't so long, I'd eat there every day. I loved the toasted bread and melted cheese that went on every sandwich. The best part about a Potbelly's sandwich, in my opinion, though, was the stuff on it; tons of lettuce, tomatoes, onions, spices, mustard, vinaigrette, and best of all, hot peppers.

The fact that Drew actually chose this for our dinner showed unbelievable thoughtfulness to me. He had done all this for me. ME. No one had ever done something like this. Sure, Max had taken me to expensive restaurants, and we'd taken lavish trips, and he'd bought me expensive gifts, but this was different. This meant more. No one had ever paid attention or seemed to care about the little things that made me happy. Except for Drew. And it made me realize that although Max loved me, Max wasn't very considerate. He didn't really know what I liked and what I didn't like. He didn't even know my favorite color, probably because he didn't care. For someone to take the time to remember things about me was foreign. And wonderful.

While unwrapping the food, I watched my date uncork the wine. "Drew?" I said.

He looked up at me. "Yeah?"

"Thanks for the sandwiches."

"Sure."

"No, I mean it."

With a cute smile, he responded, "It's just a sandwich."

"You really pay attention to things, don't you?"

"Just with people I care about," he said with a smile, "I think I get that from my mother. She was a really kind and giving person from what I remember, and she used to tell me, 'Don't just listen to people, hear them.' I never forgot that."

111

"Wow," I responded, "That's so true. How many people really hear what we say?" At this moment, I was thinking about how much my mother needed to heed Drew's mother's advice.

"Not many," agreed Drew.

"When did she die?"

"When I was ten," he said, "Car accident. She was hit by a drunk driver."

"I'm sorry," was all I said. But what I really wanted to say was that I'd experienced the same thing when I was three, and that my dad had died in a car accident, and that I too grew up with only one parent, and that I understood him better than he thought. I was afraid, though. I didn't want to get too close to Drew emotionally, given the true reason I was here tonight.

A few minutes later, just as we started eating, the most amazing thing happened. All of the lights came on. The place lit up and was as bright as it was on the night of a game.

"Wow!" I exclaimed.

Drew smiled at my reaction, and then, in the bright lights, two people sitting smack in the middle of Soldier Field, the only people (with the exception of Eddie) in the entire stadium, ate Potbelly's sandwiches, drank wine, and talked about everything.

Politics, music, movies, books. I was having a hard time understanding how I could have missed the fact that Drew was so intelligent. He knew about things. But I'd never taken the time to talk with him enough to realize that. For his career, Drew had chosen to be a camera operator, a job for which he was clearly overqualified. But that didn't mean he was uneducated or not well read. Look at me. I was the lottery girl. Did people assume I wasn't smart either? Drew Conrad was *very* smart, and I was finding that quality as appealing as his perfect biceps.

As the two of us became more and more at ease with each other, our conversations shifted to topics such as my first kiss, Drew's first kiss and the celebrities each of us wanted to have sex with. Finally, with no more wine, but with plenty of unused energy, we ended up singing every Bruce Springsteen song we could think of. And as I looked into his beautiful green eyes that lit up as much as Soldier Field when we sang *Glory Days* together, I wanted to kiss him, and touch him and hold him and yes, sleep with him. And it scared me to death, because I didn't want to do it for the money. I wanted to do it for me.

As we cleaned up the picnic and folded up the blankets, both of us were giggling, each trying to think of more songs off the *Born to Run* CD.

"Can I ask you a question?" I asked Drew.

"Sure."

"Do you know my favorite color?"

Drew thought about it for a second, and then answered, "Actually, yes. I think I do."

"What is it?" I asked.

"I'm going to go with blue," he answered with lots of self-assurance, "navy blue."

As we walked off the field, I hid my face behind the blankets I was carrying.

"Am I right?" he asked, pulling the blankets down and revealing my big grin.

"How did you know?" I asked with a laugh.

Chapter 15

After saying good-bye to Eddie, we got into the car. Drew immediately turned on the heat, since the temperature had dropped at least twenty degrees in the three hours we were out on the field, and both of us were freezing. I couldn't feel my nose, and when I looked at Drew, his cheeks were bright red. I watched him cup his hands in his face and exhale really hard to get some warm air on them.

God, he was cute! I wondered how I could have over-looked so many wonderful things about him for so long. But although a great feeling, my crush on Drew was throwing a huge wrench into the master plan, which was all about money, money, money! There was no time to throw unexpected emotions into the mix.

"Ready?" he asked me, rubbing his hands up and down my arms to warm me up.

"Yeah," I smiled, "Hey Drew?"

"Yeah?"

"This was really fun," I said with a smile. Then I did something that shocked both him and I. I leaned over and kissed him on the mouth, soft and slow. I couldn't believe

I did it. It was as if I wasn't even here anymore, and like some sweet, sexy woman had taken my place. The woman had enough self-confidence and enough courage to show what she was feeling, very unlike me, the coward who never showed her cards.

When my lips first touched Drew's, I realized how cold he truly was because his lips and even his tongue felt like ice. Not for long, though. We sat in his car and kissed for awhile. Not aggressive "I want sex" kisses, just sweet, tender kisses, with lots of holding, hugging and cuddling. And when we finally got going, the entire drive home was silent. Neither of us felt talking was necessary. I think we were both enjoying what had just happened, and let's be honest, looking forward to more of it in a warmer, more comfortable atmosphere.

When we pulled up to my building, it seemed obvious Drew was coming up to my place. It was even more of a sure thing when we found a parking spot right in front. I was sure this was a sign. My building had four meter spots in front of it, and during the six years I'd lived there I'd never seen one available until right now.

Drew quickly took the spot and when we got out of the car, he grabbed my hand and rushed me into the building and into the elevator. The kissing began the second the elevator doors closed. Now our kisses weren't the sweet, tender kisses like the ones in the car. They were, in fact, the aggressive "I want sex" kisses.

The elevator reached my floor and I scrambled to find my keys, while Drew began softly kissing my neck. The second I got the door open, he practically pushed me inside and slammed it shut. A few moments later, clothes began to fly off and we headed toward the bedroom. By the time we reached my bed (which was covered with most of my rejection outfits) we were both in nothing but our underwear.

"Um, Drew?" It felt so awkward, but it had to be done.

"Yeah?"

"Do you have any diseases I should know about?"

He stopped kissing me and smiled. "No, I promise."

"Are you sure? I mean..."

"Yes. I actually just got tested for everything. I took out a whole life insurance policy," he said, "Do you have one of those? I mean, I heard it's a good long term investment and..."

"Shut up!" I said with a giggle.

"What? I'm just curious," he laughed.

Drew grabbed my face and kissed me hard on the mouth. This was good. No diseases. The only thing I had to worry about now, was the fact that I was a selfish user, who was about to trick a really nice guy into becoming a father.

In between kisses he added, "Jamie, if you're worried about getting pregnant, we can use something."

What? Use something? Was he crazy? I thought.

"Don't worry about it," I said, putting my lips back on his. What a snake I was! Nonetheless, the snake was really enjoying his lips, even though the guilt was overwhelming. If any guy knew he was being used to get someone pregnant, wouldn't he run the other way as fast as he could? Drew didn't have that option. He had no way of knowing he was being manipulated, that he was part of a scheme. He thought I was about to sleep with him because I desired him, which let's be honest, was the case, but he had no clue that during the act, he might help create a fetus.

We made love that night and I had to say, hands down, it was the best sex I'd ever had. Around 6:00 a.m. the next morning, I got out of bed as quietly as I could, slipped on an oversized sweatshirt, and headed to the kitchen for some water. As I sat at the counter, sipping a bottled water and watching the sun come up, I thought about what a perfect night it had been. From the moment Drew came to the door, things couldn't have gone any better. And the best part of the whole thing was, the goal of the date had been achieved.

I touched my stomach and wondered if I'd made a baby. I smiled. I touched my stomach again and wondered if I'd have a boy or a girl. This time I cringed. Not because I didn't like children, because I was afraid of them.

At that moment, I felt Drew's arms hug me from behind. They were so warm, so comfortable. I turned around and began to kiss this beautiful man, standing before me in his boxers.

"I had fun last night," he whispered.

"Me, too."

I felt more at ease with Drew, the guy who'd been hanging around my office for years, the guy who I'd bypassed, perhaps taken for granted, than with anyone I'd ever known, including my ex-husband and my two-minute fiancé. He made me feel desirable and sexy, and at the same time, safe and secure. Suddenly, I thought, 'Maybe I could love this man.' Ma would hate him but who cared? She did this. In fact, I would actually get tremendous joy and satisfaction from that aspect of it.

At this very moment, something caught my eye. Sitting on the kitchen counter was a picture in a frame. Even though I'd placed the black and white photo there when I moved in years earlier, and regardless of the fact that I'd looked at it hundreds of times, I couldn't help but become fixated on it at this moment. It was a picture of my parents on their wedding day.

"What's wrong?" asked Drew.

"My mom and dad," I began, never taking my eyes off the photo, "they didn't have a big, elaborate wedding. They had a small ceremony and then dinner at my grandparent's house after. There were like thirty-five people, total, at the reception."

"Oh," replied Drew.

"My mom's dress," I went on, picking up the frame to give Drew a closer look, "it's pretty, huh?"

Drew smiled, "Yes, it is."

"This wasn't even her own dress, you know. She couldn't afford one, so she borrowed it from a girlfriend." Tears welled up in my eyes. "My mom told me there was a woman whose house they cleaned, who gave her as a gift, the money to buy her own wedding dress."

"But you said this was her friend's dress."

"It was." Tears now began flowing down my cheeks. "Do you know what my mom did with the money?"

"What?"

"She bought her mother a dress. She said the mother of the bride had to look her best."

Drew hugged me tight, and I burst into tears. "It's okay," he whispered.

"But if you knew…if you knew what my mother was doing…"

He continued to hold me. "Well, the good news is, she's got all the money she needs now."

This comment sent me over the edge. I was now semi-hyperventilating. Ma, dressed in her friend's bridal gown, standing next to the love of her life, looked so beautiful, so happy. She was such a good person back then. What had happened to her? How could a woman who chose her mother's happiness over her own, turn into a psychotic grandma wannabe, who was bribing her kids into parenthood? I just didn't get it. And it was making me crazy, and sad, and miserable. And ironically, the man holding me was making me calm and happy and blissful.

The only way I could make sense of anything was to realize that in the picture, Frankie didn't know yet that she would bear two children. She didn't know yet that her husband would die seven years later. She didn't know yet that her adult children would still be single at ages thirty-two and thirty-four. And maybe as good hearted and ethical of a person as she was, she felt because of her misfortune with her husband, she was owed the miracle of life, perhaps the blessings of her children's children. I wasn't sure, but suddenly I wanted to please my mother and give her what she wanted. Not to mention, I also wanted her eight million bucks, which is why I decided at this moment, maybe I needed to increase my odds of getting knocked up.

"Come here," I said as I took Drew's hand and led him back to the bedroom.

"I'm still trying to figure you out," he said with a chuckle, "A few days ago, I thought you hated me."

"I never hated you."

"Am I your rebound guy, Jamie?"

"Shut up and get under the covers."

Chapter 16

Sitting in a booth at Sushi Samba *with Janine was like being in prison. Nothing against Janine, she was actually a sweetheart. But there was only one girl I wanted to be with, and asshole me had just broken up with her.*

Janine was one of three prospective mothers for my eight million dollar baby. I'd met her a couple months earlier on the shoot for the "Warts-be-gone" ad campaign. Janine was the hair and make-up stylist assigned to me for the day. I know it sounds really conceited, but I could tell she instantly loved me. Just being honest. The thing about me was, yes, I was a womanizer, but I was also a really nice guy, friendly and cool to everyone I worked with. So it wasn't out of character for me to befriend Janine. While she styled my hair and applied my make-up, the two of us laughed and made jokes about the ad campaign.

"This guy needs to worry more about the disgusting things on his hands than about how his hair looks!" I joked about the character I was about to portray.

"Yeah buddy, go to Supercuts and save your money," Janine played along, "I hear 'Warts-be Gone' is pretty expensive!"

Janine and I laughed and talked a lot, but even though I found her attractive, I had no intention of asking her out, mainly because I'd just started seeing Jennifer and didn't want to cheat. I had morals, but let's be honest, I was worried about my career, too, and cheating on my agent wouldn't be too wise.

So at the end of the day, I hugged Janine good-bye and left it at that. It was no surprise to me, though, when she slipped me her business card. But as I did with all of them, I shoved the card in my jeans pocket, never to be seen again.

Now, three months later, because of my dear, sweet mother, and my desperation for her money, my memory was somehow sparked, and I remembered Janine telling me she worked at Salon Buzz on Oak Street. I called information, got the number and was connected to Janine within a minute.

"Hello, this is Janine..." she said into the phone. She told me later that she was having trouble holding the receiver because she was wearing rubber gloves that were semi covered in hair dye. She said she was in the middle of highlighting a woman's hair, and the only reason she took the call was because whoever answered the phone told her it was a guy named Danny who sounded cute.

"Janine, this is Danny," I simply said.

"Danny who?" she asked.

"The guy with warts all over his hands," I joked.

"Oh my God!" she exclaimed, "I gave up on you!"

I told her that the reason I never called was because I had a girlfriend at the time, which was the truth, and she was cool with it. In fact, she couldn't have been more delighted to hear from me. Within a minute of the conversation we had plans to meet.

The date was going pretty well, even though my heart was miles away. Still, I was pretty sure I'd be going home tonight with Janine, seducing her, and hopefully knocking her up. I felt pretty guilty, but rationalized what I was about to do by telling myself that if I was lucky enough to get Janine pregnant, she and the baby would be well taken care of financially. In fact, she and the baby would be rich beyond their wildest dreams, and Janine wouldn't have any trouble finding a husband. I hated myself, but I was doing what I thought was best. And besides, I wasn't really doing anything. My mother was. I was the victim.

The minute I paid the check, I stood up and said "Want to go?"

"Sure," she said, standing up. I grabbed her hand and led her out the door. From there, things happened exactly the way I wanted them to. We went back to her place, drank some more wine, and began taking each other's clothes off. The only curveball was my inability to get Courtney off my mind. It was suddenly hard to fool around with someone and not think of her the entire time. Not only because I felt like I was cheating (even though I wasn't), but because she was the one I wished was in my arms.

"I'm so glad you called me," said Janine, unbuttoning my pants. She seemed so happy and so into me. I couldn't have felt like more of a jerk.

"Can I ask you something, Janine?"

"Sure," she replied.

"Are you...um...healthy?"

Janine took her hands off the zipper of my pants and said, "What do you mean? Like do I have any STDs?"

"Yeah."

"No. No diseases. You?"

"No."

"Are you on the pill?" I asked, realizing most guys pray a girl will say yes, and I was praying she'd say no.

"No."

"Oh," I answered, trying not to sound too psyched.

"Don't worry. I have an IUD."

The look on my face must have confused her, because she giggled and said, "I thought that would make you happy. You look like a kid whose dog just died."

"Janine, I don't feel so great." I zipped my pants up. Then I ran back into her living room, somehow found my shirt in about four seconds, and put it on. I held my stomach and said, "I think I may have food poisoning."

Chapter 17

The second of the three girls I had dates lined up with was Ronna Bliss, who interestingly enough was a former sportscaster at WGB, where Jamie worked. My sister had introduced us a couple years earlier and we began dating. Six weeks into the relationship, Ronna told me she loved me and wanted to marry me. In true Danny style, I felt otherwise and broke up with her. I didn't want a wife. I wanted someone to have fun with. That was it.

Ronna was devastated. Jamie would tell me how she would come into her office in tears and want to talk about it for hours. She would ask Jamie, "What's wrong with me?"

And my sis would answer truthfully, "Nothing, Ronna, I promise. It's Danny. He just doesn't want to get married. Ever."

"What did I do wrong?" she would ask.

"Nothing, Ronna, I promise. It's Danny. He just doesn't want to get married. Ever," Jamie would repeat.

"Maybe if I would have been different, less demanding..." she would say, "What can I do to get him back?"

And of course, Jamie would reply, "Nothing, Ronna, I promise. It's Danny. He just doesn't want to get married. Ever."

My sister said to me with sarcasm, "I could save a lot of time by recording my response and just pressing a button every time Ronna comes into my office. Truly, though, I feel for Ronna."

I knew Jamie was sincere. I knew this because when her husband cheated on her and moved on, I saw sadness in my sister that truly made me sick. I wanted to kill my ex-brother-in-law for hurting such a good person. Jamie had married for love, and instead was lied to and then dumped. But as badly as I felt about what John did to her, Ronna and I were in a completely different situation. Yes, I felt badly about ending a relationship and being unable to commit, but at least I was letting her know upfront, before too much time had passed. And now, Ronna could move on. Although, according to Jamie, that wasn't happening too fast.

Ronna's frequent visits had started to irritate my sister and she wanted desperately for the girl to stop coming into her office every two minutes for counseling.

"I have to do something," she said to me one day, so I offered up a suggestion.

"Why don't you set her up with that camera guy? What's his name?"

"Drew?" she asked, her voice filled with surprise.

"Yeah. Girls like that guy, don't they?"

"Umm...yeah, I guess."

"Unless you like him for yourself."

"Hello...does the name Max mean anything to you?" she responded.

I wanted to tell her that no, that name didn't mean anything to me because I knew it didn't really mean anything to HER. I kept my mouth shut, though, and reiterated what a good couple I thought Ronna and the camera guy would make.

Drew and Ronna ended up dating for about a month, and then decided to be just friends. But the mission had been accomplished. Whatever the guy did, Ronna was over me. She ended up leaving the station a few months later and went to work for some sports marketing firm. Rumor was, her salary alone was over a hundred thousand. I also heard Ronna now had a serious boyfriend, but that didn't stop me from calling and asking her out in my time of desperation. I figured these things blow up so often that chances were, the relationship was over. And when Ronna agreed to get together with me, my theory was confirmed.

We decided to meet for drinks at Glascots, a local, no-frills Lincoln Park bar where they serve peanuts in baskets and people throw the shells on the floor. Ronna and I had gone there a few times when we were dating, and in Ronna's eyes, it was "our place."

We sat at the bar and sipped cold beer out of frosty mugs, talking about Ronna's new career, and my jobs, including my latest gig as a marketer for Ed Debevic's, a famous hamburger place, where I actually had to dress up like a hamburger and pass out coupons.

I found it interesting that most of the girls I went out with always asked about my acting career. Except for one. Courtney. She had spent most of our date asking me questions about my teaching job. She seemed more interested and impressed with that career than she did about acting. And that said something to me.

"Which is better?" Ronna joked, "The pretzel costume or the burger?" At this moment, thinking about the answer to that question would have made ending my life right then and there easy, had I not had Frankie's money to look forward to. Hope was on the horizon, though. If tonight went well, I'd be sleeping and impregnating Ronna, and I'd be a multi-millionaire in nine months.

The sad part was, however, that when Ronna began taking me on a trip down memory lane, talking about our brief relationship, she was beaming while I was feeling majorly relieved that it was over. It was ironic. I was trying to get this girl to have my baby, yet I was thrilled we weren't together anymore. Thanks, Ma, was all I could think.

After a couple brewskis, Ronna moved closer to me, put her hand on my thigh and whispered in my ear. "I really missed you, Danny. I'm so glad you called."

"I missed you, too," I said, trying to act as sincere as I did when I told people how great Ed Debevic's burgers were.

"You know," she went on, "I never told you this when we dated, but…"

"What?"

She seemed tentative, afraid to continue.

"What? Tell me."

"No, I can't. It's too embarrassing."

"Please, just tell me."

She looked at me shyly. "I really think I loved you. I mean…" She took a deep breath, "I wanted to settle down with you. Have kids even."

Upon hearing this bold statement, I wanted to scream and shout as loud as I could and do jumping jacks around the bar. This scenario couldn't have been working out any better. How easy everything was going to be!

"Hey, want to get out of here?" I asked, seizing the moment.

"Sure," she said with a big grin.

I threw some money down on the bar, put my arm around Ronna, and led her to the front, toward the door. I was home free, beginning to see the pay-off ahead. I envisioned Frankie handing me a check. I pictured my future clearly now, and in it were cars, expensive vacations, a nice, new condo, a Rolex, perhaps. Unfortunately, what I failed to see was the huge beefy football player-type guy who had just walked into the bar.

Ronna saw him first. "Oh my God!" she shouted, "You're following me?"

'Is Ronna talking to this big guy who looks like he could kick my ass?' I asked myself. I got an answer pretty quickly.

"Ronna, what the hell?" answered Big Guy.

"*Umm, who is this?*" *I asked Ronna, who just stood there unable to move.*

"*I'm Ronna's boyfriend, asshole,*" *said Big Guy, as he stuck his face right in mine.*

I backed away and looked at my date. "*You have a boyfriend?*" *I asked.*

Ronna suddenly looked really sad. "*Well, kind of...*" *she answered, sounding like she was six years old.*

Big Guy didn't like her answer. "*Kind of?*" *he shouted at her. People in the bar started to stare and watch the dramatic scene taking place. They all wondered if there was going to be a fight.*

Ronna spoke to Big Guy as if they were the only ones in the bar. It was as if she suddenly forgot I was even there. "*Well, you're so into your job these days. You never even look at me and I'm sick of it.*"

I then saw something shocking. Big Guy started to cry. If what was happening wasn't screwing up my plan, this would have been hilarious to me. Here was this huge, tough guy, sobbing worse than my mother did during the movie **Steel Magnolia's**. *The guy actually had big teardrops running down his cheeks. I wasn't amused, though, and I didn't want to laugh. Actually, I wanted to cry, because it wasn't hard to figure out where things were headed.*

"*Ronna, I love you. I thought you knew that,*" *Big Guy said through tears,* "*I'm just trying to make as much money as possible for both of us. That's why I've been working so much.*" *When I looked over at Ronna, the girl who had just told me indirectly that she'd have my child, I saw she was crying. Then Big Guy got down on one knee.* "*Ronna, I want to marry you. I want to have babies with you. Will you be my wife?*"

I made one last desperate attempt to get what I wanted, which was Ronna out the door with me quickly. I looked down at Big Guy, still on his knees, and said, "*Look, we were just leaving.*"

Instantly, I heard the crowd moan, as if they were upset that the villain might still win.

Big Guy looked up at me. Suddenly his tears were gone and his face turned to rage. He then stood up and pushed me really hard, knocking me down onto the floor. I looked up and watched Ronna put her arms around her guy and kiss him hard on the mouth.

The crowd applauded and the happy couple walked out the door holding hands, smiling and kissing. No one was paying much attention to the guy on the floor who was brushing peanut shells off his shirt.

Chapter 18

I had one last shot. If this didn't work out, I'd have to go back to square one and think of new girls and/or a new strategy to collect Ma's millions. That's why I really wanted date number three, Connie Kleinberg, to work out.

I'd known Connie for years, and had always liked her. I'd met her in the emergency room at Northwestern Hospital several years earlier when she'd treated me. She gave me three stitches on my chin that I needed after attempting to slide into home plate so my baseball team could advance to the Chicago Social Club World Series. We lost the game, but I still ended up getting a prize; my beautiful, sexy doctor, Doctor Connie Kleinberg.

When Connie first introduced herself as "Dr. Kleinberg," I was stunned. She was so pretty! So, I made the mistake of telling her she looked more like a Victoria's Secret model than a doctor and I swear, to this day, I think she skimped on the anesthesia to get back at me. Getting stitches hurt a ton, but Connie was worth every single suture.

She was different than any girl I'd ever met. She was older, divorced and very independent. The night of the stitches, I asked for her phone number. She told me she was flattered, but really didn't have time to date. She was nice about it, though, and told me I was sweet and adorable, which made me feel like an eight year old kid. I wanted her to know I was more than sweet and adorable! I had to get her to go out with me.

So, a couple days later, I stopped by the hospital with pink roses and a card that read, "Dr. Kleinberg, thanks for fixing my chin. How about dinner?" And that's how our relationship was born. We began seeing each other, and what was so nice about it was that Connie's busy work schedule set the slow pace of the relationship. She worked so much that we were only able to get together once a week at the most.

It was so refreshing. For a change, it wasn't me who wanted to keep things non-serious. Connie was living her own life. She didn't care if I called or not, but she was happy when I did. She didn't care if I saw other women. She saw other men (I think). She didn't care if I didn't say "I love you." She didn't want to be in love. Connie had been very clear on all this. And it bothered me a little bit, but not because I wasn't enjoying the freedom. It just seemed strange to me. No girl had ever been so non-demanding. Did I like it? I wasn't sure.

Our relationship continued like this for a few months, until we both realized we were best as friends. Connie had met a guy who she told me she could possibly see a future with, and as for me, well, is there really any explanation needed? I was just being myself, and I didn't want a future with anyone. I respected Connie and liked spending time with her, but I was okay with helping her to move on and see if she could find happiness with the other guy, who seemed to want something more serious. In the end, neither of us walked away hurt.

Over the next few years, Connie and I would call each other sporadically and get together whenever neither of us was involved in another relationship, which was usually the case for me. We always had fun with each other, and always had good sex. And Connie never had expectations about where our relationship was headed. That's why it wasn't difficult for her to become date number three. I already liked her, and even better, I knew I could get her into bed. I also knew Connie wasn't on the pill. I had always used condoms when we were together. If I was lucky enough to sleep with her this time, I'd have to figure out a way not to use one.

Connie was a bit surprised to hear from me, because the two of us had hadn't talked in almost a year. Still, she was friendly and I figured she wasn't seeing anyone at the present time because she was very receptive to the idea of going out with me.

We had dinner at **MON AMI GABI,** *a casual French place, and then headed to Connie's place, for what we both knew was going to happen because it happened every time we got together; sex, sex and more sex. Less than a minute after we were in the door, Connie flipped on her stereo and put on a Lady Gaga CD. Then she began doing a striptease act to the song,* **Paparazzi.** *All I could do was laugh. I'd forgotten how hot Connie was. My smart doctor friend had a beautiful body and she knew how to seduce me like no one else. What a bonus. In addition to making me a wealthy man, what was about to happen was going to be fun!*

I sat there enjoying the show, watching the gorgeous future mother of my child, dressed only in a black lace bra, matching thong underwear, and black sandals with three inch heels, dance to the music and attempt to drive me insane with her seductive moves.

I was practically bursting with excitement, when all of a sudden, someone else popped into my head. Another woman, who I'd recently seen dancing, a woman who wasn't half naked, and who instead of a striptease act was dancing to **Fire Burning.** *Suddenly, I got really sad. My sweet, sexy Sean Kingston wannabe. Oh, how I missed her. I could feel my smile fade as my heart began to physically ache, something that had never, ever happened to me before.*

Connie noticed the change in me and immediately rushed over, knelt down next to me, and grabbed my hands.

"*Danny, honey, what's the matter?*" *she asked with urgency in her voice. She was sincerely concerned. As much of a sexual relationship as ours was, we really did have a genuine friendship as well, and I knew Connie cared about me.*

'*Don't blow it dude,*' *I thought to myself.* "*Nothing sweetie, keep going,*" *I said, trying to smile but dying inside.*

Connie sat down next to me on the couch. "*Please tell me. Is it another girl?*" *She was now running her fingers through my hair.*

"*No, nothing like that,*" *I faked,* "*It's just...I missed you, Connie.*" *Then I began to kiss her. And as we made our way into the bedroom, I forced myself to get Courtney out of my mind momentarily, and focus on getting Connie pregnant. I felt badly for lying to the woman I was about to sleep with, but I didn't want to complicate things. Not with everything going so perfectly.*

Once we reached the bed, Connie pushed me down onto it and then went to her dresser drawer for what I assumed was a condom. How the hell was I going to get out of using birth control? I wondered. I pondered the idea of just coming clean. Why not just tell Connie what happened with my mother and see if she'd be on board with having my baby? For all I knew, she'd be fine with it. Then again, if she said no, it was all over. I had no clue how Connie would react, so I decided to continue conning her, no pun intended.

"*Hey Con...*" *I began, as I watched her search through her drawer.*

"*Yeah?*"

"*Would it be okay if we skipped the condom tonight?*"

Connie turned around and giggled. "*Well, actually, we're going to have to. I don't have any.*"

How lucky could a guy get? "*Do YOU have any?*" *she asked me.*

"*Me? No. None.*"

134

"Well, then, I guess I need to ask you, do you have any STD's?" she asked.

"No, do you?"

Connie shook her head. This was working out unbelievably well for me. What happened next practically sent me over the edge. "Danny," she said, "if for some reason I get pregnant tonight, are you ready to be a father?"

I began to stutter, trying to figure out exactly how to answer that question.

Connie giggled, "I'm just kidding."

Everything was perfect. I was about to make love to this beautiful woman and hopefully make a baby. I was going to get Frankie's money. I could feel it. And yes, there was Courtney again, popping up in my mind every two seconds. I was actually getting kind of pissed at her for stealing my heart. She had no right to come into my life right now! So I told her that.

"Get out!" I shouted. I didn't realize I said it out loud.

"What?" said Connie.

"Uh..." I scrambled, "Get out of those underwear right now!" I shouted.

Connie burst out laughing and took off her bra and underwear. We began to kiss and all I could hear was heavy breathing, both hers and mine. Breathing and kissing and more breathing, and moaning, and more kissing and more breathing... And then I heard another noise; a beeper.

"Oh, no!" exclaimed Connie, jumping out of bed and grabbing the pager off her dresser. She looked at the number. "I can't believe this!"

"What?" I asked, sitting up in bed.

Connie looked around the room, picked up a pair of old jeans that were lying on the ground, and began to put them on.

"There's an emergency at the hospital," she said.

In my life, I don't think I've ever seen, to this day, a person get dressed faster. Not even myself, during all those times I wanted out of some random girl's apartment before she woke up the next morning.

"Should I...wait here?" I asked.

Connie leaned down and kissed my forehead. "I wouldn't. I'm sure I'll be there all night."

"Can we get together tomorrow night?" I asked in a slightly desperate tone.

Connie grabbed a bag off her dresser and put it over her shoulder. "Danny, I'm leaving tomorrow for California for a fellowship for four months. I was going to tell you but..."

"Wow," I said, trying to absorb the shock.

"I'll call you when I get back," she said, "Is that okay?"

Now I was almost numb. "Sure..."

Connie paused for one more second. "Bummer, huh?" she asked with a sad smile.

I nodded and then she blew me a kiss and was gone. As I lay there in bed, I was thinking two things. First, was I ever going to get laid again, let alone get someone pregnant? And two, how had I not noticed all the suitcases lined up at the bedroom door?

Three dates. No babies. I could only think of two words. Still in Connie's bed, I yelled them out as loud as I could, attempting to sound like the Chicago Cubs umpire.

"Strike three!"

Chapter 19

The same week Danny went out on his three dates, I was with my new man. While Danny was having dinner with Janine, I was at a bowling alley with Drew (his idea, of course). While Danny was being punched by Ronna's boyfriend, I was sitting in the *Cadillac Theater* with Drew watching *Jersey Boys*, the tickets compliments of WGB. And while Danny was viewing Connie's striptease act and flipping out about Courtney, Drew and I were watching <u>The Godfather, II</u> at my place (definitely my idea).

Drew had called and asked if I wanted to go out for Mexican.

"I'm sick of going out," I said, "I have a better idea."

So instead of munching on chips and salsa, we ate popcorn, sat in front of my flat screen and watched <u>The Godfather</u>, <u>The Godfather, II</u>, and <u>The Godfather, III</u>. It was fun to have someone to veg out with. I'd never done it with John, because he was too busy going out and cheating on me. As far as Max, he always fell asleep ten minutes after hitting the couch. I could honestly say the entire time I dated Max, I watched every movie we rented by myself, constantly turning the volume up and down, depending on how loud he was snoring.

While Drew and I watched the movie, we gave each other back rubs. As I watched Robert Dinero (as young Vito Corleone) go back to his hometown in Italy and shoot the guy who killed his family, I could feel my boyfriend's hands deeply massaging the muscles in between my shoulder blades. It was hard to concentrate on the movie, since all that was going through my head was how much I loved it when this guy touched me.

I was so happy these days. But I was completely conflicted because of the guilt I felt. Yes, I was in a relationship, but it was a relationship based on a lie. Drew genuinely believed our feelings for each other had developed through fate, while in reality he was part of a plot, a greedy scheme.

As he continued to press his fingers deeply into my back, I thought about blurting out what was going on and confessing about the whole baby bribe. I couldn't, though. I knew that Drew wasn't the kind of guy who would have a child for money. He was too ethical. And it bugged me and attracted me at the same time. If he would agree to go along with the plan, my problems would be solved. But I knew he wouldn't, and I respected him immensely for that, which pretty much made me hate myself even more.

With this thought, I turned around, put my arms around him, and began to kiss him. Drew slipped my sweater over my head, and just before he was about to kiss me again he put his hands on my rib cage, looked at my semi-naked body and whispered, "God, you are so beautiful."

I literally lost my breath for a second. And then I kissed him as hard as I possibly could. I wanted him desperately, this man who I had never let myself know until now. He was everything. He made me feel sexy. He made me feel good about myself. He made me like myself. And he paid attention to what I wanted and needed. No one had ever loved me like this. To John, I was a roommate. To Max, I was a trophy. To Drew, well, I was starting to feel somewhere in between his best friend and his sexpot. It was strange. It was all there, the physical attraction and the friendship. And it was the best feeling in the world.

We made love on my living room floor while Michael Corleone was kissing his brother Fredo on the lips and saying, "I knew it was you Fredo…you broke my heart." We'd been having sex all week, but for some reason tonight seemed more intense. It meant more.

Afterward, we were both sprawled out naked in exhaustion, and we turned our heads to the TV to watch Fredo being taken to his death in a boat, while Michael stood at the window watching. I thought about what a manipulator Michael was. He was a liar, the lowest of the lowest. And I couldn't deny, I was just like him, although I can say with certainty that I would never kill my own brother.

"Are you up for watching number three?" asked Drew.

"Definitely. You?" I asked as I got up and put my clothes back on.

"Sure," he said, following suit.

Just then, the phone rang. Since no one ever called me this late, it was a bit alarming, so I hurried to answer it. I saw private caller; my mother.

"Hi, Ma," I answered, "Everything okay?"

"I can't call my daughter after ten o'clock?" Frankie asked sarcastically.

"Of course you can," I said while motioning to Drew to put in the DVD, "What's up?"

"Is there a man over there?" asked Frankie.

As usual, the psychic knew. She was so in tune with me it was scary. "No, Ma," I lied, "there's no man here." Out of the corner of my eye, I saw Drew smile.

"Yes, there is," said Ma, "But you don't have to tell me about it. I called to tell you I'm going on vacation on Monday. I'll be gone for two weeks."

This shocked me. Ma had never left town, let alone take a trip. I panicked. "What? Monday? You mean, two days from now?" I asked, my voice filled with anxiety, "With whom?"

"No one," she replied confidently, "I'm going alone. It's time for me to travel, and now that I have the money to go places in style, I'm going for it." She went on to tell me about a European cruise she was going on, and how her friend had just returned from the same ship, and how great she said it was.

The whole thing sounded a little strange, and something didn't seem right, but I could say that about a lot of things Frankie was saying and doing these days. That's why I dismissed my feelings but told her to give me all the information and details about the ship before she left.

After we hung up, I tried to focus on the hot guy who was waiting for me to start our third movie of the evening, but I couldn't stop thinking about Ma's strange travel plans. A woman in her late fifties, who had never even been on an airplane, was going to Europe on a cruise by herself. Why wouldn't she ask a friend to go with? Or even better, why wouldn't she ask her daughter? I wondered. Money was certainly no issue. The only thing I could think of was, maybe my mother just wanted to be alone. And if that was the case, I was happy for her, happy that she now had the means to do whatever the hell she felt like doing.

Frankie had never traveled. As a matter of fact, when I thought about it, Ma had never done anything fun in her life. She was always saving, saving, saving. Sending Danny and I to college was her main reason for being so conservative. She once told me that no matter what, I would have a college degree. She'd find a way to pay for it, but I would have to find a way to graduate. Ma was so selfless back then. When exactly had my mother turned from selfless to selfish? I wondered. All my life, she'd wanted what was best for me. Now, she wanted grandchildren, and she was stopping at nothing to get them.

"Ready?" asked Drew, his hand on the remote, ready to press play.

"Sure."

"Are you okay?"

"Yeah, I just think it's really strange that my mother's going on vacation. She's really changed."

Drew smiled, "money changes people."

"You don't know the half of it!" I wanted to shout out. I didn't, though. I just answered, "I guess you're right."

And while I watched an older Michael Corleone dance with his seventeen year old daughter, I found myself thinking about the changed Frankie Jacobson. And then I realized something. Who was I kidding? She hadn't changed. Just as my mother was psychic when it came to me, I realized I could read her, too. Ma had not changed. Something weird was going on. And my gut said that something was very, very wrong.

Chapter 20

The next morning was Sunday. Drew had to get up early and go home because he had to work. After he left, I drank a pot of coffee, read three newspapers, and then started a new movie script. The idea: a woman who offers her son and her daughter millions of dollars to have babies. Pretty clever, huh? Essentially, it was a fictitious adaptation of what my nutty mother was putting Danny and I through. I figured this whole nightmare had to have a silver lining, so why not write about it? A person bribing her kids for grandkids was so far-fetched, it seemed like fiction. People would think that was funny, right? I didn't think it was funny in the least, but I figured, why not capitalize on it?

As I typed away on my laptop, the words flowing easier than they ever had with any script I'd written, the story as compelling and engaging as it was in real life, I felt I was writing something that would surely sell. The irony was killing me. My crazy, unethical, messed up life was the root of an amazing movie script that might make me a ton of money. Maybe I wouldn't need Frankie's after all!

JACKIE PILOSSOPH

Later in the morning I called Ma to get more details about the cruise. To my dismay, Frankie rushed me off the phone, saying she had a lot to do before the trip, such as last minute shopping, packing and cleaning.

"Can I help?" I asked.

"No, thanks. I'm good."

"Can I at least drive you to the airport tomorrow?"

"Thanks, honey, but you have to work, and I have a limo coming at eight."

This made sense to me. A multi-millionaire was getting a limo to take her to the airport. That's why I didn't push it. I said good-bye and hung up, but just as I had the night before, I felt very uneasy about the way my mother was acting. Was her extreme uncharacteristic behavior a byproduct of being nouveau riche or was I missing something?

I decided to call Danny.

"What do you think?" I asked him.

"I think it's great," he exclaimed, "Maybe Ma will start traveling and get her mind off becoming a grandmother. Who knows? She might end up realizing how nuts she's being and how much she's screwing with our lives."

"Maybe you're right," I told him, "But still, something's fishy. It's weird."

"Look, I think you're reading into things too much. Relax. Be happy for her. More importantly, are you pregnant yet?"

"Danny!"

"What? Isn't it a valid question?"

"I guess," I said with a shrug, "I could be pregnant. I don't know yet."

"Boy, that would be nice for you, huh?"

"Sure. I'll be rich."

"Look, Jamie, I really do think you'll be a good mother. I mean it."

"Thanks," I said to my brother as I stared at the living room floor and daydreamed about what I'd done there about fourteen hours earlier. Danny had no idea that I'd fallen for Drew and I was scared to tell him, as if saying it out loud might make it more real. But who was I kidding? It *was* real. My feelings for Drew Conrad were about as genuine as they could be. Baby or no baby, I was falling. Hard.

"How are things with you?" I asked.

"Not that good. I never realized how hard it is to find a girl to have sex with, let alone find one to get into a relationship with."

"What do you think you're going to do?"

"Well, I've been on the computer all morning looking into adoption."

"Any luck?"

"It's just too long of a process. I highly doubt someone's going to give a single guy a baby within the next two and a half months."

I took a deep breath. "Look, Danny, if I do end up getting the money, I hope you know I'm happy to help you out financially."

"What? No thanks. I don't need any handouts."

"That's not what I meant. I just mean…"

"I'm a big boy. I don't need my little sister supporting me. I'll get my own baby and my own money!"

"I didn't mean to offend you."

"I've got to go," he said.

"Are you mad at me?"

"No, Jamie," he said sadly, "I'm mad at myself."

I hung up the phone feeling really sad. Sad for Danny, sad for Drew, sad for myself, even sad for Ma. What a bad situation we were all in. The upside was, in my case the bad situation had a really great side effect. I was Drew Conrad's girlfriend. And I was anything but sad about that.

I was about to get in the shower when suddenly I got a sharp pain in my stomach. Did my conversation cause so much stress that I was experiencing stomach pain from it? Or maybe I'd had too much coffee? The pain began getting worse. I found myself holding my stomach. Seconds later, everything made sense. My pains were period cramps.

I ran to the bathroom and sat on the toilet. Within seconds, I had tears in my eyes. My life was so messed up. Here I was, upset because there was no little Jamie (or Drew) on the way, and my reason for being disappointed was sickening. I didn't care that I wasn't going to be a mother in nine months, I cared that I wasn't going to collect eight million dollars. My morals had gone bu-bye.

Why couldn't I bring myself to just tell Frankie I wasn't interested in her contract, and that she could keep her money? Where were my values? Where was my pride? They were in my wallet. I wanted to make movies, I wanted to be wealthy, I wanted out of WGB. Maybe I wasn't such a bad person. Maybe I was just a desperate person. And maybe desperate people did desperate things. Ma was a perfect example.

So being my mother's daughter, I pulled myself together and decided that I knew what I had to do. I popped two Advil, showered, and headed to Walgreen's. Once inside, I slowly and cautiously walked down the feminine hygiene aisle, praying I wouldn't run into anyone I knew. What I was looking for would have shocked my friends. Not my family, though. Thanks to my baby-loving mother, I was in search of an ovulation kit.

I had to face it. I was a little bit older. Getting pregnant might actually pose a challenge, which was a weird mindset to a girl who had spent her entire adult life trying *not* to get knocked up. If I really wanted a baby, I needed to go to the next step, which was to actually pinpoint the days I was ovulating. Then I would seduce Drew on those days.

When I made it to the ovulation kit section, I was overwhelmed at how many brands and kinds of kits there were to choose from. There was a huge market for this. I giggled bitterly as I thought about the fact that everyone was willing to pay for babies, although not to Frankie's extreme. I settled for the *One-Step* brand and quickly put the other two finalists back on the shelf. Then I paid and got the hell out of there.

Once outside, I felt relieved I didn't see anyone familiar. I also felt a sense of accomplishment, like I'd just done something that might make a difference in my life. As I walked down the street with my new little friend in its bag, my thoughts drifted once again to the living room floor and to Drew; sweet, hunky, adorable Drew. I didn't deserve him. But I had him and that's all that mattered right now.

"Jamie?" I heard all of a sudden, my name snapping me out of the romantic daze I was in. I looked up. Standing there was none other than my ex-fiancé. "Hey girl," Max said playfully. He was trying so hard to be cool and nonchalant, but it wasn't working for the guy. It would *never* work for him. Ever.

I decided to play nice. "Hi Mr. Engaged man," I said with a grin, "How's it going?"

"Not bad...not bad..." Max said in that same tone. His cockiness was unbelievable. Hadn't he gotten enough revenge last time I'd seen him? Obviously not. He wanted to rub it in more. "Just doing a lot of wedding stuff. Picking out my tux, planning my bachelor party, you know…" Then he stopped for a second. "Well, I guess you *don't* know," he said sadly and with some drama.

Now I became annoyed. Was he patronizing me? Was he actually forgetting the fact that *I* was the one who ended it, and that because of me he was marrying the person he was marrying? I felt like he thought I was devastated about him being off the market. All I could think about at this moment was how much I wanted to burn him.

"So, what are you up to?" he asked.

Suddenly, I realized that the object I was carrying in my bag was a ticket to revenge. I pulled it out and held it up. "This!" I exclaimed. "I'm trying to have a baby with the man I've fallen madly in love with." I wondered for a split second if perhaps what I just blurted out was actually the truth.

Max stood there with his jaw on the ground.

"I've got to go," I continued, "My honey's waiting for me at home…" I put the kit back into the bag and then stood on my tiptoes and put my lips right in Max's ear. "In bed," I whispered. Then I waved, turned around, and walked away. I never looked back to see Max's reaction, but I felt it. I knew I had really shocked him, and deep down I knew I'd hurt him. And it didn't make me feel good. It made me feel like crap, actually.

Instead of going home, I decided to take a walk. It felt nice to stroll without being in a hurry, and since I was feeling so many different emotions, I needed to clear my head. I felt angry with my mother. As far as Drew, I felt happy because of him, sad because of him and alive because of him. Drew Conrad was the unexpected lucky penny who had come into my life. So how could I be angry at Frankie? Because of her, I was with Drew.

As I continued down the street, my mind drifted from Max to John and to every other man from my past. I thought about them individually and actually labeled them in my head. Max was the nerd, John, the stud. Then there was Eric, the father figure, Miles, the artsy guy, Adam, the boy toy, and Ken, the uptight closet gay guy. There were many more, all different, but all with one thing in common; wrong for me. Was Drew wrong for me too? I wondered. Initially, (before I was dating him) I labeled him the blue collar guy. Now I hated myself for thinking this way.

Was there something wrong with someone who didn't have a college degree? Drew Conrad was smarter than any Northwestern grad I knew. Plus he had a good heart. Wasn't that worth more than anything? If Drew was anywhere near me at this very moment, I probably would have jumped into his arms and hugged him like a little girl whose dad just got home from a business trip. I missed him. All the time now.

I kept walking, feeling somewhat dazed. A couple blocks further down, I stumbled upon a store I'd never seen before. I was thinking it must be new, because I seemed to remember some kind of shoe repair place in this spot, which was now gone. Stopping to take a closer look into the windows of the store, I was captured by the display of lacy bras and underwear in a rainbow of different colors. I suddenly felt very sexy, which made sense when I looked up and read the sign, "YOU SEXY THING YOU-Sexy Lingerie for Sexy Women." I giggled when I read the bottom part of the window that read, "And by the way, all women are sexy." I was so intrigued now, I had to go inside.

I walked in and began looking around. Dozens of racks with beautiful lingerie were all around the pretty store. I smiled, realizing I was definitely in the market for something in this shop.

"Hi. Let me know if I can help you," said a very attractive woman, "My name's Courtney." Miraculously enough, it never clicked that this was Danny's Courtney.

"Okay, thanks," I answered, still feeling sexy, but not as sexy as her. A lavender lace teddy caught my eye. I picked it up and examined it for a few seconds. Then I examined the price, a hundred and twenty five dollars. I put it back immediately and moved on. I was thinking about walking out, but I didn't for two reasons. First, I didn't want Miss Sexy to think I was cheap, and second, I wanted to see more. All of it was so pretty.

A brown leopard bra with matching underwear were the next things that interested me. I picked them up. Sixty-five for the bra, thirty-five for the undies. Ouch. They were nice, though. 'Drew would love them,' I sold myself.

'Sixty-five dollars for a bra you can buy at Target?' I could hear Ma saying. And that was it. Sold. I didn't even try them on. Besides, now that Ma was Miss Millions, maybe she wouldn't have that attitude anymore.

"I'd like to buy these," I said to Miss Sexy, who in my eyes was now Miss overpriced. Then I headed to the counter.

"Cute…" said Courtney, "Want to look around more?"

'Not unless I want to spend a quick five hundred bucks,' I felt like saying. "No thanks. I think I'm good."

I set the bra and panties, as well as my Walgreen's bag down on the counter. As Courtney started to ring up the sale, I noticed something else on a nearby rack. It was a chocolate brown, long, silky nightgown, the top of it a halter that tied in the back. I picked it up and loved how soft it felt. It was so elegant, so classy.

"Isn't that pretty?" said Courtney, "It goes so well with what you're buying."

I looked at the size. Medium. Perfect. I looked at the price, one seventy-five. Not so ideal. After hesitating for about two seconds, I decided I loved it, and had to have it. "Okay, I'll get this too," I said.

"You'll be glad you did. It's really something."

She was right. It was beautiful. More importantly, I knew Drew would love it. I started to think about him touching it. And touching me. Suddenly, I felt happy and very very very sexy.

"Two ninety-nine o six," said Courtney.

I must have gasped without hearing myself, because after I handed Courtney my credit card, she did something really nice.

"Listen," she said, "I was going to put that nightgown on sale in a few days..." She re-rang the register. "How does two thirty-one even sound?"

"Are you sure?" I asked.

"Yes. You seem like you're buying this for a special occasion. Am I right?"

I thought about the words special occasion. Every night with Drew was like a special occasion, most of the dates better than any Valentine's day I could ever remember. I smiled at Courtney and answered, "You could say that."

"I can tell. You're glowing."

"Are you the owner?"

"I am," she said, as she wrapped the things in tissue.

"Well thank you so much. I'm sure you're going to do great here."

Courtney smiled and handed me the bag. "You think so?"

"Of course I do."

I walked out of the store. In my left hand, I held a bag with a bra, undies, and a beautiful nightgown in it. In my right hand I held an ovulation kit. And in my heart, I held Drew Conrad, the camera man whom I'd pursued for a baby and for money, but whom I couldn't deny any longer, was instead taking my breath away more and more with each passing day.

Chapter 21

I kept walking down the block. For some reason, I didn't want to go home yet. I began to notice little things I'd never taken the time to see before, like an elderly couple walking peacefully hand in hand, a younger couple sitting on a bench, feeding each other ice-cream, and two college-age kids passionately kissing.

What made relationships work? I wondered. When I was with any one of my old flames, we'd never been as happy as these people seemed. Then I saw something that made me think maybe the previous three couples were flukes; not the norm. I noticed a guy and a girl standing in front of a store arguing. They were shouting at each other. I watched intently. 'See?' I thought to myself, 'This is what eventually happens in relationships.'

I pretended to look in the window of *Banana Republic* so I could get closer and hear more of their fight. The yelling was getting louder. Now the girl looked as if she might cry. It reminded me of my relationship with John. I thought to myself, 'I rest my case.' Maybe no one was truly happy in a relationship.

All of a sudden, the couple stopped shouting and silence ensued for a moment. What was going on? The suspense was killing me. It was like watching a movie. I was waiting for the girl to run off. That didn't happen, though. Instead, both the guy and the girl burst out laughing.

I stood there baffled. I didn't get it. They seemed so angry at each other just seconds ago. Now they were laughing so hard that the girl actually had tears streaming down her face. The laughing went on for a couple more minutes and then they hugged.

"I'm sorry, honey," said the guy.

"Me, too," answered the girl, sniffling.

Then I watched the guy wipe away his girlfriend or wife's tears with his finger. It wasn't until he and I made eye contact and I realized he caught me spying on them that I quickly turned and continued down the block.

I couldn't believe it. Was everyone happy? Strangely, I found myself angry. I was resenting these people and feeling bitter about everyone who was fulfilled in their relationships. And then I realized, why begrudge them? Join them! With Drew, true happiness was in my grasp. All I had to do was reach out and take it. And forget about the baby for money scam, of course.

But even if I did that and told Drew the whole story, there was a chance he might never speak to me again. And as much as it disgusted me to question it, was I really willing to give up eight million dollars? What if I ended up with no money *and* no Drew? I needed answers and I needed them fast. A second later, I saw an opportunity to get them.

I was staring up at a tiny storefront with nothing but a dark curtain in the window. A small handmade sign was scotch-taped to the door. It read, "Tarot Card Reader." With zero hesitation, I opened the door and walked in.

The place was literally as big as my bathroom. It was dark and it smelled like burning incense. As I took a couple steps further inside, the wood floors creaked loudly. The door I had just come through swung shut, and instantly, an old woman appeared from behind a large, velvet, mahogany curtain. She looked Middle-Eastern. Her dark skin was wrinkled and her long black hair had streaks of gray running through it. Her eyes were the brownest I'd ever seen. They reminded me of Greek olives.

The woman wore a long full skirt and a white blouse, and on her feet were wooden clogs. As she approached me, all I could focus on was how strange it was that her footsteps weren't making any noise. It made the woman seem sort of magical.

"Would you like a read today?" she asked me in a heavy accent, which confirmed that she was from somewhere like Egypt or Syria.

"Umm, okay…sure."

The woman eyed me over. "Come," she said. She didn't seem mean, but she wasn't warm and fuzzy either.

I followed her behind a curtain and into another room, and I found my heart beating faster. I was about to get some valuable information! Maybe the cards would tell me how to get out of my potentially explosive situation, or better yet, when exactly I should sleep with my boyfriend to conceive.

The room I was in now was even smaller than the reception area. I'm not lying when I say it was literally the size of my shower. The only furniture in it was a tiny round table with cards on it, and two wooden stools with cushions on them. Several lit candles on the floor were burning.

"My name is Sarina," the woman said softly, "Sit please."

Suddenly, I loved Sarina! After all, wasn't she holding the key to Frankie's cash register? I put the bags down next to my stool and sat down.

"I've never had my cards read," I said, nervousness enveloping me. "In fact, I've never had any type of psychic treatment before."

Sarina, who was slowly mixing the deck of large cards did not respond.

"So, how much is this?" I asked, my voice slightly shaking. The second the words came out of my mouth, I regretted them because now I felt like Sarina was going to judge me and/or be annoyed by me, and I was afraid that might affect my reading. "Never mind," I added quickly, "It doesn't matter."

"You pay later," said Sarina, putting down the deck of cards. "Let me see hands," she then said with authority, as she pulled both of my hands toward her. She turned them over to view my palms, closed her eyes, and began feeling them with her palms. This was getting a bit weird for me, but desperate times called for desperate measures, and this sweet, old woman hardly seemed like a lesbian to me, so I figured I should just let her do her thing.

After what seemed like a long time, Sarina opened her eyes and let go of my hands. "We begin," she said, picking up the deck of cards.

Out of nervousness, I cleared my throat.

"You cut cards," she said, putting the deck in front of me. I did what I was told with enthusiasm.

Sarina then laid out five cards on the table. I looked at her face to try to read her expression, but there was none. She just kept staring at the cards.

"So?" I asked.

"The magician," she said.

It was hard to keep silent. I was extremely anxious and wanted to say, "Can you pick up the pace?" but I didn't. I actually had to bite my lip to prevent myself from speaking again while I waited for Sarina to make a comment.

"The magician represents the conscious mind," she finally said, "It focuses on an idea, or a goal."

"I definitely have a goal!" I exclaimed.

"The conscious mind brings these ideas into action."

"Does it say how?"

Now this sweet, gentle, old woman looked annoyed with me and I felt like a complete idiot.

Sarina looked right at me. "The table in front of him has all the tools to make this possible."

"I don't mean to be rude, but you're being a little too vague," I said, "What's on the table?"

"What do you see?"

I couldn't take it anymore. Sarina was speaking too metaphorically for me. I didn't want theoretical advice, I wanted a practical solution. The bottom line, I wanted to know specifically what I needed to do to get knocked up. "Okay...you're not really helping. What's the next card?"

Sarina shot me a look and suddenly I felt judged, and I guess in a way, I didn't blame her for that. She turned over another card and said, "This is the lover's card. Are you in love right now?"

"No!" was my gut reaction.

"The lover's card represents relationships. It symbolizes the union of opposites."

"Well, we're definitely opposites," I said, trying to sound cute.

"Opposite, but compatible," said Sarina.

"Yes!" I responded. Things were looking up. Maybe Sarina would be able to help me. "I have to admit," I said, "the sex is great."

No reaction from Sarina.

"What I really want to know…the reason I'm here…is to find out if I'm going to get pregnant anytime soon."

"You are looking for the sun, the giver of life."

I stood up, about to burst. "Yes! Please!"

Sarina looked back down at the cards. "I'm sorry. It's not here."

"It has to be!" I said, sitting back down. I picked up the deck of un-dealt cards and handed them to Sarina. "Please…deal me another card."

"This is not your read," she said sadly, "it won't work."

I didn't want to believe her. "Come on…hit me," I said, practically shoving the deck in her face.

"This isn't black jack. This is your life."

Now I was exasperated. "Look, I need a baby, and I need to know if it's in the cards, so to speak." I found myself pleading with this woman. "Please, help me."

Sarina continued to study the cards, and suddenly I felt like a stand-by passenger watching a gate attendant type away on a computer while waiting to see if I was getting on the next flight.

"Well?" I said, after a few moments.

Sarina looked at me and I knew something was wrong. "What is it?"

She pointed to the next card and said, "This card…"

"Yeah?"

"This card represents the fool."

Chapter 22

It was almost dinner time when I got home, and I realized I hadn't eaten all day. The whole tarot card experience pretty much took my appetite away until I got far, far away from that awful place. So, the first thing I did when I walked in the door was order an Italian salad from *O'Fame*. It came with fresh Italian bread and olive oil, and I always asked for extra bread. Pinot Noir went perfectly with this meal, so I opened up a bottle while waiting for the food.

I took my glass of wine into the bedroom and sat down on my bed, sipping it while examining the ovulation kit. While reading the directions and general information about it, I thought about how incredible science was. In my hand, I held a test. All I had to do was pee on a stick everyday for seven days and it would tell me the days of the month I was most likely to conceive a baby. The concept was unbelievable to me. I thought about what a great way it was to help people, people who really wanted children for the *right* reasons.

I had spent so long not wanting to get pregnant that I'd never considered the opposite problem; infertility.

Ma had told me about some of her friends' kids who'd taken fertility drugs, or who'd gone through in-vitro fertilization to have babies, but I'd never really thought about how heartbreaking it must be for couples having difficulty conceiving a child. At this moment, Courtney, the girl Danny told me he really liked popped into my head and I felt badly that I wasn't more sympathetic when he told me about her.

I stored the ovulation kit, (which I planned on using in seven days like the box said) in the bathroom cabinet and returned to my bed, where the *You Sexy Thing, You* bag sat. I pulled my beautiful new nightgown out of the tissue paper, held it up to my body and looked in the mirror. Seven days from now I'd wear this for Drew. I couldn't wait.

Drew was either reading my mind or he had put a hidden camera in my bedroom last time he was here, because right at this moment, he called. I thought the call was from my doorman, telling me *O'Fame* was here, so when I heard Drew's voice I was pleasantly surprised.

"Hi," he said.

"Hi!"

"What are you doing?"

I looked at the nightgown, now lying flat on the bed. "Thinking about your hands all over me," I wanted to say. "Um, nothing. Waiting for my dinner. I just ordered…"

"Let me guess," he said, "*O'Fame?*"

I looked up at the ceiling and all around the room for the hidden camera before realizing once again, how well Drew really knew me.

"Yes."

"I knew it," he said proudly. "Listen, I'm going out of town for a few days. I'm leaving tomorrow morning."

"Is everything okay?"

"It will be," he said. Then he hesitated again before finishing, "I'm going to Arizona to see my dad and Monica."

Now I understood. Since the night Drew had told me about his dad pretty much stealing his girlfriend, the subject had never come up again. I'd wanted to ask him about it several times, but the timing never seemed quite right. I knew nothing about the situation other than the fact that his Dad and Monica were married and lived in Arizona.

"Jamie, I don't know what it is about you. Maybe I'm just happy because you're in my life now, but I feel like it's time for me to reconcile with them."

"Are you saying you haven't spoken to them?"

Drew took a deep breath. "After Monica and I got back from our trip to Arizona, she ended our relationship. I found out later she had been sneaking around with my dad the entire time we were visiting. How I didn't see it is unbelievable," he said, "I felt so stupid."

"No, Drew, you weren't stupid. That's how I felt, too, with John."

"My dad called me a couple of weeks later and told me Monica was moving down there to be with him. Three months later, they were married."

"God, I'm so sorry," was all I could manage. I was blown away. I felt for him immensely. This poor guy's girlfriend cheated on him. With his own father! "I have to say something, though. It's pretty amazing that you're not bitter about it. In fact, you're not bitter about anything."

"No, I'm not bitter. I'm just commitment-phobic," he joked.

"That's understandable."

"Anyhow, my dad and I haven't talked for more than two minutes at a time since the whole thing happened. He tried to make amends, but I just couldn't deal."

"I can't say I blame you."

"The thing is, he's getting older and it's time for me to let it go and just let him be happy. Her too, I guess. So, I'm going to go down there for a nice visit, basically to give them my blessing."

"I think that's really great."

"I know this sounds really strange, but a lot of how I feel is because of you," he said, "You're making me really happy, Ms. Jacobson, and I guess my heart's wide open and ready to forgive and love my dad again."

"I'm glad. How long will you be gone?"

When he told me a week, I was instantly saddened. Don't get me wrong. I was truly happy for him and knew his trip was a good decision, but I would miss him terribly.

"Can I come over and say good-bye?" Drew asked.

"Right now?"

"Yeah."

"Sure," I said with a wide grin, "Come share my salad with me."

Twenty minutes later, Drew was at my door and when I opened it, he put his arms around me and hugged me for a long time.

I led him to the kitchen table, where salad, wine, and lots of bread were waiting for us. While we ate, Drew told me more about his mom and how devastated his dad was when she died. He also talked about his brother, Mark, who lived in California, and how the whole Monica scenario had driven a wedge between not only Drew and his dad, but between all of them.

"So, I called Mark, too, and he's going to meet me in Arizona."

I held up my wine glass and said with a smile, "So, it's a true family reunion."

"I guess so," Drew smiled.

We ate in silence for the next couple minutes and then Drew did the sweetest thing. He put his hand on mine and said, "I've had the best time with you the past few weeks. I'm going to miss you."

I then had an out of body experience. I put down my fork and leaned over to Drew. Smiling through tears, I cupped his face in my hands and looked right into his eyes. "I'll be here waiting for you when you get home."

At that very moment, all I could think about was that me, Miss Manipulative-money-hungry-user, hadn't trapped Drew into fatherhood. I had instead trapped *myself* into a relationship. Drew was my boyfriend and I cared about him deeply. And admitting that didn't seem so hard all of a sudden.

After dinner, we cuddled on the couch for awhile, watched *Curb Your Enthusiasm* and of course, the WGB 9:00 news. Drew was lying behind me, spooning me. I eventually drifted into a consciousness that was half out of it, half awake. It was the awake half that heard the words that would change everything.

"I love you, Jamie," Drew whispered.

The fake sleeper lie still. My heart was pounding and I wanted so badly to say it back. I didn't, though. I just kept pretending I was sleeping. In the never-ending war between courage and fear, fear had just declared victory in this battle.

Chapter 23

Jamie and I had a bond. We'd always been close. We had had only each other for as long as I could remember. Our dad was out of the picture so early on and Ma was always working, so we took care of each other. We helped each other out. I'd help my sister brush her teeth. She'd help me with math problems. I taught her how to tie her shoes. And she taught me every word to the song, **The Devil Went Down to Georgia.**

Of course, as we got older we drifted apart a little bit and had separate social lives. I hung with the cool crowd, my sister tended to befriend all the nerds in school. But as adults, we became close again. It was an unwritten rule that the two of us would be here for each other if needed. And we would help each other, just as we did as kids. That's why Jamie had promised me the lead if she ever got funding to make a movie.

Jamie and I were close. Jamie and Ma were close. Ma and I, not so close. I loved my mother dearly, but she drove me nuts. My sister did too, actually, but she was my little sister and I'd always be her big bro.

So, I wasn't angry with her for offering me a handout if she ended up coming through with a baby for Ma's money. In fact,

JACKIE PILOSSOPH

part of me felt grateful. But, boy, did she strike a nerve. My ego was having a really hard time with my baby sister giving me money for the rest of my life. I was perfectly capable of obtaining the inheritance myself. And that was the thought that led me to the W Hotel on Lakeshore Drive.

The bar at the W is famous for two things; its Cosmopolitans and its reputation for being the easiest pick-up joint in Chicago. So, here I sat, dressed in my Lucky Brand jeans and a navy Polo shirt, ready to find myself a woman. Not just for sex, though. Well, yes, for sex, but specifically for sex to lead to a pregnancy.

Already on my third martini, I decided the bar wasn't living up to its expectations, and I'm not referring to the drinks. Girls weren't so easy to seduce under these times of extreme pressure. I'd already talked to three women and had been unsuccessful in wooing any of them into bed for the night.

The first girl turned out to be meeting her boyfriend there. After buying the second girl two Grey Gooses (or is it Geese?) on the rocks, I found out this hopeful mother of my child was a lesbian. And ironically, the third girl was pregnant! I found this out when I went to buy her a drink.

"What can I get you?" I asked.

"Just a Coke please," she said with a smile.

"Aww, come on, let me buy you something that costs more," I flirted, "How about one of these?" I asked, motioning to my Cosmo. And that's when she broke the news to me.

So here I sat, still alone and still desperate and determined to find someone. I told myself I wouldn't leave this place alone tonight, no matter what. Suddenly, to my unexpected surprise, my luck changed. A very attractive woman sat down next to me.

"Hi," I said to this beauty with the prettiest pink frosted lips I'd seen all night.

The girl gave me a courtesy smile that was a bit standoffish. Then she waved the bartender over.

"What can I get you?" the bartender asked her.

"Whatever she's having, I'm buying," I said.

"You don't have to do that," she replied. Then she looked at the bartender and said, "I'll have a vodka and cranberry please."

The bartender went off to make the drink.

"Thanks," she said, shyly.

"No problem. I'm Danny," I said, holding out my hand.

She shook my hand and said, "Look, I don't mean to be rude, but I'm not looking to meet anyone."

"Neither am I," I charmed, "Tell you what. Let me buy you the drink and we'll just sit here and not talk."

"Why would we do that?"

At this moment, I noticed her pretty cheekbones. "Because then neither of us will be meeting anyone new, since we're both not looking to do that." I was trying really hard to be funny. "We'll just sit here and drink by ourselve, since that's the only reason we're both here."

"I'm sorry," she giggled, "I didn't mean to sound like a bitch. It's just..." She paused and put her head down.

"Did you just get out of a relationship or something?"

"How did you guess?"

"I could just tell. I'm in the same situation. My girlfriend just dumped me, like last week."

"I'm sorry," she said sweetly, "you must be hurting."

The second her drink came, I made a toast. "To two people who recently got dumped, one who happens to be a complete knockout."

"Thanks," she said with a big grin.

"...And then there's you," I joked.

The girl cracked up and we both laughed as we toasted and sipped our drinks.

Over the next round of cocktails, I found out a lot about frosty pink, whose name was Susan. She was thirty-five, she worked for an advertising agency, and she had moved here from Cincinnati four years earlier. The most important thing I found out about Susan was that she really wanted a baby! Even better, Susan told me that she was completely frustrated because she didn't make enough money. "The bottom line," she said, "is that I want to be wealthy."

Now I knew I'd just hit the jackpot with this one. That's why I wasted no time and decided to get right to the point. After a few martinis, it wasn't hard to be blunt. "Can I be honest with you, Susan?" I slurred.

"Sure."

"No, I mean brutally honest."

"Please..."

"I need to have sex with someone."

The look on Susan's face transformed so quickly it was frightening. She looked like she wanted to kill me.

"This drink is about to be thrown in your face, so I would get up pretty quickly if I were you," she said in a very low voice.

I pleaded with her, "No...no...listen to me."

Susan picked up her glass and began tilting it in position to toss it in my face.

"Seriously, Susan, listen! If I don't get a girl pregnant in the next two months, I won't inherit any of my mother's money!"

"What are you talking about?"

"Look, this is serious. I have to have sex, lots of sex, until I get someone pregnant."

She grabbed her purse off the bar and stood up to go. "Sorry, this is just a little too weird for me."

I had to make her understand, so I stopped her. "I have a proposition for you," I said, "If you sleep with me and get pregnant, I promise you, you'll get rich. Plus, you'll have a baby! This couldn't be a more perfect situation for you."

"What are you talking about?"

"I'm talking about millions of dollars. I'm willing to give you a million dollars to have my kid."

Susan took a big gulp of her drink. "Let me get this straight. Did you say A MILLION DOLLARS?"

"Yup," I said, feeling more confident than I did a minute earlier.

"So, what do we do? Start trying tonight?" she asked.

I looked down at Susan's lap. Her legs were crossed and there was a slit in her skirt that was exposing one of her thighs. I found myself so focused on baby-making, that as nice of a thigh as it was, it was barely turning me on.

"Absolutely," I answered. Now I knew I was in.

"So, will you give me some of it tonight?" Susan asked, throwing me a curveball.

I was confused. "What do you mean?"

"I mean, if I sleep with you tonight, I want a thousand dollars."

Now I was a little weirded out. "Are you joking?"

"No," she said, "If I'm going to have sex with you, I deserve to be paid."

I didn't know where this was headed, or what just happened here, but all of a sudden I got this strange feeling about Susan, almost like she was a prostitute. I knew I was being ridiculous for thinking this way, however, because the girl had been so descriptive when talking about her advertising position. My head was spinning, combination confusion and alcohol, but I knew Susan was my last prospect of the evening so I decided to bypass her bizarre behavior and just give things a shot.

I stood up, put my hand in my pocket, pulled out a wad of cash and counted it. "Okay listen, I've got two hundred fifty bucks. What do you think?"

"Can I see it?" she asked.

I handed her the money and within about two seconds, she took it, grabbed her purse off the bar, and pulled out a badge and a pair of handcuffs. "You're under arrest for soliciting a prostitute," she said in a very different voice than she had been using all night.

Before I could even speak, I was being handcuffed. Several bar patrons watched my arrest as Susan, now known as Officer Kay Olson of the Chicago Police Department special crimes unit escorted the suspect out of the bar. I sobered up quick, especially when we got outside and I saw the police car that would take me to jail.

"Are you crazy? I was totally set up! This is entrapment!" I yelled.

Susan, with the beautiful lips and high cheekbones opened the squad car door. "Get in," she said.

Chapter 24

At 6:00 the next morning, I was awakened by the faint ringing of my cell phone. I jumped out of bed, wearing sweats and a t-shirt Drew had left at my place. I wouldn't tell him I loved him, but I was so attached I had now taken to sleeping in his clothes.

I ran around the apartment searching for my ringing phone, wondering who could be calling so early. It was either Drew or Frankie, both headed out of town today and probably calling to say good-bye or give me some last minute details. I finally located my *Blackberry*, which was hidden under a stack of unread mail on the kitchen counter.

"Hello?" I answered.

"Where have you been?" asked Danny. His voice was very loud and very urgent. "I've been calling you for hours!"

"I must not have heard the phone. What's up? What's wrong? Is it Ma?"

"No. I'm in jail."

"What?"

"I'm at the police station at 44th and California. Will you come get me?" he asked.

I stood there in shock.

"And call that guy, Alan, Ma's lawyer," he added.

My head was spinning. Where was 44th and California? Where was Alan's phone number? Most likely it was attached somewhere on the "baby for money" contract.

"Danny, what did you do?"

"Nothing. I'm innocent. I'll explain when I see you."

"Okay, I'll be there as soon as I can."

"And Jamie?"

"Yeah?"

"Bring your checkbook. You know…for bail. And whatever you do, DO NOT call Ma."

"Gotcha," I said, before ending the call. I stood there deciding what to do first. Call the office and tell them I might be late? I could call from the cab. And did the police actually take checks for bail?

Quickly, I took off the sweats, threw on a pair of old jeans and headed out, wondering what on earth Danny could have done to have gotten arrested. In the back of my mind, I somehow knew that the whole baby thing had something to do with it. That's why I had a strong urge to call Ma and let *her* deal with the mess she'd created. But Danny told me not to. Plus, my baby-loving mother was probably at the airport drinking mimosas, waiting for her first-class flight to board.

The first thing I did when I got in the cab was call information for Alan's number. Seconds after I was connected, he answered. I was shocked. I expected to get his voice mail at 6:10 a.m.

"Alan speaking…"

"Hi Alan, this is Jamie Jacobson. I…"

"Hello, Jamie, how may I help you?"

He was being extremely courteous. In fact, the way he was treating me was making me realize how much he really liked my mother. Of course, it didn't hurt that his client was worth millions.

"Well, my brother's in jail. Apparently, he was arrested last night. He's at 44th and California, wherever that is, and I'm on my way there now."

At this moment, I noticed the cab driver checking me out in his rear view mirror.

"Okay, Jamie, slow down," Alan said, "First of all, do you need directions?"

"No, I'm in a cab."

"Okay, good. Now tell me what's going on with Danny. Where and why was he arrested?"

"He didn't tell me anything. He just said to come get him and to call you."

"Okay. One of my colleagues will meet you there shortly to represent Danny and to bail him out. You just get there and don't worry about a thing." Now I surmised that Ma was paying him well.

I thanked Alan, hung up and then realized my cab driver was lost. He proceeded to drive around for a half hour looking for the place. When we finally made it there, Danny and some guy, who I presumed was Alan's lawyer buddy, were standing in the lobby talking.

"It's about time," Danny said with hostility, "First you don't answer your phone, and then it takes you an hour to get here!"

"My cab driver got lost. Excuse me!" I replied.

"Hi, I'm Stan Warshawsky," Alan's guy said, extending his hand.

"Jamie Jacobson."

173

"Nice to meet you. I play the lottery every Monday, Wednesday and Friday," he said, sounding like an infatuated groupie.

I secretly enjoyed the attention.

Danny exploded. "I'm glad. Can we talk about me for a second, please?"

"Yes, let's," I said, "Are you going to tell me what you did?"

"I told you, I'm innocent!" he practically shouted, "Can we go? I'll give you the whole story on the way home."

We got a taxi and headed north to Danny's apartment, during which time he told me all about Susan, A.K.A. Officer Kay Olson of the Chicago Police Department, special crimes unit.

"It's funny," he said, "If you're a guy, you live your life in fear that you might get a call from some girl you slept with one night, telling you she's got a little problem and that the two of you need to talk."

"Now, you'd love to hear those words, huh?"

"Yeah," he chuckled.

"Danny, don't worry about this, okay? Alan will get you out of this mess."

He looked at me and smiled sadly. "Listen, Jamie, it's over for me. I don't want the money."

"Really?"

"Well, I do want the money but what I'm saying is, it's not worth it for me. I'm a really good teacher. Plus, I'm a good actor. I have a lot going for me. I don't need Ma's money so much, that I have to go to this extreme to get it. And by the way, I'm not judging you in any way. You should do what you want to do. But for me, I know what I want."

"Courtney?" I asked.

Danny smiled, "Yeah, Courtney."

I put my head on my big brother's shoulder and I said, "That makes me happy."

Chapter 25

The second I got home from jail, I walked straight into my bedroom and plopped down on the bed. The instant my head hit the pillow, I was out. I slept deeply. And I dreamed. I dreamed so vividly I was sure it was real; the person I was dreaming about was someone I rarely, if ever, dreamed about: my father.

In the dream, there was a knock at my door. I got up out of bed and answered the door. He was standing there.

"Hi," he said.

"Dad, what are you doing here?"

"Can I come in?"

"Uh, sure. Want to sit down?"

"Okay." My dad sat on the couch and I sat on the loveseat. "Can I get you anything? A beer?"

"I can't drink anything, Danny. I'm dead."

Suddenly, I was frightened. Was I like the kid from <u>The Sixth Sense</u>*? I see dead people?*

"Don't worry, son. I'm not a ghost or anything. I just came to talk to you."

"Okay."

"First of all, I want to apologize for dying on you. The day of the snowstorm, I didn't have to stay at school so late and work. I knew a storm was coming. I could have left early like everyone else."

"Why didn't you?"

"Because I'm an idiot. If I could go back in time and change things so that I could be with all of you, you have no idea how much I would do that. But I can't."

"Why are you here right now, Dad?"

He came over and sat down next to me. Then he pulled out a picture of the two of us. In the photo, I was around two. I was dressed in a lion costume, for Halloween, I guessed. Holding me was my dad, and it was easy to see the pride and happiness in his eyes and his smile.

"Remember this?" he asked.

"Not really."

"This little boy was so full of love. He had so much to offer. Now, don't get me wrong. I'm really proud of you. My son's a history teacher for the Chicago Public school district. You can't imagine how much I respect that. All that said, for some reason, over the years, this sweet little kid turned into someone who's afraid to love. How did that happen?"

"What is this? Psych 101? I'm doing just fine Dad, no thanks to you."

"Look, I didn't come here to upset you. I came to help you. I'm sorry I wasn't here for you all these years, but it isn't my fault. I loved you. And I loved your mother and sister, too. Don't let my death scare you into thinking you can't love someone because you might lose them. Good job with that girl…Jillian. So it didn't work out. So what? Wasn't meant to be. At least you took a chance."

"What do you do, Dad? Sit up in heaven and watch me all day?"

"Yeah. And Jamie, and your mother, too. You have a problem with that?"

"I guess not."

"I have one word of advice, son."

"What's that, Dad?"

"Courtney."

"What about her?"

"You like her. Go for it."

"I think I love her."

"That's the spirit! Love's the best, isn't it?"

I smiled at my dad. He seemed a little nerdy, but really awesome. Truthfully, it was so bittersweet it was sickening. *"Yeah, Dad,"* I chuckled, *"I guess it is."* I took the photo out of his hand and asked, *"Can I keep this?"*

With a sad look on his face, my dad took it back. *"Sorry. It's not real. But if I'm not mistaken, you have this picture in a box somewhere. Sometime, if you're bored and you have time to kill, dig it out."*

"Thanks," I said with a smile, *"maybe I will."*

"By the way, Courtney's hot."

"Dad!"

"Sorry, just being honest."

I smiled. *"Is it okay to hug you?"*

"Again, sorry, Danny. I'm not real."

I was disappointed. I put my head down.

"You don't have to hug me to feel me in your heart, son."

With hope in my eyes, I looked up at my father but he was gone, and at that moment the dream ended. I woke up.

"Dad..." I was saying, *"Dad..."*

I sat up, still dazed and in deep thought about the dream I'd just had. I looked at the clock next to my bed. It was 11:14 a.m. I knew I needed more sleep, but there was something I desperately needed to do. I got up and practically staggered across the bedroom. Even though my apartment was the size of a small shoebox, the master bedroom closet was a large walk-in. Go figure. I opened *the closet door and looked around, and then spent the next twenty minutes rummaging through things and putting them back.*

I was in search of two tin boxes. The containers had once held Christmas cookies, but now housed some of my personal things, such as old letters, mementos, birthday cards and last but not least, old photos. The tins had survived every move I'd made (and there were lots in the fifteen years since I'd moved out of Ma's house), yet I never opened them unless I was shoving something new in there.

I moved a couple of big boxes, (I had no clue what was in them) out of the way to see if there was anything behind them. Nothing but some framed posters I'd never hung. Next, I got down on my knees and searched under a rack of clothes that hung to the floor. There I discovered some acting books I'd collected over the years.

There was only one more place to look. The boxes had to be on the top shelf. I got a chair, put it in the closet, and stood on top of it so I could see everything on the shelf. Bingo. There they were. Carefully, I got the tins down, put them on my unmade bed, and began to explore. I was desperate to find the picture of me in the lion costume, the one my dad had shown me in the dream.

During my pursuit, I came across lots of funny, entertaining things. A birthday card from Connie Kleinberg. "Dear Danny, Happy Birthday! Let me come over and give you your birthday gift in person! Love, Connie." This instantly brought a smile to my face. A letter from Jillian. "Dear Danny, hope this letter is finding you well and happy. I thought you should know that I am getting married next month…" Blah blah blah… Who cared?

Next came my sister's wedding invitation. "Jamie Louise Jacobson and John Patrick Sullivan joyfully invite you to share in their happiness as they unite in marriage, Saturday, May 16th…" I shook my head and grinned.

Then I came across a letter from Ma. I remembered receiving it just after college when I was moving to New York. I took it out of the envelope and began to read it.

"Dear Danny, first, I want to tell you that I am so proud of you for graduating from Syracuse. You will find out later how important your degree is and how many opportunities it will help you come across. Congratulations!"

It was as though I was reading Ma's letter for the first time. For some reason, I had no recollection of it.

She went on, "The main reason for this letter, though, is to wish you luck in the big apple. I admire what you're doing, and I have no doubt that you will be a success as both a teacher and an actor, or actually, any career you wish to pursue..."

As I continued reading, I couldn't believe Frankie would ever write something like this. She was so supportive, so optimistic. I realized that when I got this letter all those years ago, I'd chosen to skim it instead of taking the time to really read it. Suddenly, I was ashamed of myself. I read on.

"I'm enclosing this picture of you and Dad. It was taken on Halloween when you were just two years old. Dad picked out the costume. I know if he was here now, he would be proud of what you've accomplished and what you are about to achieve. I love you, Danny, and I'm here for you whenever you need me. Love, Mom."

I put the letter down and picked up its envelope, and sure enough, inside of it was the photo. I took it out and stared at it for a long time. Then, all of a sudden, I began to cry. I sat there and sobbed for a long time, something I RARELY did in the life I'd created for myself, the life with all the walls I'd put up around me.

Maybe I was still grieving about my father, but there was something else. I never realized that there was a part of me who blamed my mother for not having a father. I resented her and that's why I'd always kept my distance. I'd always felt that if I got close to Ma, I was being disloyal to my dead father. In any event, I realized I didn't appreciate my family half as much as I should. I'd always been kind to Ma, like every Jewish kid is to his mother, and I'd been *the best son I knew how to be. Still, there was a certain distance I kept between Frankie and myself, between EVERYONE and myself.*

As I sat there sobbing, I realized that my dream wasn't really my dad talking to me, it was ME talking to me. I didn't really know if my dad could watch us, but I felt pretty certain that if he was up there looking down, he WOULD be proud of me for being a teacher, because I was proud of me. And my dad wasn't the one telling me to go for it with Courtney, I was telling myself that.

And then there was Frankie. Now I desperately wanted to talk to her. I wanted to apologize and tell her what a good mother she was to me all my life. I wanted to tell her how much I loved her, something I wasn't sure I'd actually ever said to her. As soon as she got home from her trip, I would say it. I would tell her I understood how hard her life must have been. And I would ask her questions, lots of questions. I now understood why Jamie always wanted to know all the details of our mom and dad's lives. They were our parents, after all. And living or dead, I wanted to know them both.

I spent most of the day looking through my tins that contained lots of pictures of me and Jamie growing up. Birthday parties, Thanksgiving, Hanukkah, high-school football games, prom, graduation... And what I realized was that Frankie was in every picture. My mother was always there for me, supporting me, encouraging me, and most importantly, loving me.

Yes, she had gone totally overboard with her whole grandchild bribe, but maybe I needed to talk to her about it. Maybe she and I needed to understand each other more. I suddenly wondered how the hell I was going to wait two weeks before seeing her. I was dying to tell her about my eye-opening realizations. I'd have to wait though.

In the meantime, there was someone else I had to have a little chat with, a girl who I was certain my mother would love. More importantly, a girl I was beginning to think I couldn't live without.

Chapter 26

"Pretzel boy! What are you doing here?" cried Vito, when he saw me walk into his shop, "You're not working today."

"No. I'm actually here to buy something."

"Fantastic!"

"I'll take two dozen pretzels, just mix them up."

"Sure, no problem!" said Vito, happily preparing my order, "Nice to see you actually believe in what you sell."

I stood there smiling, but what I really wanted to do is tell Vito to shut up and ring me up quickly.

"Here you go," he said, handing me a box with a big blue bow around it, "forty-o-nine."

I handed him my credit card and a couple minutes later, I headed out the door. "Thanks, Vito," I said.

"See you next Saturday, Pretzel boy!" he said loudly.

"Don't call me that!"

I could hear Vito laughing as I left the shop.

'What an asshole,' I said to myself with a chuckle, as I hailed a cab.

My next stop: You Sexy Thing, You. *I knew Courtney closed her store at 6:00, so I wanted to get there right around then. I figured that would be the best time to talk to her.*

At 6:04 I was standing outside, peeking through the window. There didn't appear to be any customers in the store. All I could see was Courtney reorganizing some nightgowns on one of the racks. God, she was beautiful, and I don't just mean hot-looking. I missed her sweet demeanor, her quirky jokes, her smart, sexy personality, her lips on mine, and her giggle when I teased her about Sean Kingston.

What could I possibly say to get her back? Would she give me another chance? Did I deserve one? I wasn't sure. I just knew I was going for it. I had been in love once in my life. The outcome had sucked. Now, I was being given a second chance and I was going to do everything I could to un-screw up everything I'd done with her. I ate an Altoid, fixed my hair with my fingers, and took a few deep breaths. Then I went into battle.

The minute I walked in the door, I knew I was screwed. Courtney saw me and I watched the relaxed, peaceful look on her face instantly transform to uncomfortable.

"Hi," I said with a nervous grin.

"Danny, hi..." she said. She seemed so nervous, it was painful.

Right then, some dude walked out of the bathroom.

"Who's this?" the guy asked.

Courtney turned to him. "Matt, this is a friend of mine, Danny Jacobson. Danny, this is Matt Hill."

The guy extended his hand to shake mine and had the nerve to say, "Nice to meet you. I'm Courtney's boyfriend."

"Really?" I asked.

"We've known each other for four days," Courtney answered.

"I don't think that really matters," answered Mr. P-whipped.

"Courtney, can I talk to you for a minute?" I asked.

"Sure..."

We both looked at Matt, expecting him to walk out of the room, but he just stood there. "Dude, I'm thinking you should go outside for a minute," I said to him, "Is that cool?"

Matt looked at Courtney. "Is that okay?" she asked him.

"Sure." He looked pissed, but he did it.

The second he was gone, I said, "You already have another boyfriend?"

"He's a little bit of a stalker, I have to say, but he really likes me."

"Do you like HIM?"

"Why are you here, Danny?"

I handed her the box of pretzels. "I came to apologize. I was such a jerk. I'm so sorry."

"What is this?" she asked, holding up the box.

"Chocolate covered pretzels."

"Thank you. That's thoughtful."

"Sure."

"Listen, you weren't that bad. You just did what you felt was right."

"See, that's just it. I DIDN'T do what I felt at all. I was selfish and a complete idiot. Look, here's how I feel..." Then, I kissed her, and I mean hard on the mouth. I pulled away after a minute and said, "I like you, Courtney, in fact, I like you more than anyone I think I've ever liked."

"What about Matt?" she asked.

I looked at my watch. "It's 6:10. Maybe you can have a little chat with him, and then I'll meet you for dinner at 7:00? Where should we go?"

"You're unbelievable!"

"Not really. I just know I like you and I think you like me. And I don't want to waste one more minute being without you. I don't want to scare you and I don't want to be a stalker, but I feel

a connection I don't think I've ever felt before. And I think you do, too. Don't you?"

"Can I ask you something?"

"Sure."

"My not being able to have kids, are you really okay with that?"

I gave her a huge grin and said, "More than you can imagine."

Courtney's face lit up. "I'll meet you at Las Pinata's at 7:00."

I went to kiss her again, but this time she pulled away. "Go. I don't want Matt to see this."

"Okay," I said with a smile and a wave. Then I walked outside and told her boyfriend he could come back in. I did feel kind of sorry for the guy, but I felt great for myself!

As promised, Courtney showed up at Las Pinatas at 7:00 and we ended up having a couple margaritas, chips, salsa, and tacos. It was a really fun night and I couldn't have been more sure that I did the right thing giving up the cash and going for my girl.

After dinner, we ended up back at her place, where I spent the night. And yes, we slept together. I knew we weren't making babies, but I didn't care. What I felt for this woman far outweighed my desire to knock up some chick and get my mother's money. Screw it. I was done.

Eventually I would tell Courtney about Frankie's contract, and even though the thought of it made me cringe, I would also have to let her know I got arrested for solicitation of prostitution. I wasn't looking forward to that, but I would figure out the right time to tell her about everything. Right now, I just wanted to enjoy her and get to know her better. I felt like we had all the time in the world now. And it felt amazing.

For the next week, I pretty much lived at Courtney's apartment. Besides going home to get more clothes, or going to my job, I was a new fixture at her place. So uncharacteristic of my personality, I felt extremely at ease there, and other than the tremendous fear I felt *every time I got off the elevator and passed Jennifer's door, I was truly enjoying co-habitation.*

Every morning, both of us would go to work, and like some whipped dude, I'd constantly think about how great it was going to be when we both walked through the door that evening. I found myself smiling all day, like some love-struck idiot. Even my students noticed.

"Mr. Jacobson, what's up with you?" asked Corinne Keller.

"Mr. J., you're different," said Will Jones.

"Mr. J. has a girlfriend," said Angela Walker, smiling from ear to ear, "I can tell."

I smiled back at my number one, bright, beautiful student, who looking at these days made me depressed as hell, since she was planning on leaving school in the next couple of months. Angela was job searching and was set to drop out of Martin Luther King as soon as something came through. And as much as I'd tried to convince her not to quit school, her mind seemed to be made up. She was going to be a mom and a high-school dropout, and she was going to give up her dream career in marketing and public relations. I couldn't understand why she didn't think she could do both.

But as frustrated as I was about my student, I was on cloud nine for myself. I did some very romantic things that week. I just wanted to do nice things for Courtney. I felt like she deserved it. On Tuesday, I sent a dozen red roses to her store. Thursday, I gave her my high-school basketball jersey (which really meant a lot to me) so she would have something to sleep in besides lacy lingerie. And on Saturday, after my miserable day of dressing up like Mr. Salty, I ordered Ranalli's pizza (which besides being good pizza was sentimental) and had dinner on the table when Courtney walked in the door at 6:15. The table was set, candles were lit, and a Nora Jones CD was playing on the stereo.

"What's all this?" she asked.

"Dinner."

"You did all this for me?"

"Sure."

"Why?"

"Because I…" The words I love you were dying to come out. They were festering inside my body, trying to escape the frightened idiot who never had the guts to use them.

"Because you mean a lot to me," I said.

Courtney threw her arms around me and told me I meant a lot to her, too. I was pissed at myself. 'Did I have any balls at all?' I wondered. As my girlfriend held me in her arms, I told myself that I'd tell her I loved her soon. Very soon. I would tell her lots of things very soon. Very soon…

Chapter 27

Rarely do I start my day at 5:30 in the morning, but today I was so excited that I popped out of bed. This was a big day for me. According to the directions of my ovulation kit, I was supposed to start testing myself six days after my period. Today was that day. Today was also the day I was seeing my boyfriend for the first time in almost a week. Drew had gotten home late the night before and would be at work this morning. I was so excited to see him I could barely stand it.

The week he was gone, he texted me a few times and called twice, but both times I could tell it was hard for him to talk because his family was around. What I got from him, though, was that he was having a good time and that he was glad he'd chosen to go there.

"I'll give you more details when I get back," he said during one of our conversations. Other things he said and texted during the week were, "I miss you," "I can't wait to see you," and "I can't stop thinking about you."

My response to all of those sentiments was the same every time. "Me too," I'd say or text.

Drew did tell me he loved me one time during his trip. My response was not "me too." Instead, I went with, "Okay, well, have fun! See you soon!"

He chuckled and then said, "Sleep well, honey."

Honey did sleep well, thanks to the Xanax I felt like I desperately needed as a result of hearing "I love you" again. I knew "I love you" wasn't going away. I felt sure that Drew really did mean it. As far as my feelings, they were all over the map. Yes, I was pretty sure I loved him, too. But what about the plan? What about the baby? The money? My desire to be wealthy and make movies was still a big priority. Couldn't I have it all? I wasn't sure, and I felt like I was in too deep to tell Drew the truth.

At 5:35 a.m., I had my official result of the ovulation test, which was that I, Jamie Jacobson, was in fact in baby-making mode. I was ovulating! According to the doctors who commented on the pamphlet, it was highly unusual for a woman to ovulate on "day 6," but possible. My heart began to pound. This was it! My egg was ready to be fertilized! Cha-ching! And at the same time, the thought of tricking Drew into having a child was causing extreme guilt, and I don't just mean the typical Jewish person's guilt, I'm talking major, major shame and disgust in what my ethical standards had become, and what I was setting out to do. Still, eight million dollars was far outweighing any amount of reason. In fact, it was tipping the scales against morality and integrity as well.

I decided that in any event, I had to look spectacular for work today. I wanted to look my best when Drew saw me for the first time in a week. So, I wore a light pink silk dress with a matching jacket and gold sling-back sandals. I also flat ironed my hair much more than usual, I made sure my nails and toenails were done, and I took lots of extra time putting on my make-up. Just before I headed out, I sprayed two sprays of Chanel Allure on my wrists. I can honestly say, it was the first time I'd ever worn perfume to work.

I got to the station around 8:30 and saw that my boyfriend was already there. He was sitting in the equipment room training a new audio guy named Gerard. He looked so cute! Drew, that is, not Gerard.

Drew was wearing a white Polo and khakis, and I had this strong desire to run in there and squeeze the crap out of him. I couldn't, though, because I didn't want anyone to know about Drew and I yet. I'd never been a big fan of the whole inner office romance thing. In fact, I'd always thought it was a little cheesy to date someone in the office. But I was doing it, and was oh-so-happy about it.

As I spied on Drew, watching him teach Gerard, and at the same time crack jokes in an effort to make the guy feel at ease, I thought about his gift of always being able to find something to smile about, even in a serious situation. I thought back to an incident that happened at the station a couple years earlier. One of the reporters, Samantha Banks was being stalked by some weirdo, who would call and e-mail her dozens of times a day. Samantha tried to let the guy know in a nice way that she wasn't interested, but he was obsessed and wouldn't let it go. Finally, one day, he showed up at the station, and to this day no one can figure out how he got past security.

When Samantha got back from lunch, the stalker was waiting for her in her office. When she walked in, he closed the door behind her, locked it, pulled down the shades and began to attack her physically. Samantha tried to scream but he covered her mouth and began lifting up her skirt. The whole thing was so bizarre because this was happening in broad daylight with everyone going about their daily business, not knowing a rape was about to occur just a few feet away.

Luckily for Samantha, our news director, Larry, had just returned to the office, as well. Larry was a guy who frequently enjoyed a few cocktails during his lunch hour. He headed to Samantha's office to talk to her about a piece she did on Vince Vaughn. Actually, rumor has it that Larry was planning on giving her an earful about how bad he thought the story was.

He knocked on the door and when he realized it was locked, he began pounding on it. Had it not been for Larry's aggressive drunk behavior, God only knows what would have happened. Larry heard noises coming from Samantha's office and began screaming her name while continuing to bang on the door. This apparently caused the attacker to become nervous and lose his concentration, and Samantha was able to let out a scream for help. Larry now knew for sure something was wrong. A few people had begun to gather around Samantha's office door, not knowing what to do, until finally, Chuck, one of the editing guys, grabbed a fire extinguisher and started hitting the door until it broke open.

Drew had just walked by and realized what was going on, so when the psycho guy started to run out, he was able to grab him and hold him down. The whole experience was a nightmare for Samantha, and for everyone in a way, but what I remembered so clearly was Drew making jokes about the attacker to ease the tension and make all of us laugh.

After the cops took the stalker away, Drew went over to Samantha and said, "He really did seem like your type. Want me to call the police station and get his number?" Some people thought it was funny. Even Samantha laughed. At the time, I thought his joking around was annoying and inappropriate. Now, however, reflecting back, I saw it as a sweet gesture, and an effort to make things easier by comforting everyone.

As I continued to watch him and think about how many times I'd misjudged him, he looked up, saw me, and happily waved through the glass. My heart skipped a beat. I smiled and waved, and our eyes stayed locked for a few moments until I heard I was being paged and had to go back to my office.

I sat at my desk doing three things. First, I was talking on the phone. The woman who'd had me paged was Marcy Rosenberg, Public Relations director for The East Bank Club. Marcy and her team wanted me to appear in a commercial. I would be working out while speaking. My line was supposed to be something like, "It's harder to win the lottery than it is to have a good body." I thought it sounded stupid, and I really didn't want to do it. Plus, I felt like being in the commercial and saying that line would make people think I was conceited and thought I had a good body. It was really making me uncomfortable, and what I really wanted to do was give Marcy my brother's name and number. He was the actor, after all. My station manager was insistent, however, that I do the commercial.

The second thing I was doing was browsing through my e-mails to see who was rejecting my screenplay today. As always, it was frustrating and depressing, but the good news was I was almost finished with my new script (the truth-based one) and it was turning out outrageously funny. I actually couldn't wait until it was done so I could start sending it out. I truly believed I could sell it.

The third thing I was doing was thinking about my cutie in the equipment room.

"Can I call you back, Marcy?"

"Sure," she said, "But I really need to know when you're available for the shoot."

"I'll let you know by tomorrow, okay? The thing is, I just got called into an emergency meeting." I crossed my fingers, as if that would make the lie acceptable.

"No problem."

"Thanks," I said, "And just so you know, I'm really excited to be a part of your ad campaign."

"We appreciate that."

When I hung up, I grabbed my purse and headed toward the elevator, pretending to be on my way to the *Starbucks*, which was in the lobby of the building. I had to pass the equipment room on the way. The door was halfway open, and for some reason I sensed Drew was still in there and that he was by himself. I walked in. Sure enough, there he was, on his knees, cleaning the lens of a camera with a piece of cloth.

"Hi!" I exclaimed.

He looked up and smiled. "Look at you..." he flirted.

"What about me?"

"You're hot," he said, "And you're wearing perfume. What's the occasion?"

I grinned and said, "You."

He stood up and slowly walked toward me. Watching him, I couldn't move. Or talk. Or breathe, for that matter. I was frozen with fear, excitement and desire. Drew reached behind me, closed the door and locked it, and that's when my heart started to pound furiously. He kissed me hard on the mouth, and I felt as if I might actually melt in his arms. I was truly lost in his embrace, and all I wanted to do was touch him. I lifted off his shirt. He already had his hands under my dress and was taking off my panty hose.

What we were about to do was so hot and so sexy, and would be a memory that would surely never leave me. I'd never been more attracted to someone in all my life. This was purely erotic and heart pounding. At the same time, though, it was so much more than just random sex in a semi-public place. This was Drew, and this meant something. *He* meant something. And he loved me. It had been a long week without him and I'd missed him terribly. So I guessed I was making up for lost time. In fact, I felt like, perhaps, I was making up for a whole lifetime of lost time, an entire life of never having this kind of closeness and comfort with anyone.

"Who the hell locked this damn door?" I heard next, along with pounding on the door.

Drew and I both burst out laughing, and in less than ten seconds, I was fully dressed again and trying to act normal while opening the door. "Oh, sorry, Larry," I said, "I have no idea why this is locked."

"Larry, buddy," Drew called out, "Come in, dude, I'm just cleaning this lens for that promo we're shooting this afternoon." I had to hide my giggle when I looked at Drew and noticed sweat dripping down his forehead. He had practically jumped back into the position he was in prior to our little escapade.

Larry looked at the two of us for a second, trying to figure out what was going on. Then he shot us each a dirty look and grabbed a tri-pod. He motioned to the door on his way out. "This stays open!" he shouted. Then he stormed off.

With a giggle I asked, "I'm going to Starbucks. Interested in a latte?"

"I'm interested in a latte more than what just happened," Drew joked.

"Bye," I said with a smile.

"It was fun," he said with a wink.

And as I waited in line at Starbucks with a stupid, silly grin on my face, I kept thinking about Drew, sitting there happily cleaning the camera lens with his shirt on inside out. I thought about what we'd just done, and how desperately I needed more.

Not long after returning to my desk I got another rejection e-mail. I couldn't have cared less, though, because the next e-mail was the best e-mail. It read, "To be continued... tonight at your place?"

I giggled and hit reply. "Come over at 8:00."

A few hours later it was time for the lottery. I walked into the studio, my mood the same as it had been all day: cheery, happy and giddy. I gave Drew a little smile and a wave, and he smiled at me, practically sending me into cardiac arrest. There he sat behind the camera, shooting me. It was so hard to focus and I felt like everyone in the room could see my heart bursting out of me.

When we went on air I tried to act professional, but as I pulled the balls out of their bins and announced the numbers, I knew I was being a bit flighty. But I was also peppy and enthusiastic, and for the first time, I wasn't acting. My demeanor was genuine.

I pulled out the last ball and saw it was a seven. "Seven," I exclaimed, "Lucky number seven!" I was so pumped up, I felt like I could fly. It was as if I'd been in a deep sleep for so long and I'd just woken up. And my alarm clock was the guy behind the camera, shooting me.

I was smiling so wide my cheeks were hurting. "There you have it," I continued, "Four nine nine seven for the pick four, and six three eight for the pick three." Ordinarily, I would have gone with one of my usual phony sign-offs like, "Thanks so much for watching WGB, the official station for the Illinois Lottery. Have a wonderful afternoon and remember, somebody's got to win. Why shouldn't it be you?" or "Thanks so much for watching WGB, the official station for the Illinois Lottery. Have a great day and keep taking chances." Today, though, nothing was fake or phony. I wasn't going through the motions anymore. Not with my job, and definitely not when it came to Drew.

"I don't know about you, but I feel lucky lucky lucky today!" I exclaimed into the camera. Truly, I was speaking to the guy behind the camera, but no one knew that except for me (and the camera man, of course.) "I hope everyone gets lucky today," I continued, knowing full well that my producer, Richard was probably cringing right about now, "and tonight!"

Drew's face was behind the camera but I could tell he was laughing. I signed off with a giggle, "For WGB, I'm Jamie Jacobson."

"We're clear," yelled Richard to the crew.

Drew's face appeared from behind the camera, his wide grin melting me.

"What the hell, Jamie?" I heard Richard yell.

"What?" I asked him.

"Are you on drugs?"

"I think she's drunk," replied someone from the crew.

"Shut up," Richard yelled back, not even knowing who said it.

"I'm just happy," I said, looking right at Drew, "Is there something wrong with that?"

"We don't need any drug addicts at the station," grumbled Richard.

"Me too," Drew mouthed to me.

God, he was dreamy.

Chapter 28

There was no conversation, no small talk. In fact, there wasn't even a hello. When I answered my door at about 8:05, wearing my new silk nightgown, there stood Drew with his beautiful green eyes and his kind smile. Without so much as one word exchanged, he took me in his arms and began to kiss me.

We kissed and kissed and made our way into my bedroom, where we did a lot more than kiss. The nightgown was off in literally three minutes, and as far as Drew's clothes, within six seconds, they were on the floor, spread out like a path of bread crumbs leading to my bed.

We made love for a long time, and he whispered how much he'd missed me, and how beautiful I was, and how lucky he felt that we were together. And though I felt all those things, no words came out of my mouth. The feel of his body was taking my breath away, but that wasn't the reason I didn't say anything. At this moment, I felt as if I was in a dream, and I never wanted it to end. I wanted to feel him and touch him and hear him breathe and look in his eyes, and there wasn't one word I could say that wouldn't take away from the overwhelming sense of passion I was feeling at this very moment.

"Are you okay?" Drew asked me.

"Yeah, why?" I whispered.

"Because you're crying," he said, wiping tears from my eyes.

"No, I'm not."

He gave me a gentle smile. "Yes, you are. Tell me why."

I looked into his eyes so directly that I almost felt like I was trying to look into his soul. And then I whispered, "I love you," and I realized that for the first time in my life, I actually meant it.

Drew gave me a smile like the one you get from your best friend and said, "What did you say? I couldn't hear you."

"You heard me," I giggled through tears.

"No, I didn't."

"I love you," I said a bit louder.

"Huh?" he joked, "Speak up!"

"I love you," I shouted with a laugh.

In an instant, he grabbed me and gave me a huge bear hug. "I love you, too," he said, "But you already knew that."

A little while later, we decided to make our way into the kitchen and eat.

"So I want to hear about your trip," I said, standing over the stove, cooking scrambled eggs and cheese, and now wearing Drew's t-shirt and a pair of sweats.

"My trip was great. We did a lot. We played tennis and golf, and we swam and went out for nice dinners…it was nice."

"And what about your dad? Did you guys talk?"

"Yeah. He apologized for what happened and so did Monica. I have to admit, it's really weird, but we all need to get over it if we want to start acting like a family again."

"I think it's great. I'm happy for you."

"Thanks. I just want my dad to be happy. He's almost seventy, and he likes her. He loves her, I guess. And she seems like she's nice to him. She'll never take my mother's place, but as long as my dad's happy, that's the most important thing."

I stirred the eggs and then left them for a moment to fetch some orange juice from the fridge. "You know what I love about you?"

"Wow..." he joked, "Now you're throwing out the L word like nothing! It's so good to see!"

"Shut up," I giggled.

"Sorry. What do you love about me?"

"You always see the good in people. In everything, come to think of it. How do you do it?"

"Well," he said, taking the juice carton from me and pouring some juice into two glasses, "Take you, for example."

I grinned.

"You were a total bitch to me for what? Two, three years?"

"That's not true!"

Now he took my hands. "I know people, and I know what's inside of you."

"You do?"

"Yes. I know you, Jamie. I see you. I saw how you suffered, and how you gave up on men. And I understand that. You were trying to be tough. You tried to play the game. But I saw through it."

"Wait a minute..."

He continued, "Jamie, I'm glad I saw through it. I feel lucky that I saw through it."

Tears welled in my eyes and Drew gently kissed my lips.

"I want you," he said softly, "Not just in bed. I want *you*. All of you."

"I hope so," I said softly.

"I'm here. Not just for a few days or a few months. I'm here for you long term. Do you understand that?"

I sat there nodding my head slowly, believing perhaps for the first time that true love really did exist. And then I put my arms around him and I hugged him for a long time, wondering how the hell I was going to tell him the truth about how our whole relationship began. I knew now that I had to be honest with him. If I loved him, he deserved to know. That being said, the thought of losing him over it was almost unbearable.

"I love you," I whispered again, "I love you."

We stood in my kitchen embraced in a hug, and it felt so good, like I belonged in his safe, strong arms. We stayed like that for a long, long time. Actually, until the smoke alarm went off. The eggs were burned.

Chapter 29

When I first noticed Angela Walker's pregnant tummy, I was in the middle of having a discussion with my students about the German occupation in France in 1941. I was trying to convince a couple of them that the movie, <u>Inglorious Bastards</u> was in fact, a work of fiction, when the reality of seeing Angela's bulging stomach set in, depressing me beyond belief, not because I didn't want her to have the kid, but because this extremely intelligent, gifted and promising student was giving up her education.

So, when the bell rang and all my students dashed out of their seats and toward the door, I decided I wasn't giving up on her. "Angela..." I called to her as she passed my desk.

She stopped and turned to me, "Yes?"

"Can I talk to you?"

"Okay..." she said, seeming apprehensive, I think because she knew how I felt about her decision and didn't want any more confrontation regarding the subject.

"Can you stick around for a minute?"

"Um...I'm meeting my girlfriends out front."

"It'll only take a minute."

"Sure."

I waited until all the students were out of the room before I began. "Angela, I just want to appeal to you one more time. Think about what you're doing. You're seventeen years old. You have your whole life ahead of you…"

"Mr. J., I appreciate what you're saying," she said with a sad smile, "but my mind's made up. My parents think this is the best thing for me, and Terrence is even okay with it now." With fake enthusiasm, she added, "I think we're going to get married."

Now, I seriously felt like puking. This beautiful, smart woman was going to throw her life away! I had to do something. "Listen, this is YOUR life, not mine. And maybe I have no right to get involved like this, but I can't help it."

Now Angela's eyes filled with tears. "I really do appreciate what you're trying to do, but you don't understand. I can't go against my parents. I don't have a choice."

"Yes, you do!"

Now Angela started to cry and I was actually happy about that because I realized right then that she did want to stay in school, and that she was afraid of her parents and what was expected of her. And her parents seemed like an easier obstacle than trying to change HER mind about getting her high-school degree and going to college.

"Angela, what are you doing right now? Can I take you somewhere?" I asked her.

"Um…where?"

"I want to show you something," I said with a grin, "I'll have you home in an hour, I promise."

Twenty minutes later, my student and I pulled up to You Sexy Thing, You in a taxi. I paid the driver, we got out of the cab, and then I led her to the entrance where she said to me, "Mr. J., why are you bringing me to a lingerie store?"

"Because I want you to see what you can do with a college degree."

202

The minute we walked in the door, the hot owner approached us. I'd texted her on the way to tell her we were coming.

"You must be Angela," said Courtney, extending her hand out to shake my student's, "I'm Courtney."

"Courtney owns this store," I said, "I wanted you guys to talk. Courtney graduated from Northwestern and worked as a buyer for Bloomingdale's before starting her own business."

"Wow...that's so cool," exclaimed Angela.

"Angela wants to own her own marketing and public relations firm someday," I told my girlfriend.

"That's exciting," Courtney exclaimed, "What made you decide you want to do that?"

While Angela told Courtney about how she had always been interested in commercials and billboards, I decided to browse the shop and leave the two women alone to chat. I was hoping Courtney would have some kind of impact on Angela and cause her to reevaluate her situation.

As I examined bras, underwear, teddies and nightgowns, which don't get me wrong, I was truly enjoying, I was mostly watching what I hoped would inspire Angela and make her realize the value of an education. Semi listening to my smart girlfriend telling the young girl about how much her education had done for her, both financially and personally, I could see she really wanted to help Angela. I could also see that Angela was impressed by Courtney, and that was exciting. I was crossing my fingers she would see the light.

After a few minutes and with customers waiting, I knew Courtney had run out of time. I walked Angela outside.

"Look, Angela, I've been teaching at your school for a long time. You're not the first girl I've seen get pregnant and drop out, and you won't be the last. I don't know how the lives of the women who dropped out have turned out, but I do know about some of the men and women who have graduated. Some of them have contacted me *and asked if they could put me down as a reference for jobs they're trying to get." I took her shoulders, looked right into her eyes and said with passion, "Jobs with IBM, and Motorola, and Discover, and Schering Plough, and Nordstrom, and even DDB Needham. It's all possible. Especially for you, Angela. You can do anything you want. Even with your baby. I'll help you. But you have to want to help yourself."*

"But my parents..."

"I can talk to them, but only if you'll let me. You have to want this. Then, we can do our best to convince them. Just think about it, okay?"

"Thanks, Mr. J., I will," she said with a smile.

I hailed a cab, paid the driver, and told him where to take my student. Right before the taxi pulled away, Angela's window came down and she said to me, "Hey, Mr. J.?"

"Yeah?"

"How come YOU don't have any kids yet?"

The irony was killing me. All I could do was give her a big grin. "Think about it, okay, Angela?"

"Sure," she smiled.

I waved and watched the cab drive down the street, and then I went back into You Sexy Thing, You and asked my girlfriend if I could take her to dinner.

"I want to tell you something," she said to me, gently taking my face in her hands, "You're a good teacher."

"I hope so."

"I have a lot of respect for what you just did, no matter how it turns out."

"You know what?" I said with a big grin, "You're hot."

Courtney giggled.

I looked right into her eyes and said, "I can't play it cool anymore. You got me, Courtney."

"How do you know I want you?" she joked.

"Maybe you don't," I said, "But either way, you got me." I nodded my head slowly and said it again, this time, to myself. *"You got me."*

"Don't worry, Danny," she said, "I want you."

"Good," I said again, "Because you got me."

Chapter 30

Drew popped his head into my office. With his cute little grin he asked, "Want to go out for dinner with me tonight?"

I looked up from the rejection e-mail I was reading and said playfully, "Drew, let me give you a friendly tip. You don't have to wine and dine me all the time. You'll still get me into bed."

"I want to wine and dine you, *and* I want to get you into bed."

"Well then, sure, I'd love to go out tonight.

He winked at me. "I'll call you later, hun," he said, and with a wave and a smile, he was gone.

Hun? What was that all about? I wondered. I sat there at my desk trying to absorb *hun,* but then realized the old Jamie was coming out and that I needed to pipe down and let the new Jamie enjoy her sweet boyfriend. *Hun* was good. *Hun* meant comfort. *Hun* was a term of endearment.

The new Jamie began thinking that tonight might be a good time to tell Drew the truth and end the Frankie nightmare. If I really loved him, I needed to tell him exactly what was going on. So, that became my goal for the evening.

A few hours later, as we walked down the street headed to dinner, I was a wreck.

"What's wrong?" Drew asked.

Did I want to tell him before dinner? Maybe that was the way to go. Get it out of the way and then we could enjoy our evening. Why wait?

"Last night…" I began, "Was…"

"Amazing," he finished.

"Yes, it was."

"So, is that what's wrong?" he asked.

"No, it's just…"

"Hey, I can't believe I forgot to tell you this."

"What?"

"My dad called today…"

"That's nice."

"You're not going to believe this one."

"What?"

"Monica's pregnant."

I froze. Had I just heard correctly? I wanted to shout, "Is everyone in the world but *me* having babies?" Instead, I just said, "Wow."

"I know, I can't believe it either," he said. We continued down the block. "I mean, it's unbelievable," Drew went on, "I'm going to have a new brother or sister, whose mom is my ex-girlfriend!"

"So, were they trying?" I asked. I was dying to add, "Because God knows, it's not easy."

"I really don't know. Why?"

"I was just wondering."

We walked a bit more in silence. "Can I ask you something?" he asked me.

"Sure."

"What kind of relationship do you think I'll have with the baby?"

"Well, what kind of relationship do you want?"

He thought about it for a minute, "I guess I want to be a really good big brother."

"I think that's great."

"I mean, as weird as the whole thing is, family's family right? Someday I'm going to have kids, and I definitely want my dad in their lives."

"So you think you might want kids someday?" I asked.

"Sure, don't you?"

"Um..." Suddenly I couldn't take it anymore. I *had* to come clean. "Drew, I have to talk to you about something."

"Sure, what is it?"

I couldn't find the words.

"What?"

"I can't find the words."

"Jamie, just tell me."

"I think you'll make a great big brother *and* a great father."

"Thanks, but that's not what you were going to say."

"I know," I said with a nervous giggle.

"Please tell me."

I took a deep breath, and just as the first word of my confession was coming out of my mouth, I saw Danny walking toward us. He was holding hands with a girl, who I was sure was Courtney, and oddly enough, she looked vaguely familiar.

"Here comes Danny," I exclaimed.

"Your brother?"

Danny saw us and waved. I waved back and within seconds, they were standing in front of us.

"Hi!" said my brother.

"Hi," I grinned.

"Drew, right?" asked Danny.

"Yeah," he replied, shaking my brother's hand.

Then Danny introduced us to Courtney.

"Weren't you in my store last week?" she asked me.

"Yes! On Armitage," I exclaimed. It was all coming back.

"You bought a night gown, right?" she asked.

"Yeah."

Drew piped in. "That came from your store? My girl-friend looked amazing in it," he said with a grin.

"Can we not talk about my lingerie with my brother standing here?"

"Good idea," joked Danny.

"Where are you guys headed?" Drew asked them.

"We don't really know," said Danny, "We're just restaurant browsing. "How about you?"

"I'm thinking *Japonnais*," Drew said, "Hey, do you guys want to eat with us?"

"Sure!" said Danny at the same time as Courtney said, "We'd love to."

I smiled and said, "Great!"

As the four of us walked down the block making small talk, Drew whispered, "Will you tell me what you were going to tell me later?"

"Sure," I replied. Thank God for my brother.

Chapter 31

As I sat on a bar stool next to my brother's girlfriend, listening to how she got into the lingerie business, I watched Danny with Drew. They seemed to be getting along great, which didn't surprise me because Danny really was a sweet guy, and as for Drew, he could strike up and hold a conversation with any person who had a pulse.

As for Courtney, I was really enjoying her. She wasn't anything like all the girls I'd seen my brother with over the years, each one skinnier, blonder, and more airhead-ish than the one before. Courtney was different; her dark, wavy hair and sparkling eyes making her a natural beauty in my opinion.

There was more to Courtney than just physical beauty, though. She was really smart, and I had respect for her career. But even more importantly, she seemed genuine. I liked the way she looked at Danny every time his name came up in conversation, and I loved the fact that she loved his teaching career. It was cute how she gushed about it. She seemed to see all the good things in my brother, and that made me feel good.

An hour and two martinis each later, we finally got a table. Courtney followed the hostess who was seating us, followed by me, Danny, and then Drew. It was extremely loud in the place, so when Danny tapped my shoulder on the way to the table and said, "Drew is a great guy," I wasn't worried Drew would hear. I nodded and kept walking.

Once seated, we began to truly enjoy the ambiance of *Japonnais*. This place was the place to be, according to *Check, Please*, which had featured the restaurant on the show a couple weeks earlier. The music was blaring, so we found ourselves almost yelling our conversation. None of us seemed to care, though.

I was truly enjoying the people I was with. It was fun to see Danny and Drew interact. Mr. Full-of-Himself meets Mr. Laid-back. I also liked watching my brother and his date. I'd never seen him so into a girl. He seemed so happy, and that made *me* really happy. Of course, what was going to happen when she found out about Danny's arrest and Frankie's bribe? It was hard to say, just like it was hard to say how Drew would react. I decided not to think about it.

As the appetizers came and went, the four of us sampled different kinds of sake. Hot, cold, milky, sweet, bitter... You name it, we drank it. And as we drank, we talked and laughed a lot. It was hard to believe this was our first time out together as a foursome. Things felt so comfortable, so natural.

After my brother's third little cup of sake, he pulled out a picture of my dad and himself dressed as a lion for Halloween. In the photo, Danny couldn't have been more than two. "I found this in a box," he said.

"You look so much like Dad," I said. I'd seen dozens of pictures of my father, many of which I looked at frequently, and I'd never really noticed how much Danny resembled him. Maybe I'd always been apprehensive about making the connection because it was just too sad. Now, though, I saw the resemblance as a really good thing, especially when I thought about how my mother probably felt about it. It probably gave her comfort and happiness to see her husband in her son.

"Do you really think so?" Danny asked proudly, "I can't tell."

"Ask Ma."

"I will," he said with smile, and I could tell he was thinking about her, which made me happy since there had always been tension between Ma and Danny. I never really understood why, and the two had always gotten along okay, but Danny always seemed to be a little bit angry with her. Now, however, when I saw the way he was smiling at the thought of her, I sensed something was different.

If someone would have told me Danny was seeing a therapist, and had just had a major breakthrough I would have believed it. But I knew better. Not in a million years would my stubborn brother seek professional help for his issues. I realized right then, Danny's therapist was sitting next to me. And now I liked her even more, because whether she meant to or not she was helping my brother. He was changing for the better, and my gut feeling was that Courtney had a lot to do with it.

The photo led to some hilarious conversations about Frankie. We began telling Courtney and Drew all about our nutty mother. Of course, we omitted any mention of her hideous contract for babies. But there were so many cute little things about Frankie Jacobson that made for great entertainment, like how she cooked the best steaks, but how her lasagna was so bad, we always had to pretend not to feel well so we didn't have to eat it. We also talked about her ridiculous gifts.

"Last year, she bought us Snuggies for Hanukkah," I said.

"She's also a big fan of the Chia Pet," Danny joked.

"If you come to my apartment," I said with a giggle, "I can give you guys a lifetime supply of Suzanne Somers' sweetened cookies."

Danny added, "If you come over to my place, you'll receive one of the six blow-up beds Ma bought for me over the years, just in case anyone ever spends the night."

We laughed and laughed, especially when Danny did his imitation of Ma. When he was done, I joked, "You really have become a great actor!"

"Your poor mom!" said Courtney.

"No," defended Danny, "We're not making fun of her. All of this, I do with love."

I sat there thinking the same thing. I did love my mother dearly. Was I angry with her at this moment? Yes. But besides becoming a psycho, hiring a lawyer, and bribing us to reproduce for money, was she a bad mother? Definitely not.

"How is your mom handling all her new money?" Drew asked Danny, "I mean, has winning the lottery affected her life much?"

"Um…" he struggled. He looked at me and said, "Yeah, you could say that." Then he chugged the rest of his sake.

"What am I missing?" asked Drew.

"I think we should order our main courses," I said, "What looks good?"

Thankfully, Drew let it go. Danny and I were safe for now. But our guilty secret was looming in the air and we both knew the truth had to come out at some point. Not tonight, though.

After dinner, Drew insisted we get the dessert that was featured on *Check Please*, fried bananas with vanilla ice-cream. We also ordered the flourless chocolate cake. I don't remember how it came up, but as we all dug our forks into the desserts, Drew and I started talking about Larry, our drunken news director. Together, we told the story about how one morning, a massive snowstorm had made it impossible for me to get to the station on time to do the lottery. Larry, who had probably had a few screwdrivers that morning volunteered himself to fill in. He was stumbling across the floor and slurring his words into the mic. Drew did a funny and very accurate imitation of him.

"Larry even dropped a ball!" I said.

"Yeah, it was the third number for the pick four," added Drew.

I could tell we were thoroughly entertaining my brother and his girlfriend. Both of them were laughing heartily. What a great night this was! I couldn't remember the last time I'd had so much fun. The four of us were great together, and let's be honest, both couples were great with each other. I loved seeing Danny happy, and I could tell he enjoyed seeing me in a good relationship, too.

When the check came, Drew and Danny fought over it, and Courtney gave me this cute little giggle. In the end, Danny agreed to let Drew pay under the condition that Drew had to play in Danny's Tuesday night poker game the following week.

Walking out of the restaurant, Courtney led the way, followed by Danny, me, and then Drew. This time, I tapped Danny on the shoulder and said loudly, "She's a great girl." Again, because of the noise level, I wasn't worried that Courtney would hear.

Danny responded with a wide grin, "Funny, huh? Both of us fell in love at the same time."

I gave my brother a big smile, "Is it that obvious?"

"Yeah," he replied with a chuckle, "But good luck introducing him to Ma!"

Chapter 32

I can only speak for myself, but I was feeling no pain when I walked out of the restaurant. I suspected that the other three people who drank just as much if not more, felt the same way.

"Hey, there's a new club just a couple blocks down. Anyone interested?" asked Danny.

I'm pretty sure we all said yes at the exact same time.

As we walked down the block, the four of us were engaged in a conversation about the US Air flight attendant guy who drank a beer and slid down the slide, when all of a sudden, we noticed a stroller coming toward us.

"Wow, what a cutie!" I heard Danny say.

The parents stopped in front of us and I looked down and saw a little girl who looked no more than a year old. I found myself somewhat in awe of the beauty of the child, a very different reaction than I'd ever had in the past. Something had changed within me. Usually, I'd roll my eyes when I saw a baby and try to avoid any contact at all costs. But tonight, I found myself drawn to her, interested, infatuated almost.

Drew looked at me and said, "She kind of makes you want one of your own, doesn't she?"

This was unbelievable! The irony was making my head spin more than the drinks. Here I was, trying to get pregnant by a guy who didn't think I wanted kids. Standing next to me was a woman who couldn't have kids, dating a guy who she had no idea had just given up millions for her.

"She's really beautiful," I whispered, feeling tears well up in my eyes.

Courtney put her arm around me and said in a comforting tone, "Someday..."

The parents told us all to have a nice evening and strolled on. When I looked at Drew, he was smiling. "Maybe you're more ready for kids than I thought," he said.

"I don't know," I replied.

He whispered in my ear, "You'd be a *great* mother. You know that, right?"

I couldn't have felt worse at this moment. I *had* to tell him the truth. I *had* to.

We continued down the block, and the second we walked into the club, Danny shouted, "Hey, listen to the song!" He and Courtney burst out laughing. I heard Sean Kingston's *Fire Burning* blaring.

"What's so funny?" Drew asked.

"You've got to show them!" Danny said to Courtney.

"No way!" she shouted.

"Please?"

"Fine," she agreed with a giggle.

"Come on," Danny said, taking her hand and leading her onto the dance floor. He turned around and said to us, "Watch her!"

Drew took my hand and pulled me onto the dark, crowded dance floor. While we danced, we watched

218

Courtney do a PERFECT imitation of Sean Kingston in the Fire Burning video. It was truly hilarious! She was great! Plus, it was so cute how she was laughing at herself while she did it.

As for myself, I was so enjoying my dance partner. He was sexy, sexy, sexy! Drew wasn't that great of a dancer by any means, but he sure looked good. His perfectly sculpted body helped matters immensely.

All of us stayed on the dance floor for a long time, and before I knew it the waiters were serving last call. I couldn't believe it was almost two in the morning.

Once outside the bar, Drew offered the first cab that stopped to Danny and Courtney. I kissed my brother on the cheek, and then came the shocker; Courtney was hugging me hard.

"I'm so glad we ran into you guys!" she exclaimed, "I had so much fun!"

Being extremely tired and drunk, I said, "You too." I immediately regretted the response since there was so much more I wanted to say to my brother's girlfriend. The whole cab ride home, all I could talk about was my very lame choice of words.

"I can't believe I couldn't come up with something better!" I complained to Drew, "I'm a screenwriter for God's sake!"

"Don't worry about it," he said with a laugh, "You were fine."

"I wanted to tell Courtney how much I liked her, and how great it was to see Danny with someone so smart and so sweet and so into him. I wanted to tell her that I considered her a friend, and that I respected her and admired her."

"You can tell her all that," said Drew, "Why don't you call her tomorrow?"

"Yeah," I said with a drunk smile, "I think I will."

Then I put my head on my boyfriend's shoulder and fell asleep until the cab pulled up to my building.

We staggered inside and then up to my apartment, and the second I opened the door I made a mad dash for the couch.

"Come on," Drew said, picking me up and throwing me over his shoulder, "Let's go to bed."

That's the last thing I remember. I must have fallen asleep upside down while being carried into my bedroom.

Chapter 33

I woke up early the next morning, still in my clothes. Next to me was Drew, still in his clothes. Our shoes were off. My head was pounding. I tried to recall how I ended up this way. Bits and pieces of the previous night were floating around in my head.

Monica was pregnant, Danny was carrying around a picture of him and dad, I was eating sushi, I was chugging sake, Drew and I were talking about Larry, we were eating fried bananas, I was staring at the beautiful baby, Courtney was dancing like Sean Kingston, Drew's biceps were looking good, Courtney was hugging me good-bye, I was making a b-line for my couch. And now, I was here, in my clothes with a horrendous hangover.

It had been a great night, though, worth every pain I felt. I was in love. Danny was in love. Danny liked the guy I loved. And I loved the girl he loved. And then I remembered the dark cloud looming over everything, which was that I still needed to talk to Drew. Until he knew the truth, what we had wasn't real. And even though the thought of that was making my head pound harder, it was a conversation that desperately, matter-of-factly had to take place.

"Let me guess. You have a headache," were the first words out of Drew's mouth. Before I could respond, he started taking off my shirt and kissing my neck.

At this moment, the ovulation kit popped into my head and I realized I probably wasn't ovulating anymore, but I didn't care. I loved this man, and I wanted him, just for him, not for a baby. It was over for me. I was surrendering to love, and my days of manipulation and con games were behind me. I would have to tell Frankie when she got back that I was done with her contract and her scheme. I was in love. And yes, indirectly she'd had something to do with that, but her bribe had been wrong. Very wrong. And I had been wrong for ever considering it.

"You know, something really interesting happened last night," Drew said softly in between kisses, "We actually slept together and didn't sleep together."

"What does that mean?"

"It just means that we were actually able to enjoy each other without sex. It's cool that we just cuddled and didn't actually fool around. You know something? We might actually end up getting married and having like five kids together."

I couldn't take it anymore. This was just too much. The guilt had finally overtaken my soul. I had to tell him the truth this instant. "Drew, I can't do this anymore. I have to tell you something."

"Oh my God!" he exclaimed, "You're pregnant, aren't you? I should have known!"

"Drew…"

"You were acting so weird last night, and when you saw that baby in the stroller... Now I get it!"

I suddenly felt like someone just flushed the toilet and I was going down it. "Drew, stop."

"Oh my God! Why were you drinking last night?"

I grabbed his shoulders. "Listen to me. I AM NOT pregnant."

"You're not?" he asked. I wasn't sure if he was relieved or disappointed.

"Actually, I don't know. Maybe I could be, but it would be really early on, and drinking wouldn't matter at this point...I don't think..."

"But you might be pregnant?"

I put my head down in shame. Then I took a deep breath and mustered up all the courage I had. "Look, I've been trying to conceive a child since the first time we slept together. It has to do with my mother's lottery winnings. A few weeks ago, she gave Danny and I a contract that stated if either of us had a baby in the next year, she'd give us eight million dollars."

As I spoke, I could detect three things on Drew's face; shock, disgust and sadness. I found it interesting that I could actually see all those emotions in one look. I figured this must have been the same look he had on his face when he found out about his dad and Monica.

"So I went out with you," I continued, "and I slept with you in hopes of having your baby."

The movie, The Blair Witch Project actually caused me to both throw up and to acquire insomnia. At this moment, if I had the choice of seeing it again or seeing Drew's reaction, I would gladly have picked the movie in a heartbeat.

When he responded, his voice was cold, unemotional and distant. "So you basically used me."

I put my head down. "Yes."

"You pretended to be attracted to me and to care about me and listen to my stories."

"No, that's not true."

"The dinner at Soldier Field, all the dates we had, the other day in the equipment room, and that night...that night you told me you loved me."

"I know," I said softly.

Now his voice rose. "I trusted you! I told you things!" he shouted, "About my dad, and about how I felt, and about everything!"

"Drew please let me explain," I pleaded.

He got up and was now hurriedly looking for his socks and shoes.

"It was so wrong. I'm really sorry. I didn't want to hurt you. I was desperate."

"Yeah, you must have been," he shouted, "And now, I can only think of one word for you." He stopped shouting and stood there for a moment. I waited for the word. He looked up at me with a frosty stare that literally made me shiver. And then he said softly, "evil," and headed for the door.

I went running after him and literally chased him into the hallway by the elevators.

"Drew, I'm not evil. You know me," I pleaded, "All those dates and all the times we made love..."

"We didn't make love," he snapped, "You used me for sex." He pressed the elevator button.

"That's not true!" I wasn't sure if I was lying or telling the truth. I was and I wasn't.

"It's not true? Can you honestly say that every time we were together it was because you wanted to be with me?"

"I don't know when the turning point was, but on one of those dates I fell in love with you."

The elevator door arrived and Drew got in. He held the open door button and said sadly, "With the way our relationship began, with the lying and the using, there's no way it can work." And with those words, the elevator doors closed. I stood there in my hallway and began to sob.

Chapter 34

I sat on the edge of the bed and I watched her sleep. She was beautiful. Physically beautiful, yes, but so much more. My heart started to pound because I knew what I had to do, what I had to SAY actually.

"What are you doing?" Courtney whispered when she woke up.

"Watching you," I smiled.

"I feel awful," she giggled. Then she started to get up.

"Where are you going?"

"Bathroom."

"Wait," I said, gently taking her arm.

She smiled. "What?"

I drew in a deep breath. "Yesterday I told you, you got me."

"Yeah," she smiled, "I remember."

"What I should have said was that I love you."

I don't think I've ever seen someone start crying that quickly. "I love you, too," she said through tears.

I said softly, "You got me."

"Yeah, I got you," she said with a smile.

We hugged for literally ten minutes. I just sat on the bed holding her, and it was amazing. I was such a softie now. Between wanting to make amends with my mother, making friends with my sister's boyfriend, and being in love, I was like one of those guys I always made fun of, one of those guys I always referred to as "whipped" or "wimpy" or "like a dog on a leash." The funny part was, I loved it!

I started to lift my old basketball jersey over Courtney's head when my cell phone rang.

"Sorry, this may be Vito," I said, scrambling to find my phone in my jacket pocket, "I think I might be working today." I finally found it and saw it was my sister.

"Hey, Jamie," I answered.

"Hi," she said. I could tell immediately that she was crying. Rarely had I seen or heard my sister upset, so whatever was troubling her, I knew it was probably a big deal.

"What's wrong?"

She began telling me the whole Drew saga, while I mouthed to Courtney, "Sorry, she's crying…"

Courtney nodded, "I'm going to make coffee," she whispered.

I gave her a thumbs-up, while continuing to listen to the awful details Jamie was sharing.

Her story took about a minute and a half to tell, and when she was finished she said, "What should I do?" like she wanted me, her big brother to fix it.

"Look, don't worry about it," I began, "Just try to work it out with him. He's a great guy. I really like him. Let yourself be happy. I mean, look at me. I'm with Courtney now and obviously baby-making with her isn't going to happen." I lay back down on the bed and looked up at the ceiling, as I continued. "And trust me, I have zero interest in getting arrested again, trying to pick up a woman to have my baby, nor do I feel like calling any other old girlfriends to have sex with, so I can get Ma's money."

"What?" I heard next.

I quickly sat up and saw Courtney standing in the doorway. She was holding an empty coffee pot.

"Let me call you back," I said into the phone. Then I snapped it shut. "Courtney..."

"So you got arrested picking up a women to have sex with? Interesting..."

She turned around and stormed into the kitchen. I followed closely behind. I could tell she was trying to stay calm, but I knew she was pissed beyond belief.

"Look," I scrambled, "My mother bribed us. She told us she'd give us eight million dollars if we gave her a grandchild. What was I supposed to do?"

"Oh, that justifies everything!" she shouted with sarcasm.

"Hear me out, please? She gave Jamie and I a contract. We have a year to have a child..."

"I'm sickened! How could you even consider having kids for money?"

"Well, it's not just money. It's eight million dollars."

"I don't care if it's eight BILLION!" she shouted, "It's wrong! You would actually create a life solely to profit financially?"

"It wouldn't have to be that way. I would do my best to be a good dad. But that's not even the point. The thing is...I met YOU, and..."

Courtney let out a bitter laugh. "Huh! That's the funniest part! You met me, the girl who can't have kids! Oh my God! That's why you broke up with me, isn't it?"

"Uh..."

"What the hell were you thinking?"

"I was thinking that I realized I was in love with you. That's why I came to see you and get back together. Don't you understand?! I don't care about the money anymore!"

"But before you figured that out, you had to go around and screw a bunch of women!"

"No! I swear, I didn't sleep with any of them!"

Tears were running down her cheeks. "I wish I could believe you."

"Please..." I walked over to her and tried to hold her, but she pushed me away.

"No! Don't touch me. You make me sick! You AND your sister. She's using that poor guy, Drew. Isn't she?"

"Courtney, you have to believe me..."

"I don't believe anything you say. You're a liar. Get out of my apartment!"

I went back into the bedroom and got dressed. A minute later I was back in the kitchen. Courtney had stopped crying and was putting some dishes in the dishwasher. She refused to look up.

"Courtney, I love you. I mean it. I don't want the money. I just want you." I actually felt tears well in my eyes. "You got me, remember?" I whispered.

Courtney looked up at me, her eyes filled with anger. "I don't want you."

"Really?"

"The clock's ticking. You better go sleep with some more girls."

Now I knew I'd lost. I put my head down in shame and left without saying another word.

Chapter 35

After I got off the phone with Danny, I found myself beyond depressed. Not only had I lost Drew, but I'd also probably caused the demise of my brother and the woman he loved. I wished so much that I could take back that fateful phone call, but what was done was done, and I had to live with it.

I spent the day in front of the TV, eating as much junk food as I possibly could without throwing up. While watching <u>Pretty In Pink</u>, I devoured a bag of *O'Keedokee* cheese popcorn. I managed to eat a pint of *Ben and Jerry's Chubby Hubby*, while flipping back and forth from <u>The Shawshank Redemption</u> to E! channel's *Top 100 Celebrity Break-ups*. I also finished off some left over pizza, while watching *Sex and the City* re-runs. I was using food to comfort and soothe my anxiety and depression, but it wasn't working. All it did was make me feel bloated and sick. Somewhere between when Andy Dufrane crawled through the sewer to escape Shawshank, and the break up between Jennifer Aniston and Brad Pitt, Danny called.

"Are you mad at me?" was the first thing I asked him after we said hello.

"No," he replied, "It was my fault for talking when I knew she was in the next room."

"Still, I'm really sorry. What happened?"

"It's pretty bad. I can't talk about it."

I heard street noise in the background and I knew Danny was on his cell. "Are you working?"

"Yup. Pretzel boy's handing out samples."

"Danny, why don't you quit that job? You hate it."

"I need the money."

In the background, I heard a guy shout, "Off the phone! We're losing business!"

"Plus, I love the guy I work for," Danny joked, "He's so inspiring."

Danny quickly told me about Courtney's reaction to hearing about Ma's contract. I felt horrible for my brother because I knew he was hurting, and the guilt I felt for being the cause was semi-unbearable.

"How are you?" he asked me.

"We don't have to talk about me. I know you have a lot on your mind."

"Ma really screwed things up for us, didn't she?" he asked.

"Did she?" I asked.

"Yes!"

"Think about it, Danny. She did and she didn't. It's because of her that I'm with Drew. Or I should say…*was* with Drew."

"That's true, but Ma didn't do me any favors in this whole deal. Because of her, I blew it with Courtney, plus I now have legal issues."

"I know, but maybe Frankie did something for you, too. Think about it. Without meaning to, she sort of forced you to make a choice between money and love. And you chose love. You should feel really good about that."

"Maybe you're right. Still, the girl I'm in love with wants nothing to do with me."

"Give her time. She'll realize what a great guy you are. I know it."

"Thanks, Sis. You do the same."

"I'll try. But, you know, he called me evil! Maybe I am."

"You're not evil. I promise."

I wanted to believe my big brother but it was hard. The more I reflected, the more I realized how unethical and appalling my behavior had been for such a long time. I thought about Max. Yes, he had his flaws, but the poor guy wanted to marry me and I was going to get back together with him for the sole purpose of having a child for money. We'd most likely have found ourselves in a terrible marriage, and some poor, sweet, little child would have had to live in a turbulent, unhappy household. How could I have even considered that scenario?

I wanted to blame my mother for everything, but how could I? She wasn't responsible for all those nights I used Drew. Frankie didn't plan and scheme and dress seductively to trick an innocent guy into having a child. I did that all by myself. So I was the only one to blame. And the more I thought about things, the angrier I became. Yes, I was angry at my mother, but so much more upset with myself. I went to bed angry, and the next morning I woke up angry.

It was Monday morning. I got ready for work in my usual manner, however, I did wear my loosest suit because I couldn't have felt any fatter. The second I left my place, I was a complete bitch to every person I came in contact with. I yelled at my cab driver for turning down the wrong street, I told the *Starbucks* guy who made my Grande skim, half-calf, half-decaf, no-foam latte that there was in fact a little bit of foam in it, and once inside the elevator of my office building, I purposely closed the elevator door before a sweet little old man was about to get on. And all that happened before I even got into work.

When I walked into WGB, I didn't say hello or say hello back to a single person. I thought it was kind of funny how most people didn't even notice that I wasn't saying hi. I retreated to my office, praying that on the way I wouldn't run into my now ex-boyfriend, who thought I was evil.

I sat at my desk fuming. If only I could talk to my mother right now! Boy, would I let her have it. When Frankie got back from pampering herself, I planned on sitting her down and explaining exactly how I felt. If I loved my mother, I needed to make her understand how wrong I thought she was in her decision to force something both Danny and I clearly weren't ready for. And she needed to know the price we were paying for her selfishness.

I also wanted to ask my mother why she really did it, because in my heart I felt it was completely out of character. I needed a better explanation than the one Frankie had given me. I needed better justification than, "I have waited long enough for you two to grow up. It's time for you to realize what's important in life." But talking to Frankie would have to wait until she got back. And that was frustrating. I had so much anger and rage pumping through my veins, and a serious need to vent.

"You're on in ten minutes," Richard shouted as he walked by my office.

Ten minutes till show time. Ten minutes to turn anger and bitterness into sweet and bubbly. Or not...

I realized something right then. If I needed to vent, who better to listen than the general public?

Chapter 36

Walking into the studio, I felt like a prisoner on death row, walking to her execution. As angry and belligerent as I felt about so many things, I was really scared to see Drew. I hadn't seen or heard from him since he left my place the day before. Now, not only did I have to be in the same room with him, but he would be looking at me through a big lens. In six minutes from now, he'd be shooting me, ironically something he probably wanted to do with a gun instead of a camera.

Once on stage, the nervousness intensified. Drew's face was hidden behind the camera and other than asking me to hold still so he could get a good focus, he didn't say anything to me. Not even hi. He was cold and distant, acting like a stranger. Richard and the audio guy were giving each other looks, and I could tell they sensed the tension.

"Three...two..." said Drew. Then he held up his index finger to indicate "one" silently. It was show time.

"Good Afternoon, and welcome to WGB, the official station for the Illinois Lottery..." I was acting like my usual sugary, uplifting self, but normalcy was an effort, given the fact that every time I looked into the camera I was forced to look at the guy behind it, forced to look at a person with whom I'd just spent the best weeks of my life, and forced to look at a guy who didn't seem like he was going to forgive me anytime soon.

"There you have it," I said with a smile, wrapping things up and still acting like the Jamie Jacobson everyone knew, "Once again your pick three is one nine two…the pick four…six six four three." Then came the big shock. "Let's be honest, though. Most likely, none of you will win tonight, but if you do happen to win, I have something to say to you. God help you!"

I could feel Richard's jaw drop, but still, I continued, "My mother won the lottery and you know where it got me? It ruined my life. Her money ruined my life. You want to be happy? Work hard and try to be a good person. And by the way, for those of you who think I'm *evil*, I'm not! You know what's evil? Money! For WGB, I'm Jamie Jacobson."

"We're clear," yelled Richard.

My microphone was immediately turned down and the credits rolled, as I stood there for a couple of seconds. Then we went to black.

"What the fuck, Jamie?" Richard shouted.

"Sorry," I said, my tone calm and soft, "I quit." Then I put the mic down and walked off the stage. As I walked out of the studio with my head down, I could hear people asking me questions like, "Are you okay?" and saying things like, "Jamie, wait…" I never looked at Drew. Instead, I headed straight to my office, grabbed my purse and exited WGB for the last time. I'd had it. I was done with this place.

As soon as I was out the door, I knew exactly where I was headed first. There was somewhere I felt compelled to go. I didn't know exactly why or from where the urgency came, I just knew I needed to get there immediately.

I had to stop home to grab the key I needed to get into the door of the place where I was going. When I passed through my lobby, my doorman, Rick stopped me.

"Hey Jamie, what's going on with you?" he asked. Obviously he had just seen the lottery on the little TV that sat on his desk.

"Nothing, Rick. Everything's fine. I just have somewhere to go and I'm sort of in a hurry."

"Okay, girl," he replied.

Once upstairs, I desperately searched my kitchen drawers and cabinets for a key I hadn't used in ages. I finally found it in a coffee mug, in the cabinet above the fridge. It was definitely the right key, because attached to it was a very old plastic key chain with the name *Dr. Thomas Schneider, DDS* on it. Underneath the dentist's name was his address and phone number. Doctor Schneider was the dentist Ma worked with for almost twenty years. The key on the keychain would open the door to Frankie's condo. So, with key in hand, I dashed out the door, down the elevator and through the lobby again.

"Are you sure everything's cool with you?" asked Rick, as I ran by him.

"Yeah!" I shouted, racing out the door.

I hailed a cab. The ride seemed like it took forever. I knew what I was doing was completely crazy, but I felt like I couldn't rest until I saw what I needed to see. I wasn't going to my mother's place to see my mother, since obviously, she wasn't there. Frankie was still on her cruise and wasn't coming home for a few more days. I was going there for something else.

My heart began to pound when the cab started getting close. Then, I felt like I was in a movie because the cab driver accidentally drove past Frankie's building and was heading toward a different address. By the time I told him to stop, we were a block away from Ma's building. Instead of telling him to go back to the right place, I just paid him, got out of the cab, and then ran as fast as I could back to the correct address. I felt very overly dramatic, but in my defense, I was an obsessed woman on a mission, and I couldn't wait another minute to get into Ma's condo and see the object that now occupied my mind so fanatically.

I ran up the two flights of stairs and put the key into 3G. It was a funny thought using Frankie's key. In all the years Ma had lived in this place, not once had I ever been here without her. I walked in and headed straight for the third bedroom. Hesitating only for a second, I took a deep breath and opened the door. I looked around my mother's new nursery and instantly my eyes filled with tears.

I was in awe of its purity and beauty. The walls were painted mint green, and under the white chair rail there were stripes of powder blue, light yellow, pale pink and the same mint green. A few stenciled sheep were scattered on the walls and on the wood floor was a circular crème area rug with little sheep on the edges. Two pieces of white furniture were all that stood in the room; a changing table and a crib that had a mint green sheet and a bumper pad with white, mint green and pale yellow sheep on it. Inside the crib were several stuffed farm animals, all in pastel colors. A couple tears ran down my cheeks. I reached in and took out a stuffed giraffe. I looked at it for a second and smiled. Then I knelt down on the rug, hugged my little stuffed friend and began to sob.

'This damned crib!' I thought, 'This damned room! Why did my mother do this to me?' Frankie's new money hadn't bought her any pregnancies, but it had done something to me. Without meaning to, her whole scheme had caused me to fall in love and had given me the urge to have a child.

Over and over again, John had made me feel like I wasn't worthy of being a parent. Drew had said to me just a couple nights earlier, "You know you'd be a great mother," and it had stuck. He was right! I *would* be a great mother. Drew loved me and he believed in me. And now I finally believed in myself. But at the same time, Drew wasn't mine anymore. It was unbearably upsetting to think that the person who had changed me had given up on me. How bittersweet it was.

I cried and cried for what seemed like a long time. Yes, I was crying about losing Drew, but there was more. I also felt a tremendous amount of relief. I was thankful that I was finally able to realize what I wanted, and that I was worthy of it. And now I knew in my heart that there was a chance for me to have kids someday, with or without Drew.

So I was divorced and carrying around a little baggage. Big deal. I deserved to be happy. I deserved to have a husband who loved me. Not John. I deserved to have a husband I loved. Not Max. I didn't have to settle. John's constant unkind and unsupportive words were now fading, Drew's and Danny's and my mother's all taking their place. At this moment, I felt more at peace than I had in so long.

I stood up, wiped my tears and placed the animal back in the crib. Everything was going to be okay, no matter how things turned out. I knew that now. I smiled at my good thoughts and my newfound attitude, feeling like I'd just been reborn, given a second chance, perhaps. I exhaled the breath I'd been holding in my whole life. Relaxed and ready to begin a new chapter, I gave the room one last look and turned around to head out. That's the moment I heard the front door open.

Chapter 37

Upon hearing someone entering the condo, I immediately thought I was about to be killed by a burglar. The person was going to find me in the way of his heist, and he would shoot me dead so I wouldn't be able to identify him. As he sat in his jail cell years later, convicted of another crime, he would regret what he'd done to me. But it wouldn't make a difference because I'd be dead. And what a shame that this was going to occur now, just when I realized my potential for true happiness in life.

My heart was beating out of my chest while I tiptoed out of the bedroom, made my way into the main area, and crouched behind an armchair. When I saw who had just come through the door, heart pounding panic changed to confusion. A heavyset black woman wearing a nurse's uniform quietly closed the door behind her. She was carrying a little white bag. Her presence instantly made me feel safe, calm, and comfortable. She was hardly a thief with a loose trigger finger.

I stood up. "Who are you?" I asked.

The woman jumped and gasped so hard, she dropped the bag she was holding. She recovered quickly, though, kneeling down, picking it up and responding in a calm voice. "I'm sorry. You startled me," she said, "My name is Rose. Are you...Jamie?"

Now the wheels were spinning in my head and I knew something was very wrong. "What's going on?" I asked.

Instead of answering me, she walked toward Frankie's bedroom. I practically jumped across the apartment to meet her there. When Rose opened the bedroom door, I was so shocked I literally had to put my hand over my mouth to stop myself from screaming. There was my mother, lying in bed asleep. Rose gently closed the door and put her arm around me.

"Is she okay?" I whispered, my voice shaking.

"She's going to be."

A second later, I heard a frail voice coming from the bedroom. "Jamie, is that you?"

I opened the door and walked over to my mother's bed.

"Come sit on the bed," she whispered.

Suddenly, I was frightened. Ma's voice sounded so old.

"Ma, what's wrong with you?" I asked, sitting down on the bed, "Please tell me."

"I have breast cancer," Frankie said, "My surgery was last week. I came home from the hospital yesterday."

"She got an excellent report back from the doctor today," interrupted Rose, "They got it all. Isn't that right, Mrs. Jacobson?"

"Yes, Rose."

"Oh, Ma..." I said, my eyes rapidly filling with tears.

She took my hand. "It's okay. Really. I'm going to be fine."

"Why didn't you tell us?" I asked.

"I didn't want you to worry," she said softly.

I hated myself for doing it, but I burst into tears. I knew Ma didn't want that, but I couldn't help it. I was devastated. My mother had cancer! Apparently, she'd been having radiation the past few weeks to shrink the tumor, and then she had an operation. And she went through it alone! All I could do was bawl, which I did for a few minutes.

"I'll go make some tea," said Rose, leaving the room.

"I'll let you cry for a minute or two more, and then that's enough," said Ma, "There's nothing to cry about. I'm good. I'm going to recover."

When I was finally able to stop blubbering, I looked at my frail mother, lying in her bed and asked, "Is that why you did all this? I mean, the bribing and the contract?"

Frankie slowly nodded. "All I want before I die is…"

I interrupted, "I know…grandchildren. I'm sorry, Ma. We couldn't do it. Danny and I, we both tried, but…"

"It's okay. I was wrong to do that to you. I felt desperate, though. Being sick made me have some pretty strange thoughts, and one of them was that I didn't want to die without having grandchildren."

I wiped my eyes with my forearm. "Ma, I was wrong too. About a lot of things. I was so bitter and so angry all the time. And I was afraid. Afraid to let myself be happy. I want to have babies. I'm sure of that now."

"It's okay, even if you never do. I'll always love you," she said, a tear rolling down her cheek.

I wiped it off. "I feel like I should thank you, Ma, for giving me the contract."

"Why?"

"Because through this crazy time of trying to find someone to have a baby with, I fell in love. And so did Danny."

Upon hearing both her children had fallen in love, Ma, Miss Dramatic, began to cry, which made me cry again. We both sobbed until Rose came back with a tray with three cups of tea on it. She served us and then served herself. And then she sat on a chair next to the bed and demanded to know what was going on.

Ma began telling her about the night she gave us the contract. What was so funny was that Rose began to laugh. Actually, she was howling. For some reason, she found our situation hysterically funny, which made me realize how right I was to believe it would make a great movie.

The three of us sat there talking and laughing about it for a long time, and I told them all about Danny's and my quest for fertility. And even though lots of the stories were extremely entertaining, what we did made me sad because we used people. And I was truly ashamed of that.

"I want to hear about the man you love," Ma exclaimed.

I put my head down because I couldn't even look at my mother. As if she didn't have enough going on, now she had to hear about my broken heart? By telling her that both Danny and I were in love, I'd teased her. Ma was probably expecting to hear wedding bells. Now I'd have to tell her how the people we loved currently hated our guts.

"What is it?" she asked, lifting up my chin to get a look at my eyes.

"Ma, I do love him. It's just…"

"Oh my God, he's married!"

I giggled. It was good to see Miss Drama Queen getting back to normal. "No Ma, he's not married."

"What then?" she urged.

"He doesn't love me anymore. I told him the truth about the contract, and how I began the relationship under false pretenses, and he just doesn't believe I actually fell in love with him. He told me I was evil."

"That bastard!" shouted Rose.

Ma gave me a big grin. "You, evil?" she giggled, "You, my sweet girl, are anything but evil. You're filled with so much good, and you have so much love to give. And you're finally sharing it with someone. I can tell by the look on your face. It's the same enthusiastic, warmhearted expression I see when I talk about your father and I. You've finally let someone love you the way you should be loved."

"I know, but my heart's breaking. He won't even look at me."

Frankie sat up in bed and said with determination, "If you tell him how you really feel, you can get him back."

"I don't know. He's pretty angry."

"He's also a man," Rose piped in.

"Go get him back," Ma said.

"Hey, Ma?" I said with apprehension in my voice.

"Yeah?"

"He's not Jewish."

"Huh," said Frankie with a smile, "Any chance he would convert?"

I cracked up and then I hugged my mother tight.

A few minutes later, she was ready for another nap. She told Rose to fill me in on more of the details of her condition, so the two of us went into the living room and sat on the couch, and Rose educated me on Frankie's illness. She had stage two cancer, and the doctors were very optimistic that with the radiation, the surgery, and future chemotherapy she would fully recover. Rose gave me the names and phone numbers of all of Ma's doctors so I could call them with the hundreds of questions I had.

Frankie had been so stubborn, so hard-headed in not wanting us to know she was sick, that she had carried the burden all by herself. I wondered how she must have felt telling me she was going on a vacation and seeing the world, when in reality she was having radiation treatments and then a mastectomy. She had told me she had a limousine picking her up to take her to the airport, when in truth, the limo was taking her to the hospital.

It all began to make sense. I now knew exactly why she put the demands she did on Danny and I. I wondered how I could have doubted my own mother's character. Shouldn't I have realized something was really wrong? All this time, I'd kept saying how selfish Ma was, how she wanted grand-children just because all her friends had them. Now I realized it was because Frankie felt like she was running out of time.

While Ma slept and Rose watched the news, I decided it was time to call my brother.

Chapter 38

I answered my cell, "Hey, I'm really glad you called. I need your help. I'm in a flower shop. What color roses should I send? All red or half red half pink?"

"Uh...I think half and half," she answered.

"Okay, cool," I said, "hold on." I then told the florist that I wanted to send someone a dozen roses, half red half pink.

"Um, Danny..." said my sister, "I need to talk to you."

"Sure, what's up?" Before she could get another word in, I said, "Screw it. I'm going all red. Hold on." Then I changed my order while she waited.

"Danny..." she said again.

"Yeah, sorry, Jamie. Go ahead. I'm listening. Hope you don't mind, though, if I fill out this form for the flowers while we talk."

"Look, it's Ma."

"What about her?"

"She wasn't on a trip like she said. She..." My sister then broke down crying.

"What? Tell me!" I urged.

Through tears she managed, "Look, finish ordering the flowers and then come over here, to HER place."

"Ma's place?"

"Yeah."

"What's wrong? Is Ma there?"

"Yes. We'll talk about it when you get here."

"Okay, I'll be there as soon as I can," I said. I snapped my cell shut and twelve minutes later I was knocking on my mother's door.

Jamie answered and the first thing she did was put her arms around me and start crying again.

"I'll go make some more tea," I heard a woman say. I looked up and saw some older lady in a nurse's outfit.

Jamie pulled away from me, composed herself and said to the woman, "Thank you. You're really thoughtful, Rose." Then the woman walked into the kitchen.

"Who the hell is Rose and where's Ma?" I asked.

"Asleep in her bedroom."

Now I started to shake. "Is Ma sick?"

"Yeah," answered Jamie, "Come in and sit down."

I followed my sister to our mother's brand new couch. On the way, I had a quick flashback to the day we sat on the floor waiting for all the new furniture to be delivered. Ma was so happy, so excited about all her new stuff, and her new outfit and new hair. I resented her that day. And now, not knowing what was wrong with her yet, already I felt guilty.

"Ma has breast cancer," Jamie said.

"What? When did she find out? Did something happen on her trip?"

"There was no trip, Danny. It was a lie. She didn't want us to know about the cancer, so she pretended she was going on a cruise. She's been having radiation treatments and last week she had surgery. And now she has to have chemotherapy."

As she gave me more details about Ma's prognosis and condition, I sat and listened, still trying to absorb the shock of it all and probably retaining thirty percent of the information. I asked a few questions, some of which were answered by Rose, who had come out of the kitchen and introduced herself. Rose seemed cool, and I immediately liked her and felt comfortable with her. Still, I was so stunned by learning the truth that I could barely focus on most of what they were telling me.

When Rose went to check on Ma, Jamie told me the story about how she found out the truth. As I listened, the guilt compounded. I'd been so angry with Frankie. I'd thought she was selfish and superficial and pretty much nuts for asking us to have babies for money.

"I couldn't feel worse," I said to my sister, "I'm a horrible son."

"No," she responded, "You didn't know. Neither did I."

"It all makes sense now. Ma wanted us to have babies because she thought she was going to die."

Jamie nodded in agreement. I put my head down in sadness and in shame. Just then Rose appeared in the doorway. "Your mother's up." Instantly, I got up and went into her bedroom. The sight of her was shocking. My ordinarily loud, gregarious, happy mother seemed like a quiet, frail, old woman now. It took my breath away.

"Hi, Ma," I managed, my voice almost a whisper.

"Hi, my sweet boy," Ma replied softly, "Come sit with me."

I sat down on the edge of her bed and took her hand. It felt really small, and I realized that the size of it was no different than it had always been, but how I viewed my mother had changed in an instant. She was no longer the strong, self-sufficient woman I knew. She needed me now. And that made me sad but proud of her, too. Proud because I realized that her whole life, Frankie had been a survivor. She was a single mother who raised us and gave us a good life. And I'd never appreciated that.

"I don't know what to say, Ma. I'm sorry this happened to you and I'm sorry for acting like I did."

"You acted just fine," she said, tears rolling down her cheeks.

"Can I hug you?"

"Please do."

I bent my head down and hugged my mother, and I felt like a little boy while I cried on her for a long time.

"I love you, Ma," I said.

"I haven't heard you say that in a long time."

"I know. I'm sorry."

"You know something," Ma said, "I'm not glad I got cancer, but I think everything that's gone on in the past few weeks might make our little family a lot stronger."

"Just get better, Ma," I said, "Just get better."

A little while later, we all agreed we were hungry. We decided to order Chinese. As usual, the meal was delicious. What was new at the table, however (besides the new table), was the fun conversations we were having versus the old, miserable ones, which had always been about the lack of grandchildren.

On this night, we talked about old times, old memories and the most special topic of conversation, my dad. Finally, I wanted to hear all the stories Jamie already knew. My sister had no problem hearing them again, and Rose seemed to be entertained as well. The stories about my parents were wonderful and funny and sweet and important.

"Can I ask you something, Ma?" I asked.

"Sure."

"Why didn't you ever get remarried?"

"I went on a few dates, but I knew I'd never get married again."

"Why not?"

Ma got tears in her eyes when she answered, "Your father was and will always be the love of my life. Seven years together was all I got, but I wouldn't change things even if I could. It was a great seven years."

"Weren't you ever lonely?" Jamie asked.

"If I answer that question, it's just going to make you feel badly."

"So you were," I said.

"Sometimes, but it was okay. I had you two. And hopefully, someday, on your terms of course, I'll have some grandchildren."
"So does that mean the deal's off?" I asked with a smile.
"Let's just say," Frankie answered with a big grin, "Everything's on hold for now."
After dinner, we sat in the living room drinking coffee and eating Rose's homemade chocolate chip cookies. My questions about my parents continued, and Ma told us a funny story even Jamie had never heard.
She began, "The summer before your dad died, he surprised me with a weekend getaway to Wisconsin for our anniversary. So, grandma came to watch you two, and off we went. We got off the exit to the little town where we were headed, and turned onto a dirt road, which according to dad's directions would get us to our motel. The only place it got us was lost. We found ourselves in the middle of nowhere, and we hadn't seen a car for awhile. We were all alone out there."
"Please spare us any details of any sexual activity that might have taken place," I joked.
"Daniel Jeffrey Jacobson!" Frankie scolded with a giggle. Everyone laughed.
"Continue, Ma," Jamie urged.
"We were getting more and more nervous, and then things took a turn for the worse. A tire blew. Now we were really scared. The funny thing was, though, I always felt safe with your father."
"So what happened?" asked Rose.
"So we pulled over to the side of the road, which was really the grass, and after a half hour or so a guy in a pick-up truck stopped and offered to help. He told us he would drive to the nearest gas station and get us a tow truck and that we should plan on it being there in an hour or so."
"Are you kidding me?" I asked, "I'd have forced myself into that guy's truck and made him take me with him."

"Yeah, how did you know he was coming back?" Jamie asked.

"You're missing the best part of the story," Frankie answered, "It's about what happened while we were waiting for the tow."

"Ma, I asked you not to give us any details of yours and dad's sex life!" I joked again.

She giggled and then went on, "Dad turned on the radio and found some seventies station, and we sat there listening to the music for a few minutes. Then I began to dance, and dad joined me. Then, I started doing the Electric Slide.

"You know the electric slide?" asked Jamie.

"You bet I do!" Frankie exclaimed, "I taught your father how to do it. And when the tow truck arrived, the guy found us in the middle of a dirt road doing the electric slide, The Commodores blaring in the background."

Rose teased, "No offense, but you don't seem like the electric slide type."

"Are you challenging me, Rose?" Ma asked playfully.

Jamie and I sat there listening with grins on our faces.

"I sure am," said Rose, rising from her seat and heading toward the stereo.

"There's a CD in there called Seventies Gold. *Play that," Ma requested.*

Rose pressed play, and within seconds we heard, "At first I was afraid, I was petrified...just thinking I could never live without you by my side..." It was Gloria Gaynor's I Will Survive.

A minute later, Frankie Jacobson was standing in the middle of the living room floor doing the electric slide, and with amazing rhythm and style no one would have expected. I realized right then that I'd never seen my own mother dance. Rose joined in while Jamie and I continued watching and giggling at these two cute women getting down.

"Don't even tell me you two don't know this dance," Rose called to us.

"Please, don't insult," I answered, just before joining in. *Step, slide, step, slide, step, slide, clap. Step, slide, step, slide, step, slide, clap. Jamie was next. Rock forward, rock back, rock forward, turn, touch.*

As the four of us danced together and sang and laughed, it was as if we were celebrating something. And the reality was that we were. This was the start of our new and improved family, the beginning of a closeness and warmth that had been missing for such a long time. Frankie, facing breast cancer, and Jamie and I dealing with that, not to mention our broken hearts, couldn't have been happier at this moment. Yes, we all had worry and sadness in our lives, but now our hearts were open and we were appreciating something extremely special and meaningful; each other.

As for Rose, it was obvious she was going to be a welcome addition into our little clan. She'd told Jamie earlier how much Frankie was paying her, and even though it was a ton of money it seemed well worth it. Rose was great to have around. Upbeat, sensitive, caring, funny, talented in the kitchen, and a fabulous dancer! Plus, I could see that these two women had become very good friends. And since money certainly wasn't an issue for Frankie, who cared about the cost?

We continued to dance and sing, "As long as I know how to love I know I'll stay alive...I've got all my life to live, and I've got all my love to give, and I'll survive...I will survive...I will survive."

I will survive. Wasn't that the truth? I would try to get Courtney back, but even if I didn't, I would survive. Jamie would try to work things out with Drew, but even if she didn't, she'd survive. Most importantly, Frankie would beat cancer. She would survive. She had to. Wasn't that all that really mattered? I had my family. Knowing that, I felt like the luckiest guy on earth.

Chapter 39

I got a couple strange looks when I walked past the security guys in the lobby of WGB. I actually couldn't believe they didn't stop me. I mean, I didn't work there anymore.

"Hey guys!" I exclaimed with a dashing smile and a wave. One of them waved back. The rest just smiled, all looking extremely confused.

It was two minutes before the start of the lottery drawing and I knew everyone was in the studio. I had no idea who they got to temporarily replace me, but it didn't matter. The person wouldn't be doing the lottery today. I would be. I charged into the studio.

"What the hell are *you* doing here?" I heard Richard say.

"My job," I said loudly, but without looking anyone in the eye. Then I walked on stage and grabbed the microphone out of the hands of some mousy little blonde girl who I'd never seen before.

"Thank you," I said to her.

The girl was completely stunned. Surprisingly, though, she conceded easily and walked off the set. I locked eyes with Richard, who was powerless to do anything since we'd be on-air in less than a minute. In a low, controlled voice, he said, "Don't screw up, Jamie. I'm warning you."

Instead of responding, I turned and looked at the mousy blonde, who was standing off stage looking like she might cry. Anything not to look at my now old boyfriend whose face was behind the camera that would shoot me.

"Hold still, please," he said to me, "I need to get a focus." His tone was the same as it had been the day before; cold, distant and angry.

The stress of having him ten feet away and seeing me through the lens was almost unbearable. He'd been shooting me for years, but today it felt like there was a complete stranger behind the camera. Worse, actually, because I knew he hated me. He thought I was evil, after all. And he was looking closely at me, focusing on my every move. It felt almost creepy.

"Three...two..." said Drew. "One," he motioned.

As if I'd just taken a magic pill, I fell back into my old self, performing as perky and cheerful as ever. As I pulled the balls out of the bins and called out the numbers, I wondered if the audience was surprised to see me on-air. After my performance a day earlier, I was sure they all figured I got fired. I was very wrong, and would later find out that because of my little escapade, the number of viewers on this day was up fifty percent. Apparently, the audience was dying to see what might come out of my mouth today. I have to say, I didn't disappoint.

I finished the number picking with no surprises or variations from the norm, but when I went to sign off, the audience received the drama they were hoping to get.

"Again, your pick three is two seven nine...and your pick four is nine eight one two." I paused for a second, feeling the tension of the crew, (especially Richard) each holding his or her breath, awaiting my next move. When I spoke, they didn't have the luxury of peacefully exhaling.

"Can you even imagine winning the lottery?" I began. I could almost feel people's teeth gritting, but I didn't care. I actually thought it was funny. "I mean think about it. The chance of winning is one in millions!" Next, I shot Richard a quick look. He appeared like he might blow a gasket. Still, I went on. "I want everyone to know something. Love is the same way. The odds of falling in love can sometimes feel really high. Why bother, right?"

"What the…" I heard Richard say.

Still, I continued. "Well, I'm here to tell everyone to play the lottery, both for money and for love. Take a chance. It's worth it. Especially love. I know this because I'm in love, and it's the best feeling in the world." I took a deep breath. "Drew, I don't know exactly when I fell in love with you. I think it might have been on the fifty yard line at Soldier Field. And I know you don't like me very much right now. You think I'm evil. I'm not evil, Drew. I'm just a girl who made mistakes. I'm so sorry." Now I knew the entire crew had their mouths wide open. "I'm sorry for hurting you. I love you. I think I always have. I was just too stupid to see it. And as wrong as it was, this whole thing forced me to look at you. And I'm thankful for that." I felt my eyes well with tears. "Even if you can't get past this, I'm thankful that you were mine for a little while. I love you."

I took a deep breath, suddenly feeling amazingly relieved because I'd said everything I needed to say. A very satisfying sense of inner peace and serenity came over me. "For WGB…" I began, but I didn't get to finish. Before I knew it, Drew abandoned the camera, ran up on stage, grabbed my shoulders and began to kiss me.

"Shit!" I heard Richard say, but I couldn't see him because I was lip locked. I found out later, Richard jumped out of his seat and quickly got behind the camera to take over Drew's job. The next thing I heard was applause. The entire crew started clapping and cheering.

"Sign off!" Richard shouted.

I broke away from the embrace, held the mic up, and said to the audience, struggling not to giggle too much, "Sorry about that. Have a wonderful day. For WGB, I'm Jamie Jacobson."

"Go to credits!" shouted Richard.

"Forgive me?" I asked Drew.

"You bet," he said with a big grin.

Although deathly afraid to look at the temporary camera man, I did. Surprisingly, Richard smiled and gave me a wink. When he walked out of the studio, I said to Drew, "Think they'll give me my job back?"

"Of course. You just gave Chicago some outstanding live drama. Watch out. Our ratings are about to explode!"

"I don't care about ratings," I said with a grin, "All I care about is you."

Drew kissed me again and at that moment, I realized something. I was the one who just won the lottery.

From *The Chicago Tribune, Faces and Places section, October 15, 2011.*

LOVE IS ON THE AIR

Local Lottery Host Declares Love for camera operator on air

Jamie Jacobson, WGB's mid-day lottery host, whose mother won the lottery a few weeks ago shocked viewers with her announcement at the end of yesterday's lottery drawing that she was in love with Drew Conrad, the camera operator she works with...

Chapter 40

"Let's go back to your place and have make-up sex," Drew whispered in my ear while we walked back to my office after the lottery.

We wanted to be alone. We had so much to talk about, and we had no privacy at the station since everyone had begun swarming us, congratulating us and asking us questions about how we ended up together.

A few minutes later we managed to sneak out of WGB. We hailed a cab and made out in the back seat the entire way to my apartment. The kissing even continued while we walked through the lobby.

"Jamie, nice going!" Rick, the doorman called to me as we passed the front desk.

"Thanks, Rick!" I shouted with a giggle. Then I went right back to mauling Drew. We got into the elevator and kissed all the way up to my apartment. My home phone was ringing when we walked in.

"I think we should get right down to business," said Drew, picking me up and throwing me over his shoulder, "Let's get the sex out of the way and then we can talk."

"I totally agree," I said with a giggle, having a hard time talking while upside down.

We had crazy, mad, passionate, love hate sex (although the hate part was just for dramatic purposes. We didn't hate each other, obviously.) And then we talked. I told Drew about my mother's breast cancer and how I'd found out about it.

"Is she going to be okay?" he asked.

"Yes, and she's going to want to meet you, so get ready."

"I'm up for it. The girl you marry turns into her mother as she ages. So, it's important to see what I'm going to get."

"So you think you're going to marry me?"

"Yup," he said with a smile, "Unless I hate your mother."

"You won't," I answered, tears now in my eyes, "You won't."

We fell asleep in each other's arms for awhile, and when I woke up I was so happy that this whole day wasn't a dream. What had happened at the station was real. Getting Drew back was real.

Feeling more relaxed and at peace than I could ever remember, I slipped into an old pair of jeans and a sweater, and snuck out of the bedroom so I wouldn't wake up Drew. I retrieved my *Blackberry* from my purse and giggled when I saw I had eighteen missed calls.

Frankie took the lead, attempting to phone me eight times. Danny was next with four attempts, and the rest were from friends and reporters.

I called my mother back first. "Hi, Ma…"

"Oh my God! Honey, I'm so happy for you!" The drama queen was in her glory.

"Thank you, Ma," I giggled.

"He's so cute! When do I get to meet him?"

"Soon Ma, soon."

"How about tonight?"

"Give me a couple days," I requested, "There's something else I need to take care of."

I talked to her a little while longer, asking how she was feeling and if she needed anything, to which she replied, "Yes, I need a wedding!"

My next call was to Danny. "Holy shit, Jamie!" was how he answered his phone.

"Can you believe it?"

"I'm happy for you."

"Thanks," I smiled.

"Listen, I've gotten some calls from reporters."

"I knew you would. I hope you're saying 'no comment.'"

"I have to," he said, "If I say one word to anyone, there's absolutely no chance Courtney will ever come around."

"I understand," I said, "Have you talked to her? Did she get the flowers?"

"I'm sure she did, but she still won't call me back. I've left so many messages," he said sadly.

"Keep trying."

"I am. Actually, I'm at the *Hallmark* store right now. Do you think those cards with the songs in them are stupid?"

I smiled sadly. My poor brother... "No, I don't."

"Thanks."

Just as I hung up the phone, I felt Drew's arms wrap around my waist. "What should we do for dinner?" he asked, "I'm starved."

"Listen, Drew, I have to go somewhere."

"Where?"

"I'll explain later. It's really important. Will you stay here and be here when I get back?"

"Sure," he smiled.

Fifteen minutes later, I was standing on Armitage Avenue, looking into the window of *You Sexy Thing, You.*

It was almost 6:00 and the store would be closing then. I watched Courtney working. She was showing a woman several different bras. I could tell she was trying to act happy, but she didn't fool me. She was acting robotically, seeming depressed, defeated almost.

I took a deep breath and walked in. When the door opened, Courtney turned around to greet who she thought was a last minute customer. When she saw it was me standing in the doorway, however, her pleasant welcoming smile instantly turned to a cold frown. Her eyes got smaller and it made me scared of her.

I smiled nervously and waved. She ignored me. I felt like she hated me. Could I blame her? I wondered if she'd seen or heard about the lottery earlier. If so, it obviously didn't change her opinion of me.

An older guy approached her. "I like this, but two hundred dollars? Come on…" he said, holding up a nightgown.

"How much did you want to spend?" Courtney asked politely.

"Less than a hundred."

"What a cheapskate," I mumbled under my breath, feeling sorry for the girl who was getting a gift from this guy. I waited while Courtney showed him some other options. A few minutes later, Big Bucks finally decided on a white cotton tank top and pants that were on sale for seventy nine dollars. I felt like telling him he was making a huge mistake, but for my own good I kept my mouth shut while Courtney rang up the sale and said good-bye. The second the guy was out the door, her gracious demeanor turned ice-cold.

"What are you doing here?" she asked. It was hard to believe that this was the same girl, who just a few nights earlier had said to me, "I'm so glad we ran into you guys! I had so much fun!" She had gone from treating me like a really good friend, to acting like the sight of me disgusted her.

"I was hoping we could talk," I said.

"What's there to talk about? All I have to do is read the tabloids tomorrow and I can find out all about you."

"I take it you saw the lottery."

"It's all over facebook."

"Really?"

"It doesn't change the way I feel about you."

"I understand. Can I talk to you about Danny?"

"Why bother? He's a liar, just like you."

Ouch. This was worse than I thought.

"Look," Courtney continued, "Save yourself the time and energy. I have no interest in associating with you or your brother ever again. You both disgust me."

I stood there not knowing what to do. And then, it got worse. Horrifying, actually. Courtney put her head down and began to sob. I wondered if I should hug her, but I was afraid.

"Please, just leave me alone," she managed to say through tears.

I turned to go. It was over. We had hurt this girl too much for her to ever let it go.

"I'm really sorry," I said softly. Then I walked out, feeling helplessness and defeat like never before. And that's when I saw John walking toward me, waving and smiling. My ex-husband looked different. I barely recognized him, in fact. John, who was once a hot babe was now balding and a little on the chubby side.

"Hey! It's Miss Celebrity!" he exclaimed. Then he hugged me.

I stood there frozen.

"Due, you're all over YouTube. You look amazing, way better than when we were married!"

"Thanks," I responded in an unemotional tone.

"When I saw the video I almost died!" He went on and on about how he was sure I would end up on Jay Leno, and how he hoped I wouldn't talk about him because he had a reputation to protect.

I wasn't really listening because all I could think about was Courtney, a wonderful woman who was just a few feet away from me, the girl my brother loved, and let's be honest, the girl I loved, too. I had to do something. I had to get rid of this loser in front of me and run back in there.

"Listen, I don't mean to be rude but I really have to go," I said to John.

"Alright, but hey..." he grabbed my shoulders and that's when I noticed a wedding ring on his left hand.

"Are you married again?" I asked.

"Oh...yeah" he said, nonchalantly, "But back to you. You're something else! You're famous! If you ever need a warm body in the middle of the night, I live on North Avenue and Damen, and I'm listed." He added with a creepy chuckle, "My wife travels a lot."

I was stunned for a moment, and then I got my second wind.

"John," I said with a sugary smile.

"Yeah?" he flirted.

"You're such a schmuck." Then I rolled my shoulders back, held my head high, and marched back toward the door of *You Sexy Thing, You.*

"Fame's really gone to your head!" John shouted, "Bitch!"

I never turned around to respond. He wasn't worth it. Instead, I opened the door to the store and walked back in. I looked around for Courtney and called her name. Her head popped up from across the room. She was sitting on the floor on the other side of the store folding some underwear and putting them in drawers. I noticed that she'd stopped crying, but her eyes were really red and her mascara was a little bit smeared. I walked over and knelt down beside her. Gently, I asked, "Will you go somewhere with me?"

Chapter 41

I told the cab driver the address, and then I looked at Courtney and said, "I'm taking you to meet my mother."

"Why?"

"Because if you meet her, I think you might understand things a little bit better."

Courtney didn't respond, and neither of us said a word for the entire cab ride except at one point, she asked, "How's Danny?"

Secretly, I was elated when I heard the question because even though her sadness and anger clearly showed she still cared about my brother, her asking about him confirmed it.

"Other than you two being apart, he's pretty good."

The cab pulled up to Frankie's building. When I went to pay the driver, my hand was shaking. Bringing this woman to meet Ma was just as scary if not scarier than it would be to bring Drew to meet her. Plus, I had no idea how Danny would feel if he knew I was doing this.

We walked up the stairs and then I knocked on the door. I'd called Ma on my way to Courtney's store and told her I might be bringing someone over, and that it wasn't Drew.

When Frankie opened the door, the first thing I noticed was how much better she looked. She was starting to look like herself again, recovering nicely from the surgery. Of course, chemotherapy was in her near future and she would be losing her hair and probably losing weight, and I certainly wasn't looking forward to that. However, if poison was going to get her back to normal, it was well worth seeing her look and feel bad for a few months.

"Hi Ma," I said, hugging her. I stepped back and said, "This is Courtney. Courtney, this is our mother, Frankie Jacobson."

"Hello there," Ma exclaimed with a wide grin, "What a nice surprise."

"Nice to meet you, Mrs. Jacobson," said Courtney in a very businesslike tone. She extended a handshake. Ma shook it and then gave me a look, like she thought that was weird. It was hard not to giggle.

"Come in, please…" Frankie said, leading us into the living room.

"Hi, Jamie!" said Rose, with her usual enthusiasm.

I loved this woman. She was always happy. Just the kind of roommate my mother needed right now. "Hi, Rose!" I said.

"Sit down," Frankie said, "Would anyone like something to drink?"

"I just made lemonade," offered Rose.

"No, thank you," replied Courtney, "I can't stay long."

Ma looked really uncomfortable. Rose seemed like she had no clue what to say at this moment. We were all just sitting there, the tension in the room almost unbearable.

"So, Courtney, I brought you here because I want you to know the whole story about my mother. She has breast cancer. That's why she was so desperate for us to have children."

"Not that it makes what I did okay," added Ma, "But I think fear makes people act a little crazy. At least that's what happened to me."

"My mother really is a good person. She's very selfless, and she's a great mother." I looked at Ma.

"Thank you, sweetheart," she said.

"It's true, Ma."

"I'm really sorry you have cancer, Mrs. Jacobson," said Courtney.

"Please, call me Frankie."

Courtney stood up, walked over to Ma and sat down next to her on the couch. "Frankie, I really mean it. You seem like a good person and I'm sorry I judged you without knowing all the facts." She looked at me. "And I appreciate what you're trying to do. But it doesn't make a difference for Danny and me."

"Why not?" I urged, "Danny loves you. I've honestly never seen my brother like this."

Courtney's eyes filled with tears and she stood up. "Frankie, I truly hope you get better soon. I think I should go."

"Before you leave," Ma said, sounding loud and confident, "I'd like to tell you about the favor Danny asked of me. Is that alright?"

"Okay," replied Courtney.

"My son called me and asked if I was willing to donate a large amount of money to the Endometriosis Association of America."

When I saw Courtney's reaction, I felt the first glimpse of hope for Danny.

"Really?" she asked.

Ma nodded her head and smiled, and then Courtney pretty much just lost it. She broke down again and began to sob.

"It's okay," said Ma, gently taking Courtney's hand, "Really, I'm happy to do it, but I just want you to know what a good person Danny is."

Courtney looked up at her and nodded, tears streaming down her face. "I know he is."

The two women hugged and it was the best feeling in the world. I looked at Rose and she winked at me.

"You seem like a wonderful girl," Ma said to her, "I hope I get the chance to get to know you better."

"I hope so, too," said Courtney, "Just give me a little time. Let me get used to everything."

"I understand," said Frankie.

We all headed for the door, and just before leaving Courtney turned to me. "Are you going to stay?"

I nodded.

"Thank you for bringing me here."

"Sure," I smiled.

Courtney dug through her purse, pulled out a business card and gave it to my mother. "Please call me if you need anything. I mean it."

Ma looked at the card. "Bernstein is your last name? Are you Jewish?!" she asked.

Courtney and I both burst out laughing.

"Are you sure you won't stay for dinner?" Rose asked, "I'm making chicken parmesan."

"Thanks Rose. Another time?"

"Any time!" Ma practically shouted.

"Thanks," she smiled. When she opened the door to go, her smile turned to shock. Standing there with his fist in a knocking position was my brother. He had the same look of surprise on his face.

"Hi," they both said at the same time.

"What are you doing here?" he asked her. "What is she doing here?" he then asked the other three of us.

"I brought her here," I said, afraid to make eye contact with my brother.

"I was just leaving," said Courtney, "Walk me out?"

"Okay, sure."

"Good-bye, everyone," she said with a smile. She looked at Ma one last time and said, "Be well."

Ma blew her a kiss, and the second the door closed she said, "I love her!"

"Me, too," I said.

The three of us sat and waited for Danny to come back up. A few minutes later, he walked through the door, looking both sad and happy at the same time.

"So, what happened?" asked Ma.

Danny sat down. "She thanked me for the flowers."

"That's good," I said, trying to sound enthusiastic.

"And she was really happy that I asked Ma to make a donation."

"Good!" said Ma, "Anything else?"

Now he seemed sad. "She said she wants to be friends."

"Well, that's a start," said Rose.

"I can't be friends with her. I love her too much."

"That doesn't make sense," said Ma.

"Give her a little time, Danny," I said, "I can tell she really loves you."

"How?"

"She cried."

"Right," Rose added, "She cried."

"She cried hard," I said.

"When?"

"When Ma told her about the donation."

Danny looked at me. "Thanks for trying, Jamie. I really appreciate what you did."

"You're not mad?"

"No," he said with a big grin, "You're a really good sister."

I smiled at him.

"I don't understand," said Ma, "Courtney's not a Jewish name."

It was nice to see Danny laugh.

Chapter 42

I went back to Ma's place the next night, only this time, as promised I brought Drew. To say I was nervous to introduce him to Ma, the woman who'd hated every guy I'd ever brought home (except for Max) was putting it mildly.

Rose answered the door. As always, she was a delight, so socially talented, making Drew feel comfortable right away. Frankie was another story. She made her grand entrance by walking out of her bedroom singing Frank Sinatra's *I've Got You Under My Skin*, which made me pretty much want to crawl into a hole and die. Drew, however, seemed to think it was funny. Either that, or he was trying to suck up to his new girlfriend's mother.

"Ma, why are you singing?"

"I'm happy," she gushed, "happy that my daughter's in love."

"Ma, this is Drew, Drew, this is my mother."

Ma extended her hand, "Frankie."

"Nice to meet you, Frankie," Drew said with a big grin.

As embarrassing as Ma's behavior was, she was also being uncharacteristically nice and non-judgmental to Drew, so unlike her typical attitude that if a guy wasn't Jewish, he would never get her stamp of approval.

Ma seemed genuinely interested in getting to know Drew. However, she wasn't asking him a million questions about what he wanted to do in the future, or how many kids he wanted, or what kind of house he eventually pictured himself owning. She seemed more interested in just talking to him for the purpose of learning more about the guy her daughter was crazy about.

At dinner, Drew held up his glass of wine and asked if he could make a toast. "To you, Frankie, to your health and well being. And also, to your contract!"

"Why do you say that?" I asked.

"Because I guarantee that if there was no contract, I wouldn't be sitting here with you at your mother's dining room table having dinner."

"I'm sorry about that," said Frankie, "I realize now how wrong it was."

"Maybe, but a really good thing came from it. Your bribe forced Jamie into giving me a chance. I feel grateful for that."

"Well, I feel grateful that you have forgiven both me and my daughter."

The meal couldn't have been going more smoothly. There was only one moment I lost my appetite and became nauseous. It was when Ma asked Drew, "Where do your parents live?"

"My dad and his wife live in Arizona. My mother passed away when I was really young."

"Oh, I'm sorry," Frankie said happily. The enthusiasm in her response made me realize she felt death was better than divorce.

"How long has your dad been remarried?" she asked.

276

"Three years. He met Monica through me, actually."
This was the moment I thought my spaghetti and meatballs
might come back up.

"How nice," Frankie responded, "Did you set them up?"

"Does anyone want some more wine?" I asked.

"You could say that," Drew answered Ma with a chuckle.
Then he gave me a wink.

The night went extremely well, better than I could ever
have expected, far surpassing all the nightmare meetings
I'd had with Frankie and various boyfriends. I wasn't sure
exactly what made the difference, but I felt it was probably
a combination of things. Drew, first of all, was so likeable
that I couldn't imagine anyone not taking to him. And
me, I was different now. I was softer and more at ease. But
even more so, I knew my mother could feel how much I
loved Drew, and any mother would feel good about that,
right?

The biggest reason the night went smoothly, though, was
because Frankie had changed, I think. Instead of focusing
on the fact that I was with a non-Jewish cameraman who on
paper wasn't a good match for me, she seemed to put stock
in the fact that the two people sitting at her dining room
table seemed truly in love. Everything seemed so natural,
the way it was supposed to be.

The next few weeks were crazy. I would go to work
in the mornings and spend my afternoons taking Ma to
her doctor appointments and/or to her chemotherapy
and radiation treatments, and then running errands for
her.

I also spent every free minute I had sending out my
recently finished new movie script, *Jackpot!*, to producers
and agents. I knew I'd get several rejections, but I also
knew I only needed one person to believe in the concept

of it, and with how funny and sweet it turned out, I was sure it wouldn't take long. But even if it did, that was okay. I'd keep trying. Because I had all the time in the world. I had a great life. A good job, an amazing boyfriend, a dear, sweet, brother, and a mother who was on her way to getting healthy. I had it all, and anything I obtained professionally would just be gravy on my full and happy plate.

The only thing worrying me these days was my brother. He was working really hard at his job, and also working at *Pretzel Perfection* on the weekends, trying to make extra money. He seemed really distressed. Apparently, he had tried talking to his student, Angela Walker's parents about keeping the girl in school and they had shot him down. Angela's last day of school was approaching quickly and it was killing Danny.

Then of course there was Courtney. She still wanted to be nothing more than very casual acquaintances with him, and what was even worse was that she and Ma had now become friends. Courtney had gone over to my mother's twice since the night I'd brought her there. One morning, she brought Frankie and Rose a casserole to either heat up for dinner that night or to freeze. Another time, she showed up with Starbucks coffee and all kinds of scones and muffins. The two also spoke on the phone almost every day. And although Danny was happy Frankie had some more support, I could tell it bugged him.

One Friday night, Drew and I went over to Ma's for Chinese. Even though Rose offered to cook veal piccata, which sounded amazing, no one wanted to break tradition. Both Danny and Frankie had invited Courtney, but she had a meeting with her accountants and had to decline. She told Frankie to count her in for next Friday, though.

"So that's good!" I told Danny, "Maybe she's coming around."

"I don't think so," he said, "She still won't see me."

Ma put her hand on Danny's. "Give it some more time. I'm working my angle. Last time she was here, I pulled out all kinds of baby pictures of you, and if you'd have seen the fuss she made…"

"Ma, why did you do that?" he asked.

"She's trying to help you," I said.

Danny smiled at Ma. "Thanks."

"You'll see," said Drew, said, "Your mom's right. Give it some more time."

"Pass the shrimp, please?" I requested of Danny, who was in an arm's reach of it.

"Jesus…" he said.

"What?" I asked defensively.

"Hungry?" he teased, passing me the container.

"I have an announcement," said Ma, "Even though neither of you were able to give me my baby, I've decided to give you the money anyway."

"Ma, I don't want the money," said Danny, "I just want you to be around for the next thirty or forty years."

"I feel the same way," I added.

"No! Listen to me. I've made up my mind. I don't need all this money, and I want you both to be happy."

"I can't believe this, Ma," I said, "Can't you see how happy I am right now? I've changed. I have a good job, I have Drew, I have a mother who's on her way back to being healthy…"

"I know and I'm glad. But I want you to have everything you want."

I started giggling and said, "I do have everything I want." I looked at Drew and said, "Help me."

He grinned, "Just tell them."

I took a deep breath and spoke. "I'm having a baby," I announced to the table.

My mother let out a scream that was louder than Jamie Lee Curtis in <u>Halloween.</u>

Chapter 43

I didn't really look pregnant yet, but I sure felt it. Throwing up three or four times a day became the norm for me, and one would think since I was pretty much puking up everything I ate, I'd have had a hard time gaining weight. Not the case. I had put on a few pounds, to the point where I'd started to use safety pins instead of the buttons on my pants and skirts.

Don't get me wrong, though, I was truly happy to be pregnant, and ecstatic to be carrying the baby of the man I loved. Drew and I were getting closer every day, picking out baby things together and planning our future. I had given my landlord notice, and was moving in with him in the next couple of months. I had never believed in miracles until the day I told Frankie that Drew and I decided to live together (and we weren't engaged), and she was actually happy about it.

One afternoon, I sat down at my desk to check e-mail. As usual, I expected to find a couple of rejection e-mails in my in-box. As I scrolled down the list past some junk and work related items, something caught my eye; a message from <u>KThompson@sonypictures.com</u>. The message line read "Please call me regarding *Jackpot!*." Instantly, I knew they were interested in my script. "Please call me" said it all. The standard rejection letters never read "Please call me."

I was psyched beyond belief, but not surprised. I had had a strong gut feeling about the success of the script from the moment I'd started writing it. And now, I wasn't sure what would happen, but if there was interest, then selling it was a possibility. Something in me knew that my screenplay writing career had just been born.

A few minutes later, I heard "Jamie Jacobson, please come to the front desk; you have a visitor."

I walked to the lobby. Standing there, looking as beautiful and sweet as ever was Courtney, holding a box with a big white bow around it. I hadn't seen or talked to her since the day I took her over to Ma's place. I knew she didn't hate me, but the past few weeks, I hadn't spoken with her, and I'd assumed she wasn't ready to fully forgive me yet. In fact, I wasn't even sure she'd ever want me, or Danny, for that matter in her life. It was my mother she was friends with now, and I was happy for Frankie, but very sad for Danny.

"Hi," I said.

"Hi," she smiled, "Do you have a minute to talk?"

"Sure. Let's go in here," I said, walking her into a nearby empty conference room.

The first thing she did was hand me the box. "This is for you. It's something I know you can use right now."

"I guess my mother told you?"

With a grin, she nodded.

I opened the present, which was a pair of light pink silk pajamas. "Thanks," I smiled. Then I leaned over and hugged her.

"I'm really happy for you," she said.

"Are you?"

"Yes. Just because I can't have kids, that doesn't mean I don't think other people shouldn't."

"That's not what I was thinking," I said, "I'm just wondering if you think I'll be a good mother. Do you think I'm a good person, Courtney?"

Her eyes filled with tears. "Yes, I do. Plus, I know how much in love you are with Drew. That night we went out, I could see it. The way you looked at him... Your baby's really lucky. The parents really are in love."

I practically threw my arms around her, making her giggle.

"Thank you," I whispered. Then I pulled away from the hug and said, "Thanks for the gift, and for coming here. Does this mean we're friends now?"

"Of course," she smiled.

"I'm so glad."

"Jamie, do you know where Danny is?"

"You mean, right now?"

She nodded.

I remembered Danny telling me he had a shoot today at 5:30 in Lincoln Park. I looked at my watch. It was 5:15. "Yeah, I do," I answered, "why?"

Courtney broke into a huge grin and answered, "I decided it's time for me to play the lottery."

Chapter 44

Kristin was hot. She was very tall, very tan, and had long beautiful legs, not to mention huge boobs that obviously were fake, but still really nice. The only problem was, actually, there were two problems. One, Kristin's breath smelled like smoke, and two, I was still totally in love with my Courtney girl, and I couldn't even think about being with anyone else.

Kristin was sitting on my lap on a park bench in the middle of Lincoln Park. She was facing me, and I had my hands on her butt. And we were kissing. Not because I wanted to, though, but because we were posing for a shoot. I was pretending to desire her, and it was actually making me a little nauseous because I felt no such feelings.

"Nice..." said the photographer as he snapped a few shots. "A bit more passionate, yes?" he said in his French accent, trying to shoot and speak with a lit cigarette in his mouth at the same time.

'Leave it to the French,' I thought, as I continued to make out with the other person who obviously couldn't live without a smoke.

This snobby French photographer, who thought he knew everything was really bugging me, and I couldn't wait to get this shoot over with. Believe it or not, Jennifer had actually set this up for me, even though she was no longer my agent. She had called me a couple days earlier and said she wanted to bury the hatchet and that she thought I'd be great for this gig. I thanked her and felt lucky at the time. Now I decided maybe I could have lived without this job, which was a magazine ad for "Potent Plus," a male sex drive booster pill.

What had my life come to? Did my acting suck so much that all I was worth was "Potent Plus?" As I kissed the girl harder and harder, I kept thinking, 'This is the last time. I'm done.' More kissing. 'I've changed. I am better than this.' More kissing. 'I deserve more.' More kissing, only this time, something made me look up in between kisses. A few feet away, with the sun going down behind her stood the love of my life.

"Oh my God!" I shouted. Then I stood up, causing the girl on my lap to fall onto the ground.

"Hey! What do you think you're doing, asshole?" she shouted, brushing some dirt off her leg.

I helped her up and said, "Sorry," and then I called out, "Courtney, this isn't what you think! This is a shoot for 'Potent Plus,' a male sex drive enhancer." At that moment, I couldn't have felt like more of a loser, and I figured it was only a matter of seconds until the girl I truly loved would say bu-bye for good.

But Courtney didn't turn and go. Instead, she walked toward me, looked into my eyes and said, "It's okay."

"Really?"

"Yeah," she said with a giggle, "This isn't a coincidence. Jamie told me you'd be here."

"So you hunted me down?" I asked, "That's a good sign."

"Excuse me, mademoiselle," interrupted the French guy, "we're in the middle of shooting and we need to finish before the sun goes down. Do you mind?"

"Give me two minutes," I urged.

*"We don't have two minutes!" said Frenchy, clearly beginning
to panic.*

*I ignored him and guided Courtney a few feet away for some
privacy. "Are you okay?"*

"I'm great, but I have a question."

"What?"

"Do I still have you?"

*I swear to God, at this moment, I felt exactly like Charlie did
when Willy Wonka told him he was giving him the chocolate factory.*

"Well, do I?" she asked.

"Yes! You got me!" I exclaimed.

"The light! The light!" shouted the photographer.

*"One second!" I shouted back. Then I looked right into her eyes
and said it again, softly this time. "You got me." And then we
kissed, and everything was perfect.*

*A few seconds later, I heard clicking sounds. I kept kissing
Courtney, but I was becoming preoccupied. It sounded like a camera. Then I felt bright lights. And then more clicking. Both of us
looked at the lights, and quickly realized Frenchy was snapping
shots.*

Kristin shouted at him, "What the hell are you doing?"

*"I'm sorry," he said, "this is too good. I must go with it. She
is tres jolie!"*

"Un-fucking believable!" she shouted, storming off.

*"Please..." Frenchy said to us, "Keep doing what you were
doing."*

I looked at Courtney. "I don't have a problem with it, do you?"

*"Not at all. It seems like you took your 'Potent Plus' today," she
said with a giggle.*

We continued to kiss until the sun went down.

Chapter 45

The next morning, I headed to work in my pretzel costume. It was just another typical Saturday of handing out candy for my boss, Vito, but something was different. My attitude. Mr. Salty had a lot to be happy about. I'd made peace with my mother, who thank God, was going to be fine, my sister was happy and having a baby, and me, I was truly in love for the first time in my life. Life was good. I walked into "Pretzel Perfection" smiling and whistling.

"Good morning, Vito," I said happily.

"Why are you in such a good mood?" he asked, grumpy, as usual.

"Because I love this job," I joked, "How many guys do you know who get to dress up in tights, wear a pretzel pillow around their waist and hand out samples all day?" Before Vito could offer a sarcastic comeback, I continued. "Then there's the self-sampling factor. I've got to be honest with you, however. Your Snickers pretzel could have a little more Snickers on it." I was getting a huge kick out of myself. Vito wasn't amused.

"Listen Mr. Actor boy, I'm the highest grossing chocolate shop in the city. I think my Snickers pretzels are alright, and so do the thousands of customers who buy them. If you ever get a real acting

job, and you end up making movies with Dinero or Pacino, then you can cut my pretzels down. For now, shut up!"

I wanted to tell Vito to go fuck himself, but I didn't want to lose my job, so I apologized. "Listen, Vito, buddy, I was just kidding."

"Okay then, let's sell some pretzels." He managed half a smile, and I could tell he felt badly about going off on me.

I walked outside and began to diligently hand out samples.

"Delicious...mouth watering chocolate covered pretzels..." I shouted.

Michigan Avenue was crowded and I was busy. The samples were going fast. "Absolutely the best Snickered-covered pretzels you'll ever taste!" I shouted extra loud for Vito's benefit.

"Very funny, Mr. Salty!" Vito shouted from inside the shop.

All of a sudden, I saw Angela Walker coming toward me. Her belly was getting bigger, and that was a reminder that her days in school were numbered.

"Hi Mr. J.!" she exclaimed with a giggle.

"Are you laughing at me?"

"No."

"You better not tell anyone you saw me like this," I joked.

"I won't."

"How'd you know where to find me?"

"I just left Courtney's store. She told me I should come here."

"Hey pretzel boy, don't get chatty on me!" shouted Vito from inside the shop.

"Look, I have a tough boss. I can't really talk. Is everything okay?"

Angela looked like she was going to burst. "I have some news. I've decided to stay in school."

"Oh my God! That's great!"

Angela gave me a huge hug. "Thank you, Mr. J., you're the reason I have the guts to go against my family and do this."

I was overwhelmed with pride, both in Angela and in myself.

"I'm so impressed, Angela. I know you're doing the right thing. If there's anything I can do to help you..."

"You've already done so much."

"What about the baby?" I asked.

Angela put her head down and said sadly, "I'm pretty sure I'm giving it up for adoption."

"Are you okay with that?"

She nodded. "It's the best thing."

"I'm proud of you, Angela."

"Mr. Salty!" shouted Vito from inside the shop.

Angela giggled, "I'll see you Monday." Then she kissed my cheek and I felt like I could fly. She started walking down the block.

"Wait!" I shouted.

She turned around. "What?"

"Don't you want a sample?"

"No thanks," she said with a smile, "I don't really like chocolate."

"Me neither!" I said.

All of a sudden, Vito stormed out of the shop. "What the hell do you think you're doing?"

I didn't answer my boss. Instead, I put the box of samples down on the sidewalk and began taking off my pretzel costume. All I had on underneath was a brown turtle neck and brown tights.

"What are you doing?" he asked.

"Sorry, Vito, you're going to have to find yourself another pretzel boy."

I handed the costume to Vito and walked off. And as I strutted proudly down Michigan Avenue, leaving Vito speechless for probably the first time in his life, I was filled with pride and self confidence. I had made a difference in Angela's life, and I realized that every day I went to work as a teacher, I was making a difference in a lot of lives. I suddenly felt satisfaction like never before.

I didn't care anymore that I didn't have a lot of money, and I wasn't even sure I was going to try to keep acting. For the first time in my life, I realized that teaching was enough for me. It was what I was meant to do. Right then, I thought of my dad. He had probably felt the same way. And tragically, he died as a young man. As for me, I had my whole life ahead of me to keep making a difference. And I felt lucky beyond belief. A couple of people giggled at my appearance, but I didn't care. I kept walking, feeling happier than I could ever remember.

One Friday night at dinner, pretty close to Jamie's due date, I thought it was time to bring up the night Ma presented us with her crazy contract. Everyone at the table was laughing hysterically and cracking jokes about the whole thing. Even Courtney found it hilarious now.

"If it wasn't for the contract," Ma boasted, "I guarantee there would still be two single people sitting at this table, instead of two couples!"

Rose pointed to Jamie's stomach. "And don't forget about this little person!"

"I always told my children that I wanted them to realize the important things in life," said Ma.

"Yeah, we know," I interrupted, "marriage, family, children…"

"So you were listening," she said.

"Yeah, Ma, we listened," I smiled.

"Look at us, Ma," said Jamie, while rubbing her kicking tummy, "Trust me, we listened."

As we finished the meal and sipped coffee, I gave everyone the details about my court appearance regarding the charges against me for soliciting a prostitute. The judge ended up dismissing all charges since Officer Kay Olson, a.k.a. "Susan," was a rookie and really did set me up.

As everyone talked and laughed about it, I looked over at my mother. Even with no hair and all the weight she'd lost, she was a beautiful woman. A kind, compassionate person, yet strong and defiant, too. After all, she'd literally tried to force her children into having kids.

I'd always thought Ma wanted babies just for fun; to hold and to play with and hug and kiss and tickle, and to brag about. But tonight, I found myself wondering how I could have doubted Frankie's reasons for wanting to be a grandmother. Here was a woman who worked as a cleaning lady to help her mother pay the bills, a woman who forfeited her dream wedding dress to instead buy her mother a dress, and a woman who worked her entire life to make sure her children went to college. She was a truly brave and remarkable person.

Frankie Jacobson didn't want babies for herself, she wanted them for Jamie and I to enjoy. She wanted us to experience love and families of our own. The woman I thought was so selfish for putting us through such torture was perhaps the most selfless woman I'd ever known.

I looked at Jamie and Drew. His hand was on her big tummy, and he was telling everyone at the table about the time he took my sister to Soldier Field. Then I looked at Courtney, her beautiful smile lighting up the whole room. And then I looked back at Ma, sitting at the head of the table looking contented and filled with joy. She caught my eye, smiled and blew me a kiss.

From the *Chicago Tribune, Celebrations*
section, July 10, 2012:

Engagements

**Courtney Lynn Bernstein and Daniel Jeffrey
Jacobson**

Courtney Lynn Bernstein and Daniel Jeffrey
Jacobson are proud to announce their
engagement. Their wedding is planned for
November 4, 2012 in Chicago. Courtney is
the daughter of Sandy and David Bernstein
of Los Angeles, CA. Daniel is the son of
Frankie Jacobson and the late Seth Jacobson
of Chicago. Courtney is a local business
owner on Chicago's north side, and Daniel is
a teacher at Martin Luther King High School
in Chicago.

From the *Chicago Tribune, Celebrations*
section, July, 22 2012:

Birth Announcements

Seth Charlie Conrad

Announcing the birth of Seth Charlie
Conrad, born July 15th in Chicago, weighing
seven pounds, four ounces, to Jamie Jacobson
and Drew Conrad. Proud grandparents
include Frankie Jacobson of Chicago, the
late Seth Jacobson, and Michael and Monica
Conrad of Arizona.

Epilogue

Frankie Jacobson couldn't have felt more important today. She stood proudly next to Rabbi Cohen as he held baby Seth Charlie Conrad and chanted a loud prayer. Next to the Rabbi stood the baby's proud parents, Jamie and Drew.

After the circumcision was performed everyone shouted "Mazol-tov" and like all other brisses, the competition got underway. Only now, Frankie could finally be a part of it. She took her wailing grandson and happily paraded him around the room.

"Oh Frankie, he's gorgeous!" Marilyn Grazer said excitedly.

"Those eyes…" added Ester Cohen.

Frankie posed for a few pictures and then handed the baby to Danny while she dealt with the caterer for a few minutes.

"Hello, Danny," said Marcy Rothberg, "Congratulations on your engagement."

"Thank you Mrs. Rothberg. How's Lisa doing?" he felt obligated to ask.

"She's fine. Married with two kids," she answered as if she wanted him to know her daughter survived being dumped by him.

Up walked Sandy Greenberg. "Well hello there, Danny," she said with sarcasm, "Is that your fiancé?" She motioned to Courtney, who was standing a couple feet away.

Danny introduced Courtney to Marcy and Sandy, and they all stood there in an awkward silence until Danny suggested the women help themselves to the cake and coffee that had just come out.

"Nice to see you, Danny," said Marcy as she walked away.

"Nice to meet you, Courtney," Sandy said, following Marcy across the room.

They weren't more than three feet away when Danny said to Courtney, "I dated both their daughters."

When Jamie came over to take the baby out of Danny's arms, they noticed the fierce competition taking place in the corner. Marcy Rothberg had pulled out pictures of her grandchildren and was showing them to a group of about six women, including Frankie.

"You all know Lilly and Jeffrey," she said, holding up the picture for everyone to see, "Well, this is their new little sister, Sara." There were lots of oohhs and ahhhs as Marcy held up the baby picture.

"Guess who's expecting number four?" shouted Sheila Katz, who desperately wanted in on the contest, "Joshie!"

Now Danny was pissed. What was this woman doing stealing his mother's thunder? He had to put Frankie back into the race, so he grabbed Courtney's hand and quickly headed over to the group. He cleared his throat and announced loudly, "Guess who's expecting number one?"

Everyone looked up and lots of jaws hit the ground.

"Is that true?" asked Jamie.

Danny nodded proudly and Courtney pulled out a photo from her purse. There were tears in her eyes when she handed it to Frankie.

"This is our baby girl," she said happily, "She's seven months old."

"We're adopting her," said Danny, "It was a really hard process, but we just found out a few days ago that it's going through." He gleamed, "She should be ours in the next few weeks."

Frankie went nuts, screaming with joy and excitement, and as much as her drama usually irked Jamie, this time, she loved it.

"What's the baby's name?" asked Rose.

Danny looked right at his mother and said, "We're naming her Stephanie. After Dad."

This is where Frankie lost it. She started bawling on the spot.

"Don't cry, Ma," Danny said, "I want you to be happy."

"I am," she managed through tears, "I am."

It was bittersweet. Seth had been gone for more than thirty years and Frankie still missed him as much as she ever had. But the beauty was, now her children were honoring his memory. Babies Seth and Stephanie were proof that God and love and the notion that life goes on fully existed. Yes, Frankie Jacobson finally got her babies. And as she watched her happy family embrace, her eyes were shining bright, as bright as she knew her future was. And she felt like the luckiest person on earth.